The Road to Forever

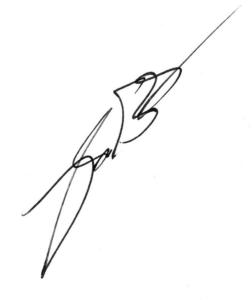

The Road to Forever

Ron Felt

Dedicated to
Alexis and Reagan

Chapter One

The cool wind swirled, carrying dirt and debris along the road, as a hint of blue appeared in the early morning sky. A low buzz radiated from the neon sign that stood at the roadside in a vain attempt to attract the attention of passersby. A pink glow surrounded the word *Vacancy*. It had been years since the white light around *No* had been lit to precede it. Raised white letters on the wooden sign, which used to be surrounded by brightly colored evergreen trees, spelled out the motel's name, *The Pines*.

Few travelers stopped these days. Independent, roadside motels had given way to hotel chains that provided better comfort, better locations and better service for a competitive price. Now the clientele at *The Pines* consisted mostly of those that did not want to be seen for various reasons. The guestbook was full of fake names written by people paying in cash. On a good night, half of the rooms would be occupied, some even for the whole night. The previous night was no exception.

Outside of room fourteen sat a small, grey car, coated in road dust. The backseat was covered in fast food wrappers from many meals eaten behind the wheel. Several almost empty coffee cups littered the floor behind both seats. Loose clothing was strewn about haphazardly and an overused map that had been folded and unfolded a few too many times lay on top of the pile. The front passenger seat was, by comparison, surprisingly clear.

A broken sidewalk led to a row of guest rooms. Rusty, gold numbers were all that distinguished one from the next. The doors were all painted pine green, but not recently. Behind each door the rooms were nearly identical. Cheap, yellow paint covered the walls. The stale smell of cigarettes and cheap perfume, imbedded in the furniture, filled the air. The curtains displayed a western themed pattern of stagecoaches, horses and cowboys swinging lassos. An antique television, complete with rabbit ear antennae sat in front of the one plaid chair which, aside from the bed, was the only piece of furniture.

At the end of the row of guest rooms was the lobby. The faint colorful glow of a television set reflected off the drab, white curtains that hung in the window. Inside, the overweight motel manager sat with his feet up on the check-in counter, sound asleep. Over the years his senses had developed to where nothing but the sound of a paying customer could disturb his slumber.

As night slowly begins to give way to the early morning, inside of room fourteen, a man stands before the bathroom mirror. The harsh light of one exposed light bulb fills the room casting curious shadows in the shower stall behind him. Leaning over the sink of chipped porcelain and rusted metal, he looks intently over the details of his own unshaven face and discovers a small scratch under his right eye.

"Huh, she must have fought harder than I thought" he says to himself.

He stares into the reflection of his own eyes, only to see that behind them lay an empty existence. This would bother him, if indeed he could be bothered. A small laugh escapes him as he considers the irony. Satisfied that he is presentable to the public, he turns out the light and walks out to the bed and picks up his jacket which lay at the foot. He takes a moment for one last look at the lifeless girl under the covers, her eyes blankly staring off into eternity. Without emotion or remorse he turns and walks out the door.

Taking in a breath of cool, fresh morning air, he pulls the door shut behind him. Making sure it's locked, he wipes the knob clean of all prints. The sound of gravel grinding under his boots escapes as he makes his way across the parking lot and past the motel office. Through the window he can make out the silhouette of the manager with his arms folded across his chest, lit by the glow of the television, still asleep. He considers asking him where the nearest diner is but decides it is better not to make any contact with someone who will eventually be questioned by the police. He decides instead to take advantage of the opportunity for a clean get away and heads for the main road. The feel of loose gravel gives way to solid asphalt and he starts walking west with nothing but open road ahead.

How long would it take this time, he wondered. It was around 5:00am and check out time was not until noon. In a small motel like this one, it wouldn't take long to clean the few rooms that were actually used the night before. He figured around 1:00pm they would start knocking on the door of room fourteen. Seeing the car still parked in front of the room, they wouldn't go in right away, not wanting to walk in on someone and find them in an embarrassing situation, he reasoned.

Impatience would get the better of them and perhaps in a half hour or so they would be knocking again, this time with the manager. There would be the yelling of warnings and maybe even threats of added fees. The manager might even consider just leaving the occupants alone and charging them for an additional night, after all, he could certainly use the business. Then it would start to eat away at him that he didn't have the money in hand. There was a strict, 'Pay before you Stay' policy. He was going to open the door.

Once inside it would not take long, maybe the turning on of a lamp or the opening of the drapes, to see that the girl was dead. There's just no mistaking that look on the face of a dead person. In truth, the man loved that look, was fascinated by it. It was almost as if the person was caught in midthought, their mouth open slightly as if to utter one final thought that would never be heard, their eyes trying in vain to see something off in the distance. Seeing them that way was part of the thrill for him.

A thousand thoughts would flood through the motel manager's mind all at once. He would stand frozen in thought until the maid would suggest calling the police. This would snap him out of it with an emphatic refusal. The man could almost picture their conversation.

"We need to call the police" the maid would say.

"No!" the manager would reply.

"What do you mean no? We have a dead body here. We have to call the police."

"Just shut up and give me a minute to think will you?"

"What is there to think about?"

"Plenty. I have a business to run here you know. Is this going to hurt us or our reputation? We can't afford to have customers turn away right now, things are too tight. How long will the police be sniffing around here, huh? You know as well as I do that half the people that stay here are trying not to be seen. You think they will show up if there are a bunch of cop cars in the parking lot? I have to think about this a minute."

"So what, are you going to throw her in your trunk and dump her in the woods? What about her car? Are you going to push it in a lake or something? What if the police come anyway, looking for her? What then?"

He would stare blankly off into space, desperately trying to sort through all of the thoughts that plagued his mind. He would conclude, but not admit, that she was right.

"I think I should call the police. Lock up the room."

Her stare would follow him out the door and back to the office as she marveled at the fact that she was working for him instead of the other way around. "I've got to get another job" she would say to herself as she locked the door and went back to work, a little afraid to open the next room for fear of what may be inside. The manager would return to his office and make the call and the police would be on the way.

The man estimated that he had until around two o'clock before the police would arrive to begin their investigation. That would give him about nine hours to grab a donut, a cup of coffee and disappear.

Chapter Two

It was two o'clock in the afternoon when Detective Simeon Jackson received the call at his desk telling him a body had been found. Twenty minutes later he was following the winding road through the woods to the secluded hideaway called *The Pines*. Though he had never been there himself, he had heard of the motel's reputation, a haven for secret lovers. Sadly, in recent years, the busiest nights were on prom weekend. It certainly wasn't the first time the police had been called, but to his knowledge, it was the first time under these circumstances.

As his car rounded one last bend, the weather-worn sign came in to view. He pulled into the parking lot and stopped behind the car outside of room fourteen. Dust from the gravel ground swirled in the air marking the trail of his car's entrance and sudden stop. Swinging open his car door, he stepped out and threw his sunglasses on the passenger seat. He stood still for a moment as if trying to soak information out of the air. The motel manager and maid could be seen in the office talking to a patrol officer and appeared to be losing patience. Jackson shook his head at the thought of the selfishness of people. The manager was upset at having to answer a few questions, most likely doing no more than interrupting his television viewing. Meanwhile, some poor soul was lying dead in a cheap motel room.

Standing in the doorway of that very room was another patrol officer, his name badge read Johnson.

"Are you the first on the scene Officer Johnson?" asked Jackson.

"Yes sir, I arrived just before two o'clock in response to a call from the motel manager" Johnson replied, pleasantly surprised by the respectful way he was spoken to. Most detectives treated him like a security guard, none referred to him as "Officer".

"And that's him in the office?"

"Right, the guy in the dirty t-shirt with the mustache."

"So what do we have?" Jackson asked as he entered the room.

"Cleaning lady says she came by about twelve thirty, knocked but there was no answer. Came back around one, same thing. Then she gets the manager, more knocking, same result. He uses the key, opens the door and they find this woman in the bed. He can tell right away that she's dead, so he calls us."

"It took you an hour to get here?"

"No, the call didn't come in until after one thirty."

"Why the delay in calling?" Jackson asks, mostly to himself. "So what's her story?" he continues, referring to the dead woman.

"He said she checked in last night, late, but he couldn't give me a definite time. She appeared to be alone, but he wouldn't swear to that either. She paid in cash for one night, then went straight to the room. Check out time was at noon."

"And no one saw or heard anything else from her" Jackson finished for him. He was now walking carefully around the bed, still not touching anything. "How many other people were staying here last night?"

"Five other rooms were occupied. The closest one to this room was two doors down. Manager says it was a family with kids so they were tucked away before the girl even arrived. Since the body wasn't discovered until after check out, most people had already left."

"Get a copy of any information the office has on anyone that was staying here, even if they used fake names. Maybe someone paid with a credit card or something we can trace. We may get desperate and need to contact them at some point. But first, go out to my car and get the yellow tape out of my trunk. We need to get this room closed off right away. Call forensics and the photographer while you're out there. This room needs to be worked before it gets disturbed." He tossed his keys to the officer. "Oh, and I want the maid and manager separated and re-interviewed. Something kept them from calling us right away and it might mean this room has been tampered with."

The officer left and another police car pulled into the lot. Jackson could faintly hear Johnson giving the newly arrived officer instructions to go in the office and separate the motel employees. Having looked all around the room, Jackson now concentrated directly on the dead woman. He leaned in and studied every inch of her face, her eyes staring back at him. The rest of her was covered by the bedspread. He wanted the whole scene photographed and video taped before he moved or touched anything. He feared that something had been moved by the manager and every detail was important until they had some idea of what happened here.

It was Jackson's opinion that every second that passed following a criminal act made the crime increasingly more difficult to solve. The more time passed, the more things were disturbed, clues disappeared, evidence just vanished. His goal was to walk into a crime scene that was exactly how it was the moment the criminal left it. That however, almost never happened. The world was constantly changing and moving, even for a dead body. The moment a person dies, the body begins to change, leaving clues as to the time and cause of death. At the same time, the area around the body would change as well. The air, dust, temperature, rodents, other people, all affecting the scene. Time changes everything.

The criminals too were smarter than ever. It seemed that they always stayed one step ahead of the technology designed to catch them. Years ago, police had to rely on eye witness accounts or sheer luck. Then there was the discovery of fingerprints and how they could be used to place someone at the scene. That was followed by DNA evidence which could use saliva, blood, other bodily fluids, hair, and even individual skin cells, to identify someone. Yet with people's fascination with crime scenes and homicide investigations, there were countless movies, books and television shows on the subject revealing the latest in high tech methods, real and imagined. All one had to do was be up on current pop culture to know how to get away with murder. Criminals were given a virtual blueprint on what methods investigators would use to catch them, thereby helping them avoid getting caught.

For this reason, among others, Jackson felt the need to take full advantage of every clue and resource available to him. Of course the greatest tool now, as it had always been, was the mind. Through training, experience and an uncommon grasp of the human thought process, Jackson had mastered the ability to read a crime scene like a movie script.

His mind was collecting the pieces of information around him and building a picture in his mind when after several minutes officer Johnson returned and snapped him back to the present. "I've sealed off the whole area around the room, including the car parked in front. I also ran the plates. The car belongs to a Dorothy Glickman of Indianapolis. The description matches the victim, from what I can see anyway. Also the evidence tech and photographer are here to process the room."

"Great, thanks Johnson. Let's get out of here and let them do their job" Jackson replied.

****

A small sedan screeched around the curve in the road before pulling into the motel parking lot and skidded to a halt next to Jackson's car, creating a cloud of dust in the air. Inside, the driver took a moment to straighten out his tie and check his hair in the mirror. His name was Bill Edwards, a young detective who had been assigned to Jackson for training. The relationship had not gotten off to the smoothest of starts. Edwards felt that he was not being taken seriously, not being treated as an equal, someone who had been on the force for a number of years. He felt like a probationary rookie all over again. It didn't help that Jackson seemed like a serious, emotionless robot that rarely spoke, at least not to him. As he looked at himself in the mirror, he secretly hoped to himself that this would be a big case, one that would make headlines and propel his career into a new level, where training would no longer be necessary.

His state of mind now in the proper place, in his opinion anyway, he opened his car door and stepped out. Walking towards the crime scene, he did his best to look important, flashing his badge at anyone who would look. As he reached the yellow police tape that now surrounded the victim's car and motel room, he began to duck under when Jackson caught sight of him and called out, "Edwards, over here. They're still photographing the room."

"Hey, sorry I'm late. I got held up…" Edwards began as he turned and approached Jackson who had just come around the corner at the end of the building.

"I don't want to hear it" Jackson said interrupting him before he could explain. "It's probably better that I don't know anyway."

"So what do we have today?" Edwards said, feeling like he had been put in his place. He tried to cling to his optimism and just get to work, ignoring Jackson's comment.

"It seems we may have your first homicide investigation on our hands." Jackson began to fill him in on the rest of what they knew up to that point, which wasn't much. Edwards couldn't help but feel a sense of excitement, already seeing himself on the evening news, suspect in hand. His legend had begun, though only within himself.

The two detectives had come to rest against one of the cars when the photographer emerged from the room. With a wave of the camera he told Jackson that his job was complete. He entered his car and headed back to the station to process the film, knowing Jackson would want it as soon as possible.

Jackson nodded an acknowledgment and watched him drive away, before turning to Edwards, who seemed anxious to get into the room. "I want you to go in the office and get all the statements from the motel employees and take them back to the station. There should be two from each of them, one when they were together, another when separated. Compare them all and look for any discrepancies. Then figure out if anything in their stories gives any indication that they tampered with anything in that room before they called us. Look for it between the lines, in what they aren't saying. Put yourself in their place and figure out what they touched. Then I want you to watch the video of the room and look through the pictures of the scene when they are ready. Make a list of anything that you think was moved, altered or messed with in any way after the perp left the scene."

"You sure you don't need me around here for a little while first? I mean I could collect evidence, look for the escape route, interview people..." Edwards pleaded, seeing his dreams slipping away and feeling dejected.

"Sorry, but you showed up too late for all of that. The interviews have been done, twice, the perp walked right out the front door and I will be the one to go through that room looking for evidence." The disappointment on Edwards face was evident. "You're the only one I trust with this. It's up to you to purify the crime scene for me and what could be more important than that?" he added. "Now get going."

It helped a little and Edwards, feeling his ego had been built up slightly, stood up to his full height, straightened his clothes, stopped by the motel office, and walked back to his car with a sense of purpose. It wasn't the first time that Jackson had seen this in a young detective. It seemed they all started out the same, with a sense of self importance, trying to get noticed and read their names in the newspapers. It wasn't until they had been detectives for a while and settled into the job that they got a sense of what it was really all about. The egos fade and eventually they just concentrate on getting the job done. He too would come around, in time.

Waving away the dust from the new cloud Edwards had created, this time by his quick departure, Jackson walked back into the motel room to find the evidence technician packing up the last of his equipment. "Afternoon Dan, you all finished in here?"

"Yep, I'm all set."

"Any luck?" Jackson asked as he began to look around.

"I was able to pull some prints. I have those of the victim and I'll get the motel employees on my way out. Depending on how well they clean these rooms and how thorough our perp is, maybe we'll get lucky and have something to run through the criminal records computer. Other than that, I haven't done much. Coroner called and he's running late. You should have some time before he arrives to look around and work your magic. Let me know if you run across anything you want tested."

"I'll do that Dan, thanks. Shut the door on your way out please" Jackson replied, already slipping into a state of deep concentration.

"Sure, see you later" Dan said closing the door, but Jackson didn't hear him.

This was Jackson's time. Alone in the room, the victim still lying there, this is when he did his best work, what he was known for. As the outside world faded away, he was able to slip into the world of the recent past and slowly see the events of the crime unfold before his eyes, as he took pieces of the puzzle from around the room and put them in their place within his mind. To share this collection of swirling thought with his fellow investigators, he removed a small, voice activated tape recorder from his coat pocket and began to think aloud. "No apparent signs of struggle. The room seems in order, nothing obviously out of place. The side of the bed opposite the victim appears unused since it was last made. The corner of the bed at the foot is still flat and smooth and the sheets and blanket appear to only be untucked from the other side. Looking to the one chair in the room, the seat cushion is not pushed back all the way, indicating someone sat in it recently, or perhaps slept in it, possibly the perp. Could be that they did not know each other or at least were not involved intimately. Moving into the bathroom, the large towels are still tightly folded and in their place. The shower is dry and shows no sign of recent use. One hand towel is unfolded and may have been used." With a gloved hand, he lifted the towel and placed it in an evidence bag. It was possible that some skin cells or hair could be found that would reveal the killer's DNA.

With one final glance around the bathroom he made his way back to the victim. Satisfied that he had drawn all the relative information he could from the surrounding area, he now drew his attention to the immediate area of the body, which usually revealed the most insight into the crime. He continued "The usual items remain on the bedside table on the victim's side and do not appear to have moved and confirm that any struggle would have to be minimal as the table is less than an arm's length from the body."

Now for the first time he reached down and slowly pulled back the bedspread that covered the girl's lifeless body. She was still fully dressed in jeans and a t-shirt. "Clothes seem intact, no sign of rape." Though tests would be performed at the autopsy to confirm this, Jackson was able to make this assumption based on how the clothes looked on the girl. When someone tries to put the clothing back on an unconscious or dead body, especially tight fitting pants, they never look the same as when a person dresses themselves.

Jackson looked over the body from head to toe before sitting down on the bed. He replaced the tape recorder in his pocket and looked intently at the dead girl next to him, willing her to give up the secrets of her death. He noticed bruising around her neck leading him to believe preliminarily that strangulation was involved and perhaps the cause of death, but this could only be confirmed at the autopsy. The pieces began to draw themselves together and in moments a scenario became clear in Jackson's mind. He stood up and placed the bedspread back how it was, and then proceeded to straddle the body. As he tried to enter the mind of the killer, he used his legs to pin down the girl's arms. From this position, the killer's mere body weight would make it difficult for the girl to move or struggle with her arms in any way and virtually eliminate their own risk of injury. It would then be all too simple to reach down and choke the very life out of the victim with little resistance.

He sat there for a moment, trying to figure out, if indeed this was the way it happened, what this could tell him about the killer that might help track them down. His first practical thought was that it stood to reason the killer weighed at least as much, if not more, than the victim for this to work without being thrown off or showing signs of a greater struggle. He looked around the room again. It appeared that the killer was allowed to share the room, but likely not the bed. There was no evidence of robbery, sex or even anything personal against this particular victim. The more he thought about it, the only motive seemed to be the act of killing itself. He turned his gaze back to the girl's face and a chill ran through him. This killer likes to look into the eyes of his victim and watch as their life slowly slips away.

Chapter Three

The detective squad was alive with activity. The usual 'Water Cooler' conversations could be heard throughout the room as detectives stood around in clumps. One group was discussing sports, another talked about the previous night's big television shows. There were actually a few people talking about cases they were working on. The squad was a large, open room, filled wall to wall with desks that were more or less in groups of four, all covered with papers and files that threatened to one day bury the computer monitors that seemed to be fighting to rise above the clutter.

One such cluster of desks was occupied by the only quiet person in the room. Bill Edwards sat staring at the screen in front of him, studying the video of the motel room. The transcripts of the manager and maid's interviews were laid out in front of him on his desk and lap, atop the rest of the papers. Periodically he would pause the tape and shuffle through the interviews trying to find any obvious discrepancies. So far he found none, and was beginning to wonder if Jackson had just given him the assignment to keep him out of the way. He knew that Jackson would be showing up soon, and either way he wanted to give him something to show his efforts. Finding nothing would hardly prove that he was ready for bigger and better things, but he feared that perhaps there really was nothing to find.

He sat back with his hands over his face, feeling nothing but frustration when he heard the thud of something landing on his desk. Dropping his hands he saw an envelope. "What's this?" he asked Jack Palmer, who had apparently left it there.

"The photos from your scene. Someone handed them to me on my way up and asked me to give them to you" he replied.

"Great." Edwards covered his face again and wished he were somewhere, anywhere else.

Jack Palmer was another detective from the squad whose desk was also part of the same cluster. He was in his mid fifties and out of shape, a long time lover of greasy food, beer and cigarettes with the physique to prove it. Behind his back, the other detectives referred to him as Heart Attack, for what they all thought was his inevitable outcome, but no one said it to his face. He was generally liked and considered a good guy, though his skills as a detective seemed to be fading with his motivation.

Dropping a grease stained paper bag on his desk, he pulled back his chair and sat down heavily with a grunt. "Did that noise come from you or the chair?" Edwards asked as he dropped his hands to his sides again and looked wearily at Palmer.

"Funny rookie, just wait 'til you're my age. That is if you make it that long, which is no sure thing on this job, especially with what I hear about you" Palmer replied.

"What are you talking about? I'm just as cautious as anybody else. I just happen to be motivated, that's all."

"Yeah, you look real motivated. Motivated to quit maybe."

"Say Palmer, you've been here a while, right?" Edwards asked, changing the subject.

"On the squad? Forever I think. Why?"

"What's the deal with Jackson?"

"Meaning what?"

"Meaning that he seems so, I don't know, distant maybe? Like he's disconnected or something. I mean he's nice enough I guess, but there's something about him. Reserved I guess might be a better way to put it."

Air escaped from Palmer's mouth as he sat back and thought for a moment. Taking another bite from his cheeseburger that was pushing its bun to the limit, he began. "So you want to know about Jackson. Well let's just say he wasn't always this way. But something you need to know is that he is one of the best cops I've had the privilege to work with, and he's a good guy. But to answer your question, several years ago, he was working on a case that involved some pretty nasty things bein' done to some kids. It was a frustrating one because things just weren't coming together and the victims were adding up. When he finally broke the case, he went after the suspect alone. It was at night and there wasn't anyone around from his shift, and at the time he didn't trust anyone else, so he decides to go alone to bring this guy in. Never a good idea, no matter who you are, especially when it's a case that affects you emotionally. Anyway, he gets to this lowlife's apartment and knocks on the door. The guy answers, like an idiot, and sees Jackson standing there holding his badge. Needless to say the badge did not impress him, nor did Jackson. The guy was maybe six foot four, weighed maybe two fifty. He looks down at Jackson who you know is what, five seven and not all that big. He says "What do you want?" in a rather annoyed tone. Jackson tells him that he's there to arrest him and starts to read him his rights. The guy gets this smug look on his face, sizes Jackson up, and tells him to come back when he has help. Then he turns and tries to close the door."

"Oh boy" Edwards sighed.

"You're darn right 'oh boy'. Not only does this completely insult his manhood and disrespect the badge, but that on top of the fact that it was all Jackson could do up to that point to control himself as he thought about what this schmuck did to those poor kids. Well he just lost it. He slams open the door and proceeds to beat the life out of this guy. I mean when he was finished, this guys own mother couldn't have recognized him."

"The guy deserved it" Edwards added.

"Well sure, but remember, Jackson's a cop, and that don't go over too good. So he ends up in court. At the trial, the guy accuses him of police brutality, and believe me, that totally killed this guy to say in public that he was beat up by this little cop."

"So what happened? Was he suspended?" Edwards asked.

"Nah, that's the funny part. The judge didn't buy it. He looks at Jackson, looks at this huge guy, and since Jackson used no weapons, he figured it was pure self defense to try and take this guy down. He figured the guy must have been injured before this whole thing since he was a lowlife anyway, and was just tryin' to blame it all on Jackson to get off on the charges against him."

"So what, he got off scot-free?"

"Almost. He got a warning and had to promise not to try and arrest a suspect alone anymore to avoid these kind of accusations."

"That's it?"

"Officially and publicly, yes. However, back at the squad, it wasn't that simple. See, we all knew what a tough son of a gun Jackson was and so did the captain. We also knew he had a mean temper. So we had no problem believing that he was totally capable of doing exactly what this guy said he did. The problem of course was that as far as the department was concerned, he was innocent. That looks better for them too. So what do you do?"

"Right, what can you do? You can't punish him for something they say didn't happen. And if they fight the ruling they are making a case for police brutality, and they aren't about to do that. You're kind of stuck."

"Basically yeah. So the captain thought he would try the honest, direct approach. He calls Jackson in to his office, closes the door and lays it straight on the table. He says officially his hands are tied on this one, but that off the record he has a pretty good idea of what really happened in that apartment building. Jackson doesn't deny a thing. Then he tells him that if something doesn't change, this kind of thing will happen again, and next time he might not be so lucky. He tells him that he will probably end up killing someone eventually and at the very least, he will lose his badge and possibly end up in jail. He says that off the record and on his own, he needs to get help, doesn't matter what kind, but something. Jackson agrees and that's exactly what he did."

Edwards sat anxiously waiting for Palmer to explain and finally ran out of patience. "Come on, what was it, what did he do?"

"Shhh. He just walked in" Palmer said with a slight nod towards to hallway. "He'll be here any second. I'll finish later."

Edwards glanced over his shoulder and saw that Jackson stopped to speak to someone. This gave him a few moments until he would be in hearing range. "Give me a hint at least, he can't hear you yet" he pleaded to Palmer.

"Look on the front seat of his car" Palmer added and then turned back to his French fries and glob of ketchup.

"What? What does that mean?" Edwards said but noticed Jackson approaching. He tried to get back to watching the video of the motel room but his mind was no longer into it. He tried to figure out what Palmer meant and what could possibly be on the front seat of Jackson's car that would be of any help.

Jackson had run into Dan Besson, the evidence technician, on his way into the detective squad. Reaching into his jacket, he pulled out the hand towel from the motel bathroom and handed it over to him. "I'd like you to analyze this for hair and tissue, maybe blood. Looks like it was the only one used last night. Also, there is a chair in the motel room. It looks like our perp may have slept in it. Have that brought in and go over it really well. You might find something."

"I'll get on the towel and get someone over there for the chair right away" Besson replied.

"Great, thanks Dan" Jackson said and proceeded towards his desk and Edwards. He was hoping Edwards was able to find something on the video that might confirm his suspicions or at least help paint a better picture of what really happened. "So what did you find?" he asked Edwards, who was looking intently at the video screen.

"Well, I'm afraid not much of anything. If the staff touched anything, I'll be darned if I can figure it out" Edwards replied.

Edwards looked up at him to see if he looked disappointed, but his face remained expressionless. Does this guy ever show any emotion, he wondered. Jackson hung his jacket on the back of his chair and moved over behind Edwards, watching the video for a moment before continuing. "Alright, put this aside for now. I think I'm starting to get some idea of what type of person we might be dealing with, and perhaps how the murder took place. I need a couple of things from you."

"Sure, go ahead" Edwards said, but he was tempted to ask him what he was basing his conclusions on. It didn't look to him like they had the first clue.

"Check in with the coroner's office. Make sure they have the body and know who to call when they have their results. Tell them I need the usual; rape kit, defensive wounds check, cause and time of death and of course they need to check under the fingernails."

"Got it. Don't they know to do that stuff?"

"If you tell them exactly what you want, you get a report on exactly what you want. Otherwise, who knows. Plus, you never know who is working on your victim, so it doesn't hurt to be specific, even if redundant. Why give them an excuse."

"Okay, lesson learned. What else do you need?"

"Then the fun part. I want you to pull all unsolved and opened cases from the last two years that may have the same M.O."

"What M.O. is that?" Edwards asked, puzzled. Had he missed something? Since when did they have an M.O.?

"I'll let you know shortly after I confer with the psychologist. I sent him an email with my hypothesis from my car's computer and I need to go see if he shares my opinion. If so, I'll have something for you to look for."

"So you think this guy has killed before then."

"I'm almost certain of it, but don't refer to the perp as a guy until we know for sure. The most dangerous thing you can do as a detective is to start assuming things you haven't proven yet."

Edwards sat for a moment, feeling like he was completely lost and out of the loop. He watched Jackson disappear around the corner and then turned anxiously back to Palmer. When his expectant look did not get a response, he said "So?"

"What?" Palmer said, looking up from his newspaper with a mouth full of fries and ketchup dripping down his chin, as if he had no idea what Edwards was asking about.

"What did Jackson do to change?" Edwards asked, exasperated.

"Oh, that. Later, he might come back. I told you, check his front seat."

"Come on, he went to see the shrink, he's not going to be back for a few minutes. Give me something."

"You're a detective, figure it out, I'm on lunch."

"From where I'm sitting it looks like lunch is on you" Edwards said throwing a napkin at him.

"Funny." Palmer wiped off his chin and continued "I will say that, as you can see, it worked. He hasn't been the same since."

"Since what?" Edwards asked a little too loud, from frustration.

"Figure it out yourself rookie" Palmer said looking around to see if

Edwards outburst had attracted any attention.

Edwards knew he had pushed his luck at that point and would get no further information from Palmer. He sat for a moment watching him and thought he detected a slight smile under the ketchup in the corner of Palmer's mouth.

"You're enjoying this aren't you?"

"Don't flatter yourself" Palmer replied, suddenly very serious again. "I get very little enjoyment from anything."

****

Jackson went down the hallway from the detective squad and arrived at the office of Bill Davis, the department psychologist. Bill spent much of his time counseling officers who had gone through traumatic experiences, helping them to cope with the often unstable home life which resulted in a seventy percent divorce rate among police officers, and talking to victims that were under duress. On occasion, he was asked to do what he found rather fascinating, and in truth what led him to his career to begin with, and that was to try and get inside the mind of a killer and try to bring him to justice. Fortunately for society, these types of cases were not as common as television or the movies might lead people to believe, but every once in a while a detective would come to him and ask him to help a killer betray himself with his own mind.

When the email arrived from Detective Jackson, he could just sense that it was going to be something interesting. He set his other work aside and immediately submersed himself in the details Jackson had sent him. There were however two things about Jackson that differed from the other detectives, one good and one not so good, at least to Bill Davis. Jackson sent more relevant details and helpful information than anyone else, which allowed Davis to get as good a feel for the killer as possible. On the other hand, Jackson was so good at his job that he often made the assessment of the killer before Davis had seen the information, and was really only looking to confirm his own opinion, not really needing Davis' help. He had developed such a great knowledge of the criminal mind over the years, that there was little he needed from Davis.

Davis' respect for Jackson outweighed his bitterness, and he still found great pleasure in discussing cases with him. As he sat in his office with the diplomas mounted on the walls and the psychology books on the shelves, he was happy to see Jackson coming down the hall.

"Do you have a few minutes?" Jackson asked as he leaned in through the doorway.

"Sure, come on in" Davis replied and motioned for him to have a seat.

"Did you get a chance to read my notes on the motel case I sent you?" Jackson asked as he closed the door and took a seat.

"Yes, I glanced through it" Davis said, down playing his enthusiasm. "Let me bring it up on my screen" he added, but it was already there. "Oh, here it is. I think you are right on track. To me it appears you are dealing with a male in his late twenties to early thirties, a loner, likely a drifter of some sort. His motivation seems to stem from the kill itself. I think the killer finds either gratification or satisfaction in the killing, possibly the moment that death occurs."

"You mean like a sense of power?"

"Possibly, but perhaps something else."

"Like what?"

"Well, could be that he is fascinated by it somehow. I'm not sure, I could be reaching. There just isn't enough here to make too many conclusions."

"What are you basing your preliminary conclusions on?"

Davis looked at him for a moment before responding. He wondered how much of this Jackson had already figured out on his own. He answered anyway. "I guess pretty much on what you've written here. There doesn't seem to be any evidence of the usual types of motive. There are no signs of a major struggle that might suggest anger or passion. Nothing of any value is missing, which leaves out robbery. I would be surprised if the victim was raped or molested in a sexual way. It seems to indicate that the killer was casual and yet intentional about it. He meant to kill her, he knew what he was doing, but doesn't give us a clue as to why. I also found your hypothesis about the positioning interesting. The fact that he was able to look the victim in the eye tells me he found pleasure in it and confirms my suspicions."

"Would you also agree that this was not the first time he has killed?"

"Definitely. This has been building for a long time. You can't be this calm and methodical about killing someone right out of the gate. This guy has previous experience."

"Thanks Bill. Let me know if you come up with anything else after you look it over some more. I'll keep you informed of our progress."

"Will do. Say Simeon, next time could you leave me something to figure out on my own? You're going to put me out of a job here" Davis said with a smile.

"I'll see what I can do" Jackson replied with a smile of his own before heading back down the hallway.

Many thoughts were swirling around his head as he walked back to the detective squad. He was glad that Davis had agreed with him. He liked Bill Davis and had a great deal of respect for him. He knew Davis would never believe it, but Jackson put a great deal of weight to his opinions. He never felt sure about his own conclusions until he ran them past Bill. Now that they were in agreement, it was time to figure out how that would be useful in catching this killer. He had two main concerns at this point. One, that it would be impossible to figure out who the killer's next victim might be, as it would likely be very random. Two, there would be a next victim.

Edwards saw Jackson approaching and quickly tried to look busy, but he realized he didn't have anything to do. He had already made the call to the coroner. In his panic he turned back to the video and pretended to be studying it.

"Forget the tape, I need you to do something else" Jackson said.

"Sure thing" Edwards responded shutting off the video and reaching for his coat.

"Forget the coat too. I need you to go through the files and pull any case that deals with hitchhikers or drifters. Also cross check that profile with anyone recently released from prison."

"Great, just what I was hoping for, more research" Edwards sighed.

"Most police work is research. If you do the right research, you save yourself a lot of time and effort in everything else."

"Yeah, but it's so boring. I just want to get out there and do something, you know?" The young side of Edwards was showing again. Jackson knew it was time to stroke his ego a little.

"You are doing something, something vital. Don't worry, you'll get to flash your badge at people soon enough" he couldn't help adding. He left Edwards sitting at his desk, mumbling to himself.

Chapter Four

Though the school bus was now only half full of students, you wouldn't know it from the sound they made. The young Simeon Jackson hated the school bus. Most of his friends had cars and on occasion would give him a ride, but it was out of their way, and today they all had plans. Crumpled pieces of paper flew back and forth across the center aisle as the younger kids tried their best to annoy each other and everyone else. There was talking and yelling, but nothing of any real interest could be heard. The few people that Jackson did not loathe on the bus, did their best to stay to themselves, reading or listening to headphones. Creating a world of your own to escape to was a defense mechanism needed for survival.

Today's escape was not a pleasant one for Simeon. His thoughts were all centered around telling his parents that he was in trouble once again for fighting in school. This was nothing new for him. He had a temper that often got away from him and had been getting him into fights since grade school. What started as childhood tantrums led to fits of anger and rage. He had three fights of note before leaving the sixth grade. One in particular was when he found out another boy had been cheating at a game during recess. Something in him snapped and the punches flew. This time his victim ended up in the emergency room. He was kicked out of school shortly after that and had to finish out the year at the school across town, where he had no friends.

His parents were not happy, but hoped that a fresh start might be what he needed. Unfortunately it only caused him to feel bitter and alone. He got in more fights. When the teachers tried to help, he fought with them too. His parents were at a loss. They were good people and loved their son. Simeon's dad had moved up on the company ladder which began to provide a better life for the family, but it also meant that he worked long hours and traveled frequently. His mother was a kind and gentle woman. It broke her heart to discipline her only son, so instead she just tried to love him through his problems. She knew that deep down Simeon was a good kid. He never disrespected her. At home he was well-behaved, though quiet. He seemed bored and disinterested much of the time. She wanted so badly to know just what it would take to make him happy.

Simeon had been trying to change. He hated hurting his parents by messing up. He especially hated the look in his mother's eyes when he disappointed her. He was dreading that look, but it was all he could see as he stared out the bus window, not seeing the neighborhood flashing by. He had a note from the school that had a phone number on it. If the school did not receive a call from his mother, they would know he hadn't given her the note. He would have to face the consequences.

His stop was coming up so he threw his backpack over his shoulder and took the handle of his saxophone that sat at his feet. As the bus slowly came to a stop he made his way through the thin center aisle awkwardly. He wondered to himself why the aisle had to be so narrow and just who they thought could pass through it comfortably as he held his saxophone in front of him and felt his backpack hit every seat as it dragged behind. He could hear some of the children making comments after being hit as he passed.

He stepped out into the open space at the corner of his block and felt the pressure of the enclosed bus drift away as the wind blew in his face. For a moment he felt better, the sun shining down on him, the air fresh and clean. Then he turned and saw his house down the block and his mother's face haunted him once more. The envelope was sealed so he didn't know exactly what she was about to read. All he did know was that he was part of an altercation in the lunch room that sent another student to the nurse with a bloody nose.

He realized that he had been just standing there for several minutes and was finally able to convince his feet to start moving him in the direction of his home. He wondered if he should bother trying to explain what happened to his mother or just let her read about it for herself. Would this mean changing schools again? He didn't know if he could handle that again. It took him two years to start building up friendships after the last time. By then he would be ready to go on to college. Whatever it took, he had to find a way to stay.

His stomach was a ball of nerves as he looked up at his front door, again finding his feet would not move. It seemed as if his entire future now depended on this note that he held in his hand. What he wouldn't give to be able to just throw it away and pretend that nothing happened. Sure he would feel guilty for a while but he would get over it. He looked down at it again and saw the phone number. Above it were the words 'CALL IMMEDIATLEY!' and he could almost hear them echoing in the air.

It was time. He looked down at his feet and willed them to move. At the top of the steps he set his saxophone down and turned the doorknob. The door opened with the sound of rubber stripping pulling apart after many hours of being sealed together. He stepped in and set down his things before closing the door. A part of him screamed to just run up the stairs to his room. He would be safe for a while under the guise of doing homework. He wouldn't have to come clean until dinner time.

He knew what he had to do. The sounds of cooking could be heard mixed with the small television broadcasting the afternoon soap operas from the kitchen where his mother was certainly hard at work. He walked steadily down the hall towards his fate. His mother called out to him as he approached. "Is that you dear?"

He continued on silently. As he entered the kitchen and saw his mom with her back to him, indeed hard at work, making a meal for the two of them since Dad was again on the road, he noticed that she was making his favorite cookies for dessert. The sensation of tears welled up behind his eyelids and he had to fight them off with everything he had. Just then she turned, smiling, and briefly looked at him as she made her way to the other side of the kitchen to retrieve something from the cabinet.

"How was your day honey?" She asked, not noticing his demeanor.

Without speaking he reached out and handed her the note.

"What's this?" she asked and then saw the phone number and those words. "Oh no. Please don't tell me you got in another fight Simeon." The first of the tears broke through despite his best efforts and rolled down his cheek. She opened the envelope and sat down as she read the note inside.

Suddenly she looked exhausted. "Hand me the phone" she sighed. He did so and she dialed the number. "This is Mrs. Jackson, Simeon's mom. I was told to call this number."

What followed was simply a series of yes's and umhum's, but nothing that gave any indication as to what was being discussed. Simeon waited silently for her to hand him back the phone to hang up. When she finally did, she simply told him to sit down, again sounding drained of all energy. Her attitude had completely changed from when he first walked in the room. It was like night and day. All of the joy had left the house and it was his fault. He sat at the small kitchen table across from her and waited for her to gather the right words to say. Inside he was screaming, dying to know what she was about to say, but he dare not speak. At last she spoke. "It seems you have once again decided that violence is the answer to your problems resulting in a fellow student requiring medical attention." This was her rather sophisticated way of saying he had gotten in a fight. He remained silent. "The boy you hit has a broken nose. His parents are not happy, but are willing to let the school handle it."

"Am I going to have to switch schools again?" he asked, no longer able to hold back. There was plenty of emotion in his voice, but it did not change his mother's expression in the least. She held his pleading gaze for a moment before answering.

"No, not yet. However, one more incident and you will be expelled."

"So it's over then? Everything is okay?" he asked, his mood beginning to brighten.

"No, it isn't over and it most certainly is not okay. I don't know what to do with you anymore. You cannot go through life fighting everyone. As for this incident, tomorrow after school you are to meet with the school psychologist. He will take it from there. Whatever he says, you better listen. If you have to give up Jazz Band or sports, whatever, I don't care."

"Mom, I'm sorry." He said it with such sincerity that she fought the urge to disregard it and instead looked deep into his eyes.

"I really hope you are Simeon. If you have any love for me at all, you will take this last opportunity and find a way to change. Next time this happens…." but she couldn't finish. Her wall of strength began to crumble and the emotions began to come through. She quickly turned away and busied herself with dinner again.

"I'll change mom, I promise" he said as he left the room, and he meant it. Somehow, he would find a way.

The next day at school seemed to pass by in a daze that dragged on and on. He found it hard to focus and more than once was caught off guard by the teacher calling on him. Finally he sat in his last class of the day and watched the clock tick in slow motion. When the bell finally rang it made his heart jump into his throat. He gathered his books and made his way into the hall. Other kids fought past him, anxious to go home. There was an excitement in the hallway as the students quickly took the books from their lockers and shoved them into the backpacks and book bags.

Simeon made his way through the crowds, to the office of the school psychologist. When he arrived, an older lady sitting behind a desk told him to have a seat. It seemed as though he had stepped out of school and into an entirely different place. So serious and quiet was this place. Even the smell was different.

"Mr. Santos will see you now" the lady said.

Simeon stood up and walked towards the office where he could hear a conversation between men taking place, but could not make out the words. He must have looked unsure of himself for a voice called out to him "Come on in Mr. Jackson. We're ready for you."

This couldn't be good. 'Mr. Jackson'? What was that all about? And what did he mean by "We"? He wasn't told that anyone else would be in there. He stepped into the musty office. One lamp sat on the desk that sent shadows to all corners of the room. Behind the desk sat a man in a suit, trying his best to look friendly as Simeon entered. Standing in the corner, leaning against the wall was a police officer. For a moment Simeon wondered if he should run. Had his Mom betrayed him? Had she known about this and not told him? Was he about to go to jail?

Seeing the panic in his eyes, Mr. Santos tried to calm him down. "It's okay son, Officer Baker is just here to talk with you." The relief was visible as Simeon relaxed his shoulders and entered the room, taking the seat being offered to him. On the desk sat a file that Mr. Santos made a point of shuffling through before speaking again. "I've been looking through your file here. Seems you have a bit of a temper. Is that fair to say?" He looked up and waited for a response.

"Yes sir." Simeon responded in a very unsure voice. It came out sounding like a question.

"And you have already been expelled from one school, correct?"

"Yes sir."

"How did that work out for you?"

"I don't know. Not so good I guess."

"How come?"

"I lost my friends and had to start over. That was no fun."

"I imagine it wasn't. And do you know that they were going to expel you from here as well?"

"No. I didn't know that." He was nervous again and he began to stiffen up. The psychologist looked over at him but let him be this time.

"Yes. They were convinced that it would be better for everyone if you got a fresh start at a different school. What do you think about that?"

"I think it stinks. I don't want to lose my friends again."

"Do you think it would help you with your problem though?"

"No, it would make it worse. I don't want to be alone again."

"I agree. It didn't help last time, and I doubt it would help now. That is why I recommended that they give you one last chance."

"You did that?"

"Yes, though at some risk to myself. You see in order for them to accept my suggestion, I had to agree to work with you personally. I am willing to make a commitment to you."

"Why?"

"Because from what I can see you are really a pretty good kid. You just need some help, some guidance. Now are you willing to make the same commitment to yourself?"

"What do I have to do?"

"You and I will get together one day a week, like we are doing now and just talk."

"About what?"

"Life, you, different things. We are going to try and get you to focus this energy you have in a more constructive way. Can you agree to this?"

"I guess so." He remembered his promise to his mother. "Yes sir, once a week. I'll be here."

"Good. Now, I've asked Officer Baker to join us this time. He would like to talk with you a little and then you can go until next time. Fair enough?"

"Sure."

The officer stepped out of the shadows and closer to the light. Standing up straight, Simeon could see for the first time the uniform and all of the equipment around his waist. The badge caught the light just right and seemed to sparkle. Then he saw the gun handle protruding from the holster looking so powerful. Simeon's fear subsided as he filled with awe. He was ready to listen to what this man said regardless of what it was.

"Simeon, I've seen boys like you before. Good kids who make mistakes. But one day you make a mistake that goes too far. You know what happens then? I'll tell you. You end up in jail or maybe even dead. Jail is no place to be son, believe me. And I have to tell you, the streets are getting more dangerous every day. You never know who might be carrying a knife or a gun these days. You pick a fight with the wrong person and you could find yourself lying in the street bleeding to death. If this sounds harsh to you, good. I want you scared. Not because I don't like you, but because I don't want to see you end up that way. You're very lucky. You had someone care enough to take an interest in you before it's too late. Not everyone gets that chance. Don't blow it."

Simeon had heard what the officer said, but it sounded distant, like he was wearing earplugs that didn't block everything. The feeling of respect for this man was overwhelming. He managed to respond "I understand sir."

He was dismissed, or so he hoped, and as he walked away his mind was filled with thoughts of a bright future indeed. He had finally seen the light. The officer that stood before him had at once represented every television show and movie about police officers that he had ever seen. Now he knew unequivocally what he was going to do with his life. He was going to be a cop.

From that point on his grades improved and so did his attitude. He had found the sense of purpose that he had been missing. The motivation to fulfill his plan helped him focus and everything started to fall into place for him. Where once there was nothing but apathy, came a sense of energy and determination that propelled him through the rest of high school and into college.

Being a police officer had become very popular and people stood in line to take test after test just to get their name placed on a list to one day be considered for any openings a particular department may have. This didn't discourage him like it once would have. Instead it just made him determined to get every advantage he could. He earned a bachelor's degree in criminal psychology, which was partly inspired by the meetings he had faithfully kept with Mr. Santos, a man he had also grown to respect and admire. He minored in criminal law. In him had grown the desire to one day hunt down the worst of the worst. If a criminal made headlines, he wanted to be the one to arrest him.

The meeting that day with those two men was a turning point in his life, one that left a permanent mark on him. It would be years before he would realize just how much of an influence they had on him. Looking back he would one day understand that he had built his career with them as the pillars. It would however, take something far greater for him to build a life and truly change who he was.

Chapter Five

The grass along the roadside ranged from mowed to ignored and was littered with garbage carelessly discarded from passing cars. After walking through it for nearly ten hours with nothing in his stomach but a doughnut and a cup of coffee, the man felt it was safe to stop and eat. Another business district lay ahead full of gas stations and fast food restaurants and he could feel the emptiness of his stomach calling to him. He figured he was a good twenty-five to thirty miles from the motel and he knew the police would only search a five mile radius from the crime scene. Past that there were just too many places to check. Besides, if they had any clue what they were doing, they would figure that he was probably on foot and wouldn't expect him to get far, not without help anyway.

He spotted a McDonald's ahead, a great place to remain anonymous. So many people come to any given McDonald's, locals and travelers, that within minutes you could be forgotten, usually before your tray hits the table. He went inside and made his way to the counter. Standing inside he realized he could be almost anywhere in the world. Behind the counter, stumbling over her carefully prepared greeting waited a high school girl in a uniform with a name badge that said Judy. The man was so hungry that everything looked good. He had taken a five dollar bill from the girl in the motel figuring that so small amount would go unnoticed. That would buy him his choice of any of the ten value meals. He chose a number and paid the young girl, pleased to have over a dollar in change, and stepped to the side to wait for his food.

In moments the tray that had been set on the counter before him was covered by a sandwich, fries that were spilling out of their container and a soft drink that had been filled too much and was now dripping down the side getting the paper tray cover wet. He picked up the tray, careful not to spill his drink, turned and walked towards the sitting area. As he walked he wondered if he was already fading from the memory of the cashier.

This particular McDonald's had a children's play area. This was a red flag for him. A man alone, and looking the way he did, would attract the attention of parents who had to watch over their children like hawks in this day and age. Chuckling to himself at all of the rules he had to follow, he located an open booth in the middle of the restaurant that would do nicely. At one point he found all of those rules to be a hassle. Constantly having to think through his every little move for even the most insignificant of tasks, the things most people did without any conscious thought at all. Now he actually found comfort in them. They gave order and purpose to everything he did. Every aspect of his life had meaning. Now it all came easily like second nature and often he wasn't aware of even doing it.

He savored every bite of the 'number three' and began to think of what his next move would be. After walking at a good pace for most of the day he knew that at the very least it was time for a ride. What happened after that would depend greatly on who it was that gave him a ride. The best thing would be to find another lone traveler like himself, someone just passing through from somewhere else, who would be forgotten the moment he walked out the door.

Trying to be subtle, he looked out over his burger and scanned the other diners looking for just the right one. There were mothers watching their children who were more interested in playing then eating. In the corner sat a group of senior citizens talking over an afternoon coffee. His feet began to ache as he thought that they might continue to be his only transportation. Just then the door opened and in walked a man in a suit, alone and carrying a briefcase. The suit was cheap and the briefcase likely as much a tool to guard against the awkward feeling of sitting alone as it was for any work related purpose. That combined with the more than friendly way in which he spoke to the cashier who was only interested in taking his order, meant that in all likelihood, this was a lonely traveling salesman desperate for human contact.

A twinge shot through the man's system as he looked on, sizing up this salesman. This would be more than just a ride. Even though it had not been even twenty four hours since he last ended a life, this was too good to pass up.

This man would be his victim and it would be all too easy. All that remained was to decide who he should pretend to be. Perhaps he would be Phil, a man trying to get home to his sick mother. Yes, that would work. The salesman gave him a friendly nod as he sat down awkwardly in a nearby booth, his hands full with the briefcase in one and the tray of food in the other. A smile and a nod later, he was engaged in polite conversation with "Phil".

****

Closing the file drawer, Edwards looked up to see Jackson standing in the doorway holding two cups of coffee.

"Jeez! You startled me" Edwards exclaimed, caught off guard.

"Sorry, I didn't know you were so jumpy."

"I've been alone in this windowless room staring at pictures from homicide scenes and reading about killers all the while not seeing another human being for the last hour. Nobody comes down here. So yes, I admit I got a little creeped out."

"I thought you could use a cup of coffee" Jackson replied, handing him one of the cups.

"Definitely, thanks. I can barely force my eyes to focus anymore. Why don't we have all of these files on the computer?"

"Some of them are, the rest have to wait for the summer interns to scan them in. Anyway, I always prefer something I can hold in my hand to a computer screen. Seems more tangible to me, if a bit old fashioned. Any luck yet?" Jackson began leafing through some of the files laid out on the table.

"Nothing solid. I pulled a few files, but I'm not crazy about any of them" Edwards said nodding towards the stack that Jackson was looking through. "You still feel like this guy has killed before huh?"

"Hmm? Yes I do" Jackson replied after a moment. He seemed to be lost in thought. "I'd say give this another hour or so, then head home and get some rest. We won't solve this thing tonight and I want you fresh for tomorrow."

"Why, what are we doing tomorrow?"

"You'll see. Not sitting in the file room all day if that's what you're worried about. Say, is there any word on the sweep of the area around the motel?"

"They checked everything for five miles but came up with nothing."

"I figured as much. How about forensics?"

"Not yet. He's going over the chair now. As far as the autopsy, they won't get to it until tomorrow."

A solemn look came across Jackson's face as if a storm cloud had developed just under his skin and again he was lost in his own thoughts. He stared off into the distance until Edwards noticed and spoke.

"What's up? What are you thinking?" he asked.

"I was just trying to come to terms with the fact that we are probably going to have to wait for the killer to strike again before we get any closer to figuring out who they are. I only hope there is more evidence next time."

"You seem pretty sure there will be a next time."

"I'm afraid so. For whatever reason, our killer needs to kill. I'm almost certain of it. It will keep going until we stop it. I'm going to take these home and look through them. I'll see you in the morning." Jackson took the stack of files and left with a slight wave.

Edwards sat still for a moment, just thinking about everything that had happened to this point. He realized that if Jackson was right, and he probably was, they had better start making some progress soon. It didn't seem like they knew much of anything to this point, and because of it, someone was likely to lose their life, and soon. This job was not as fun as he thought it would be.

****

Jackson arrived home about forty-five minutes later. He entered his humble apartment and was greeted with silence. Setting the files down on the coffee table in the living room, he made his way to the kitchen to get a drink. As he reached for the handle on the refrigerator he saw a picture of his daughter held in place by a magnet. A feeling of love came over him. He sensed the irony of his life. He worked so hard at his job because of his daughter. He wanted to protect her from all the violence and crime that he was all too familiar with. Yet it was his obsession with that job that broke apart his family and separated him from the daughter he loves.

He grabbed a bottle of water from the fridge and picked up the phone. After a few rings, the voice of a teenage girl answered "Hello."

"Judy, its Dad. How are you honey?" Jackson asked, his face alight with love.

"Hi daddy. I'm alright. How are you doing?"

"Actually I'm a little tired. We just started a big case and it looks like it may be a tough one." Jackson had promised her long ago that he would always be honest with her, so even though he wanted to just tell her he was fine and not burden her with his problems, he chose to tell her the truth.

"How's the new guy working out?"

"He's young, but unlike some of the guys I've worked with, I think he actually has potential. It depends on when he forgets what television has taught him about being a cop and opens up to the truth."

"Is he cute?"

"You are too young to ask me that."

"Dad, I'm sixteen. Like it or not, I like boys."

"To me you will always be my little girl. Besides, he isn't a boy he's a man."

"But is he cute?"

"I have no idea. Can we talk about something else please? How's school going?"

"Okay I guess. Math is a pain but my grades are still pretty good."

"Like I've said before, some subjects will come easy for you, the rest you have to work harder at. But you're smart enough, you'll do okay."

"So are you going to ask about Mom?"

"Of course, how is she?"

"Funny you should ask, she's right here. Hold on."

"Wait, Judy...I love you" but it was too late. There was silence and then a different voice.

"Hello Simeon."

"Oh, hi Irene" he replied, still disappointed at the abrupt end to the conversation.

"You sound happy to speak to me" his ex-wife replied with sarcasm.

"Sorry, I just didn't get a chance to say goodbye to Judy. How are you?"

"Making it I guess. Judy makes me feel old. She's hard to keep up with these days."

"I can imagine. I want to ask you something and I would appreciate an honest answer."

"Sure, what is it?"

"Is she happy?"

"For a teenager, I guess I'd say she's pretty happy. She has a lot going on and she's growing up very quickly, sometimes that can be difficult. But overall, I'd say yes. Why do you ask? You sound worried."

"No, not worried. She means so much to me. I know I haven't always been there for her when she needed me. You're a great mom, but it can't be easy to deal with everything yourself. I'm sorry if I'm rambling, I guess I just want to be whatever she needs me to be and help when I can. Most of all I just want to be sure she's happy after all she has gone through."

"She's a tough girl, gets that from here father. She'll be fine."

"From her mother too."

"Thanks Simeon. I'll have her call you soon, okay?"

"Thank you. Please tell her I love her and let me know if you need me."

"Will do, goodbye."

Simeon had been a patrol officer for a short time when he and Irene got married. They had met through mutual friends and hit it off right away. She was finishing up college herself and would soon find herself teaching history to reluctant high school students.

She thought she would love teaching, but it didn't take long for the novelty to wear off and reality set in. The lessons were the same year after year and though the students themselves changed, their attitudes toward history rarely did. Soon it was just another job, but she worked hard and every once in a while was rewarded with a student that truly wanted to learn. She cherished those times.

They had only been married a year when Irene got pregnant. It was at a point where they had begun to grow apart. Careers had taken precedence over their relationship. The news of the pregnancy brought them closer together, if for but a brief time.

Nine and a half months later when Judy was born, Simeon was working and missed it. Irene sat in the hospital, surrounded by family and holding her newborn child, but in her mind she began to realize that her marriage was falling apart. She began to think that Simeon was using work as an excuse to avoid her and now their child. In truth, he was suffering from an inner turmoil. His career was headed places, but he was constantly exposed to the worst things human beings were capable of and it began to weigh heavily on him. When he looked into the eyes of his helpless baby girl, he was more determined than ever to stop crime. It never seemed like anything he did made the world any safer. He became bitter and at times suffered from depression for weeks at a time. His anger returned.

Police officers have one of the highest divorce rates of any profession, as high as seventy-five percent. Eventually Irene decided to join that statistic. Her husband was almost never around, and when he was they only fought. This was not the environment she wanted to raise her child in. She filed for divorce.

To Simeon, this came as a surprise. In his mind he was giving everything he had for his family. He knew Irene didn't understand this. She wanted him to be around more and help with the baby. She didn't understand what it was like to be a cop. She hadn't seen what he had day in and day out. He still loved her and especially hated to leave Judy, but eventually he signed the papers and moved out.

****

The small sedan continued down the highway at a steady seventy miles an hour. Dark, cloudless skies full of stars hung over the farmland on both sides of the road, nothing but fields and trees for as far as the eye could see. The car's headlights revealed nothing but more open road. The driver shuddered suddenly as he realized he had begun to drift off to sleep watching the white lines blur into one line. In an attempt to stay awake, he broke the silence that he noticed filled the air. "So Phil, you say your mother is ill huh? That's too bad. How serious is it?" he asked fighting his way through a yawn.

"They don't really know yet. To be honest she doesn't take care of herself that well and she has this fear of doctors. She has always believed that you really only get sick after the doctor tells you that there is something wrong. Therefore, if you don't go to the doctor, nothing will ever be wrong. So the fact that she called me at all tells me this isn't just a cold" he said with a slight humorless chuckle.

"I'm sure glad I could help get you to her sooner at least. I hope she'll be alright."

"Thank you, and thanks again for the ride. I know it's not exactly popular to pick up strangers these days, but…"

"Actually I'm glad for the company. I travel so much for work and rarely get to speak to someone unless I'm trying to sell them something." The lines on the road started to blur once more. "If you don't mind, I think I'm gonna stop at that rest station up ahead and stretch my legs. I need to get the old circulation flowing again."

"No, that's fine. You're saving me so much time as it is. Besides, I wouldn't mind using the bathroom myself."

The exit came up quickly and he followed the ramp to the vacant parking lot. Off in the distance there were two semi trucks, but no people or other cars could be seen. As the driver got out and stretched, Phil made his way to an oversized map and appeared to be checking on their progress. Out of the corner of his eye he could see the driver make his way to the men's room. The driver entered and noticed that half the lights were broken or burnt out. He wondered to himself why all rest stops smelled the same. The smell of stale urine and well water filled his nostrils and he decided to breathe through his mouth instead. His feet stuck to the floor as he walked across the room to the urinal. He was wondering when the last time someone actually flushed or cleaned the urinal he was using when he noticed Phil had entered the room. The door closed followed by a click, but he thought little of it.

Walking over to the sink he noticed that the trash cans were full of paper towels but of course the dispensers were all empty. He didn't like the hand dryers because they took too long. For a moment he considered just not washing his hands but with Phil coming over he didn't want to seem unsanitary to his guest. He pumped some liquid soap in the palm of his hand and called out, "So Phil, how far are we from your..."

His voice was silenced as he felt a leather belt tighten around his throat and could no longer breathe. He tried in vain to squeeze his slippery wet fingers between the belt and his throat but it was too tight. Looking in the mirror in wonderment at what was happening to him he saw the reflection of his own reddening face, eyes watering, gasping for air that would not come. Over his shoulder he could see Phil, staring back at him, looking intently into his eyes. There was an excitement, a thrill in Phil's eyes that was not there before. That thrill grew as he watched the life drain from his victim.

The salesman's body gave a final twitch and went limp. Phil let it drop to the floor with a thud that echoed throughout the room. He regained control of his breathing which had accelerated with his heart rate and took a moment to stare now into his own reflection. He watched as that brief moment of stimulation faded away and his face returned to it's normal, lifeless existence.

Looking down at the lifeless form that now lay at his feet, he put his belt back on and headed towards the door. He covered his hand with his shirt sleeve and with a click, again turned the lock before walking out into the cool night air. Taking a lung full he looked in every direction and saw that there was still no one around. The trucks were where he had last seen them and in truth, someone could have come along at any moment and tried to enter that bathroom. They still could. The very thought of that had added to the thrill. The risk made everything more intense and he liked it.

As he stood alone in the silence of night, the thrill faded and his more practical side took over. He had no way to predict his time table this time, there were too many variables, too many unknowns. He was not ready to be caught and therefore needed to get moving. The main road was not a good choice. By now they would know he was a drifter and he would be picked up quickly once the body was discovered. He made his way around the building and headed into the woods. It was going to be a rough night.

****

Taking one last bite of the frozen pizza he had heated up, Jackson leafed through the last of the files spread out before him on the coffee table. After spending the entire evening going over pictures, records and histories of various criminals and their crimes he felt no closer to his goal. Each of them had something in common with who they were looking for, but none of them were the whole package. Strange as it seemed, even to him, he felt that he had a very clear understanding of this latest killer. In some way, he could feel the passion, the need behind the killing. He reminded himself to be careful. It was far too early to form such strong convictions and that almost always led to narrowing the search without properly eliminating other possibilities.

He thought about what he had said to Edwards when Bill had referred to the killer as a "he". Sure the odds were that it was a male they were looking for and he had mostly said that as an educational tool and a way to humble Edwards, keep him in his place and show him how little he knew about actual police work. But it was more than that. It was actually good advice and he decided to take it himself.

As he closed the file and sat back on the sofa exhausted he had the strangest sensation. Perhaps it was just that he was reminded that to narrow the search the right way, someone else would likely have to die, or maybe it was just his mind filled with all the information he had looked through for the last two hours. Whatever it was, the feeling was undeniable. He felt that somehow he knew, the killer had struck again.

He tried to shake the feeling and with his eyes burning from overuse, sleep began to take over. Slipping off his shoes he took one more swallow of the now tepid water, lay down and awkwardly reached up to turn off the lamp. His hand fumbled around with little strength or effort but his eyes lost the will to stay open and the arm fell to his side before accomplishing its goal. It didn't matter though, he was already asleep.

Chapter Six

The alarm went off. It was not loud, but had a tone that was just irritating enough to make it nearly impossible to ignore. Trevor Simmons was not asleep, but lay in his bed staring at the ceiling. It was a plain white ceiling, no tiles with holes to count, but he was quite familiar with even the slightest imperfections. He reached over and shut off the alarm. No need to hit the snooze button. Even though he had plenty of time before he needed to get out of bed, he hadn't snoozed in weeks. Sitting up in the dimly lit bedroom he looked out the window to see the sun beginning to rise over the gray roof of his neighbor's house, a house very similar to his own.

Trevor lived in a "good" neighborhood surrounded by "good" people, whatever that meant. That's what he'd been told by the real estate agent and again by his neighbors when he had moved in. To him they were just slightly different versions of the same people, much like their houses. Sure, crime was low, but so was the excitement. In truth, nothing much happened in Trevor's neighborhood, nothing worth mentioning anyway. As he looked out at the row of houses that looked more like the repeated reflection in a mirror than unique homes, it occurred to him that whoever wrote that story The Stepford Wives, was able to predict the future every bit as well as Nostradamus.

With a sigh, Trevor pulled the covers off his lower half and swung his legs to the side of the bed where his slippers awaited his feet. The house had hardwood floors in almost every room, and though he agreed that they look nice, they can be cold on bare feet first thing in the morning. Slipping them on he made his way to the bathroom to use the toilet and brush his teeth. He had showered the night before, hoping the warm water would sooth him into such a state of relaxation, he would not be able to have anything less than a good night's sleep. It didn't work. Insomnia is a strange thing. Sometimes people cannot sleep because they have too much on their minds, other times, like in Trevor's case, they have too little. Nothing was keeping Trevor from sleeping, literally.

On the floor at the foot of the bed sat a suitcase and garment bag, packed the night before. He was afraid that if he put it off until morning, his mind would go over the list of what he needed to take again and again and he would be denied sleep. Another plan with less than positive results. He looked at the clock then down at his luggage and sank to the bed asking himself "Is this really it? Is this all life has to offer?"

A suit lay on the bed next to him, complete with tie, shirt, socks, underwear and a pair of shoes on the floor. It looked almost as though someone had been wearing it and then just disappeared, leaving just a lifeless shell. Trevor could identify with the suit and wondered if it would actually have any more life in it even after he put it on. He went through the motions of getting dressed, feeling like a robot could live his life and it wouldn't make a difference to anyone.

Once you earn a degree, get a decent job, buy that fancy car and a house in a good neighborhood, what do you hope to achieve before retirement? What is supposed to fill the adult years once the typical goals have been met? Trevor could not answer those questions. He figured that the opportunity for marriage had long passed him by. He liked women, had asked out a few at one time or another, but nothing panned out. Now he was set in his ways and didn't think he could change to accommodate another human being with their own plans and ideas.

He traveled too much to have a pet, though he found he envied the life of a dog. Dogs live life to the fullest for ten or fifteen years, then they die. They make their own entertainment and find dry biscuits to be a major source of enjoyment. Many times if they get sick or hurt, they get to go to the doctor and just fall asleep, forever. No worries, no time to become bored with life, wanting nothing more than a pat on the head.

On occasion, one of his neighbors would invite him over for a cookout or party of some kind. He would sit and listen to other people have conversations, most of them couples or families with whom he had nothing in common but an address. The awkwardness of feeling completely out of place compounded by watching children running around screaming and ignoring their parents would not only prompt him to make an excuse to leave, but strengthen his resolve to never have children of his own.

The few dates he had gone on never went as he had pictured them. Seeing movies and television shows made dating seem so easy, but in reality they were hard work, for him at least. Were they supposed to be? Trying to keep a conversation going was on the verge of painful. He didn't have the kind of personality to be entertaining and had no clue what women liked to do on a date. The date would end politely with both knowing a second one would not be coming.

There was a woman at work that he had become interested in. She was not particularly attractive but she seemed nice enough. She was a bit overweight, and Trevor thought this might mean she had not been asked out very often and may be more open to the attentions of a male suitor, even if it was him. Day after day he tried to find things about her that he liked and eventually willed himself into having feelings for her. In his mind he pictured himself walking up to her and asking her out. She in turn would be so flattered and grateful for his attention, she would of course say yes. He worked up the courage to ask her out right before going on one of his many trips, figuring that would give him several days to plan the date with a good excuse for why it must be delayed. Filled with confidence he made his way towards her desk only to find several of the women standing around her talking excitedly. He stopped in his tracks and tried to take in the scene. On her desk was a bouquet of beautiful long stemmed roses. Then it happened. She held out her left hand and all the other women leaned in and said oooh and ahhh. It was clear that she had just gotten engaged. He was too late. Swallowing his feelings he turned and walked away. Now he would be dwelling on something else on his trip. She wasn't that attractive anyway he thought to himself, bitterly.

He had very few friends and none of them close. Those at work that he knew best, like him, traveled frequently and weren't much more than acquaintances. Trevor was an auditor for a major corporation with locations all over the United States. At least once a month he would drive to another state and spend several days going over the financial records of that particular branch. People there were generally friendly to him, but it was obvious that he was an outsider. At the end of the day they would go home to their families or go out with friends and he would go back to the motel room or catch a movie alone. At first, this bothered him a great deal, but as the years went by he got used to it. Now that was what bothered him. He was used to being alone and bored.

As he stood before the mirror, straightening his tie before leaving for this latest business trip, he resolved to figure out what it would take to feel alive again, to stop merely going through the motions of the life he had been sold. There had to be a way.

Luggage in hand, he went out the front door, locking it behind him, and made his way across the lawn to the driveway. Sitting before him was a blue Ford sedan. It was a company car that he used for traveling and routine driving. Inside the garage sat a fully loaded, polished and clean late model Lexus, the reward of his labors. It was reserved for special occasions and as such, it had not been driven for some time. At least the mileage stayed low he figured.

Perhaps he should reconsider the whole idea of marriage. If he was worried about someone coming into his life and changing everything, well that might be just what he needed. Something had to change. He needed that spark to ignite him and give him life. If marriage was what made everyone else happy, maybe it would work for him too. That was a thought. It would take courage to overcome his fear of rejection and put himself on the line like that again, but maybe it was time.

He placed the luggage in the trunk and tossed his briefcase on the passenger seat. Sitting behind the wheel he double checked the directions and then turned the ignition. With one last look at the row of houses, reflective of the days of his adult life, not being able to distinguish one from the other but for the number, he knew one thing was for sure. One way or another, by the end of this trip, he would have a plan to make some changes and begin to really live his life.

****

In another bedroom, in another town, a very different man with very different circumstances took full advantage of every minute he had to sleep, and even a few he shouldn't have. Detective Bill Edwards was someone who wanted to get the absolute most out of life, even if it killed him. Always on the go, he couldn't stand sitting still. He loved women. He loved excitement. From an early age he knew that spending his days sitting behind a desk would likely kill him. What he needed was a job where he was never in the same place or doing the same thing from one day to the next.

There is a cycle that television goes through that determines what type of shows will be on. Someone will have the idea for a show and get the right combination of writers and stars and before long, every network will follow with their own version, trying to outdo the original. In this way, genres were created that reappear over time. Medical dramas will be popular for a while, then are replaced by court room dramas, and in turn are replaced by shows about police officers. It was during one of the latter that Bill grew up. Every show in prime time was seemingly about the lives and adventures of police officers. It was only natural that this would appeal to him. Every episode had them in a new place with different people solving interesting cases and always demanding respect. They looked so powerful in their suits, guns on their belts and flashing a badge. Women seemed to be drawn to them. If he became a cop, he would have everything he wanted in life.

As a senior in high school he spent much of his time looking through the local papers to find out which police departments would be testing and what the requirements were for each. Half way through the year he turned eighteen and the testing began. The first one was difficult for him. In his mind he felt it would just come natural to him, after all, he had watched every police show religiously for years. The test was more like a real test, similar to a final at school. He did not make the list of acceptable candidates.

After that he had a better idea of what he was in for and although the tests varied slightly from one department to the next, they were all basically the same thing. He became an expert and it paid off. The city department was testing, something they only do once every two or three years. There were two positions open in the near future, everyone else would go on the list and have to wait. Ten thousand applicants showed up. Bill was so discouraged that he almost turned around and went home. It was his dream to be a big city cop and one day a detective. He decided to stay.

All the tests he had taken at other departments were great practice and he used every bit of knowledge he had gained to his advantage. When all was said and done, he came in fifth place once the points were totaled. Now he had to wait. The top two went on to more testing, moving him into third on the waiting list. One of the first two failed the physical. He moved up to number two. A health concern forced an officer to retire early, number one. A year later, while working as a security guard at night and going to community college during the day, Bill received a call. Another position had opened up. He was on his way.

While completing his associate's degree in criminal law, he took the final three tests. Those included a physical test which he passed with ease, a psychological test which was more difficult and finally an interview with a panel of police officers and city officials. This third test was where many men crumbled. However, Bill was so full of enthusiasm with his goal right there in front of him that his confidence won them over. He made it.

The academy came next. It was not the same as college. Although he remained optimistic, during most of the time he spent earning his degree, he had no real prospects for becoming a police officer. He preferred the classroom to his night job and enjoyed feeling like he was working towards something. Once he was in the academy, he knew that it was all that stood between him and finally getting where he always wanted to be. His mind wandered, always on the future, and he found it difficult to pay attention. As a result he became somewhat of a class clown, though usually not on purpose.

The social aspects of the academy were more to his liking. He flirted with the women and dated a few of them. He was part of a group that formed and began going out after a long day of training. They sat and talked about their day, what they had learned and what it would be like when they hit the streets for real. They studied together, drank together and graduated together, swearing eternal friendship.

Of course it didn't take long for that to become a faint memory. For a while they got together once a month or so, but when you are a new police officer, you work many different shifts, have different days off and trying to make plans is nearly impossible. Several new police officers from different departments trying to coordinate a time when none of them are working can't be done. It went from the whole group, to a smaller group, to phone calls and eventually nothing. After they had been on the force longer than they were in the academy, it no longer seemed worth the effort.

After graduation and a party that lasted two days, it was with great eagerness and anticipation that Bill walked through the doors of the police station. His brand new uniform pressed and cleaned, his badge and shoes polished, he was ready to go out and fight crime. He expected them to hand him the keys to a patrol car and let him hit the streets. The shift began with a meeting to let all the officers know what was happening in the city, who to look for and give a general idea of what was expected of them that day. Bill took notes furiously so he would be ready to hit the ground running. The meeting came to an end and Bill headed for the door.

"Hey rookie!" someone shouted. Bill didn't pay any attention, his mind focused on getting to work. "Rookie! Edwards, I'm talking to you." It was the shift commander who had led the meeting. This time he had Bill's attention. Stopping in his tracks and turning towards the voice, Bill noticed people were chuckling as they walked past him.

"Yes sir?"

"You see any other rookies in here?"

"No sir" Bill replied without bothering to look around.

"So either you're deaf or stupid enough to try and ignore me, is that it?"

"No sir. I'm just anxious to get started and I'm afraid I didn't realize you were talking to me. I apologize." Bill was making his way towards the podium where the shift commander was joined by an older officer with gray hair.

"Whatever, Rookie. I don't know where you think you were headed, but this here is Sergeant O'Toole. He's our resident training officer. Do you know what that means?"

"Nice to meet you sergeant" Bill said to O'Toole, "No sir, I'm afraid I don't."

"It means that he has the misfortune of training young punks like you."

"But sir, I already went to the academy." This was met with great laughter by both of the other men. Bill half smiled, but was bewildered.

"They don't teach you squat at the academy. Your real training starts today. You will be spending the next sixteen weeks with Sgt. O'Toole here. He's going to show you everything you need to know to be a cop."

Bill's heart sank. He thought the training was over. He was ready to live the dream. He wanted to fight crime, make a name for himself, make a difference. How could he do that riding along in a car with an old man? His thoughts were betrayed by his face.

"Come on son, it's not that bad. I may even let you drive, someday" O'Toole said, which brought another round of laughter at Bill's expense.

It *was* that bad. Bill's every move was watched and graded. O'Toole treated him like a kid, not a cop. He called him son, sonny, lad and other names that made him feel more like he was spending the day with his grandfather than fighting crime. As the newest officer on the force, he found little sympathy and few friends. The only thing pulling him through was knowing that at the end of sixteen weeks, he would finally be on his own. Then it would all be worth it.

It wasn't. With a pat on the back and one final condescending comment, Officer Bill Edwards was finally unleashed on the streets, criminals beware. It took less than a week for him to figure out that cops spend most of their time driving around the same streets over and over, day after day. They hand out speeding tickets and assist at accident scenes, but do very little in the way of real police work, as he defined it. Every part of his day had to be logged, there were reports for everything which meant hours of every shift were spent on paperwork. This was not what he signed up for and he wanted out.

He had worked too hard to let it all go to waste by walking away. It was then that he saw a posting at the station that read:

Detective test
Must be a sworn officer for at least five years
Need recommendation of current detective
Degree preferred

It went on to give the time and date of the test and other relevant information. This could be the answer he was looking for. It would be a few years before he could test, but with a new goal in mind, he could bide his time and make it through day by day.

Over the next few years he spent his time building up a reputation as a decent police officer. Meeting his quota of traffic tickets every month, handling his fair share of accidents, taking four hours out of his shift occasionally to process a drunk driver and providing back up when needed showed that he could be part of the team. He worked with the detectives every chance he got and built up contacts that he would use later as references.

Friendships were harder to come by. He had gained the trust of the other officers, but they knew his heart was not with them. Dreams of leaving them behind for the glamorous world of the big city detectives filled him and it shone through. The closer he got to taking the test, the more he placed himself in the no man's land between his present and future. The detectives didn't accept him as one of them because he had yet to earn it. The patrol officers felt insulted and offended at his attitude towards them as most of them would never progress any further in their own careers. He was alone.

Finally the day arrived. Everything was in place. He had his recommendations, had fulfilled his five years of service and had studied until his brain felt so full he thought information would soon drip out of his ears. With little sleep but plenty of caffeine he arrived at the station and along with several other applicants, entered the room usually used for briefings. Several tables had been set up. Test booklets with a proper distance between them to prevent cheating had been placed throughout the room. Bill took a seat with one of the booklets in front of him, written clearly on the front were specific instructions not to touch it before being told to do so. Almost as an echo to Bill's thoughts, a man at the front of the room welcomed people into the room, asked them to take seats and instructed them not to touch the booklets. Bill thought to himself, "If they plan to be detectives, shouldn't they be expected to figure these things out for themselves?" He chuckled to himself.

It was not a pleasant two hours, but Bill was ready. He worked his way through the questions, able to recall much of the information he had studied so hard at in the previous weeks. When it was all said and done, his finger sore from pressing with the pencil, he wiped the sweat from his head and confidently closed the booklet. Sometimes it is hard to get a feel for how well you do on a test. There were generally questions with more than one interpretation and it all depended on whether yours matched that of the answer key. Bill felt good though. The effort had paid off and he was certain that he had passed this phase of the process.

The results would not be posted for two days. If you passed, there would be an appointment time next to your name to indicate when you would stand before the committee and face a series of questions and scenarios. If you didn't pass, your name would be followed with one word, FAIL. For the most part, the other cops were pretty good about not hassling each other for failing the detective's exam. Those who were still uniform officers had failed it themselves, were not eligible to take it or didn't have the desire or confidence to take it. Therefore they were reluctant to tease someone who put themselves on the line and gave it a shot. Those that had passed it knew how hard it was first hand, and frankly most of them didn't really care enough to make an issue of it. They had better things to do. Bill was worried that he had become so focused on leaving his uniformed comrades behind that if he failed, they would be less considerate to him.

The next two days seemed to last forever. Thoughts of failure haunted his waking thoughts and entered his every dream. It got to the point that if he didn't make detective, he would likely walk straight into the Chief's office and resign on the spot. It had become an all or nothing situation for him. It would be easier to change his life's direction than to stop where he was. He was too driven to become idle.

Two days later he tried to keep his mind clear from the time his alarm went off until he was walking into the station and for the most part it worked. When he stepped through the door and made his way up the half staircase to where the bulletin board hung on the wall his heart and mind went crazy at once. A flurry of thoughts came to mind so fast he could not keep them straight. He thought of how wonderful it would be to make detective. Before that thought was complete he pondered what his next career would be if he quit. The detectives from all his favorite television shows flooded through his mind with him standing next to each of them, a smile from ear to ear, but the image was shattered with him standing before the captain and handing over his badge. His heart pumped with such fury it hurt. All of this took place in a fraction of a second as he froze momentarily before completing the stairs to the hallway that held his fate.

He raised his head in time to see one of the other officers frantically searching for his own name. His expression changed as the finger came to a stop on the sheet of paper before him. It looked to Bill like he might pass out as the blood drained from his face. Another officer from the other direction had approached and slapped him on the back while uttering some words of comfort that Bill could not quite make out.

Bill thought briefly about turning around and fleeing into the safety of not knowing what was behind his own name on that paper. As it was, his feet refused to move forward without great effort. He waited for the area to clear. If it was bad news, he didn't want to share the moment with anyone. His feet painstakingly moved him towards the wall one step at a time until he gradually had achieved full speed. He paused in front of the list, closed his eyes and took a deep breath. Much like removing a bandage from the hairiest part of the leg, he decided to just get it over with quickly. He opened his eyes, placed his finger to the paper and followed the names down to his own. His eyes had begun to well with tears at the whole experience as it had almost gotten to be too much to handle. His finger slid to the right of his name and his eyes read EDWARDS, WILLIAM; Monday 9:00am.

His brain took several seconds to decipher what that meant enough to allow the rest of him to realize just what he was seeing. Then like fog being burned away by a bright morning sun, his thoughts became clear. A smile crept its way onto his face and his heart leaped for joy. He had done it. Down the hall he faintly heard someone say congratulations Edwards. He mumbled a thank you as he stood still staring at the wall in disbelief.

It was hard to concentrate on his job the rest of the week. He was elated and could sense with his every action that this would all soon be behind him, beneath him. Of course it wasn't over yet. He still had to stand before the firing squad as they were called and show how well he stood up under pressure. But he knew that once again, with his goal laid out before him, nothing would stand in his way.

Monday morning came and again he was in a suit instead of a uniform. He fully expected that by the end of the day he would be leaving the uniform behind forever. Sitting in a chair in the hallway outside the Chief's office he anxiously awaited his turn. Some minutes after nine in the morning, the door opened and another hopeful emerged. Covered in sweat and out of breath, he looked relieved to just get out of the room alive. The Firing Squad, Bill thought to himself. Before he would allow his confidence to waver his name was called and he entered the room.

"Close the door behind you please" the Chief said to him. On the Chief's right side were a city council member and one of the detectives. On his left were two men Bill had not seen before. "Officer Edwards is it?" the Chief asked.

"Yes sir."

"And you believe you are ready to become a detective for this fine city, is that what I am to understand?"

"Yes sir, I am."

"How long have you been on the force son?" the council member asked.

"Five years ma'am."

"Is that all?" the detective scoffed. "You're not ready. Do you know how long it takes most guys to become a detective?"

"No sir, I don't"

"On average it takes ten years."

"I'm not average sir." Bill began to relax as he saw through the game. He felt certain that this was a test of wills, to see how he withstood pressure and to make sure he was confident in his decision to pursue this level in his career. Inside he smiled to himself. If he could handle the next few moments, he was in. He thought of the officer that was in here just moments ago. He felt compassion for him, but was thankful to him as well. It would only make him look that much better.

"Kind of cocky aren't you?" the detective responded.

"No sir, just confident in my own abilities."

"Interesting. There is nothing wrong with confidence young man, however, it takes a great deal more than that to be a good detective" this from one of the men Bill did not know.

"Yes sir, I agree. May I add that I don't plan to be a good detective, but a great one."

"I think you have an attitude, that's what I think" the detective said. "It's not like on TV you know, all glitz and glamour. We don't wrap up every case in an hour or less and if we get shot, we aren't guaranteed to survive just because the ratings are high. We have to work hard, deal with scum and watch our backs."

"I understand sir, it's the real deal. I'm ready." Bill tried hard to get images of Starsky and Hutch out of his mind.

"There's something else too, and from what I hear, this might be tough for you. When you're a detective you have to work as a team. You have to work with other detectives, uniform officers, other departments, you can't just hot dog it and do it all on your own. You sure you can handle that Officer Edwards?"

"Yes sir." This time Bill had to force himself to sound like he meant it. The detective had hit upon a weakness and after a moment of looking Bill in the eye, he knew it.

"Are you sure about that? You don't exactly have the reputation of playing well with others around here." The detective continued to press the issue. He saw that Bill's guard had begun to crumble, even if almost imperceptible. "In your five years on the force, do you have even one close friend that's a cop?"

Bill looked him in the eye and then quickly turned away. For the first time he did not have an immediate response. He wasn't sure what approach to take but ultimately decided that telling the truth was likely the only way he would not slip up and become inconsistent. "No sir, not close friends. I might point out that I have no enemies either. I have been able get along with those around me and do my job."

"Still, that makes you somewhat of a loner doesn't it? I mean five years is an awfully long time to not have one real friend wouldn't you say?"

"I think that is a matter of opinion and I have to let my record speak for itself sir. I am here to do a job, not make friends. However, if you feel strongly that making friends is a necessary part of being a detective I will make it a point to do so."

The detective was not quite prepared for the response and now he was the one to not respond right away. After a moment he opened his mouth as if to reply, but nothing came out. With a sigh and a smile he sat back in his chair and appeared satisfied with the results of his interrogation.

"Okay I think that is enough on that subject. I see here that you do in fact have an above average record in regards to your career here. You also did quite well on the written exam." The Chief had taken over the discussion and was leafing through Bill's file that from what he could discern had everything they knew about him right up to that very moment. "In looking at the recommendation you gave us from one of our detectives he states that you appear to be a capable officer who's ready to take the next step. He expresses some concern, which we have alluded to here already, that perhaps you are not the most personable fellow in regards to your relationship with those around you, but that you are respected among your peers."

"Thank you sir." Bill wasn't sure that it was the proper response and from the look he was given, the chief wasn't sure either, but neither spoke of it.

After that the mood in the room shifted and the real interview began. Scenarios were laid out, questions asked and after thirty minutes it was all over. With a sense of relief that hit him like the air that hits your face on a hot day when you go for some ice, Bill Edwards left the room. His fate was still uncertain, but he truly felt he had done all he could do. Now it was up to a group of virtual strangers to decide if it had been good enough. It was only as he walked away that he realized that no one told him how, or when for that matter, he would find out.

He didn't have to wait long. That evening as he sat in front of the television but not really watching it, his mind both racing and exhausted, the phone rang. He absentmindedly picked up the receiver and mumbled a greeting of some kind. He instantly recognized the voice on the other end as that of the Chief. "Edwards?" he asked.

"Yes sir" came Bill's reply sitting bolt upright.

"You can turn in your uniforms tomorrow at the supply room."

"Excuse me sir?" Bill's mind scrambled. For a moment he thought he had actually told someone of his intention to quit if he didn't pass the test. With baited breath he waited for the next words to come through the phone.

"Well you won't be needing them anymore will you?" That didn't help. He held his breath and hoped there would be more. The Chief must have sensed what was going on and added "Relax son, you made it. Welcome to the detective squad. As of tomorrow you wear a suit to work."

"Thank you sir, thank you so much" he finally exhaled.

"Nice job. Report to Lt. Ferguson after you turn in your gear."

Bill started to reply but the line went dead. Perhaps there were more hopefuls to call with good news. He had no idea how many had actually made it past the written exam. One for sure, but if there were others he did not know. He sat back and relaxed and noticed that it had been some time since he was able to do just that. The anxiety and bad thoughts melted away and his eyes closed before he even knew it.

The next morning he awoke with excitement, something he was not accustomed to. After a thorough shower, he styled his hair and put on his best suit. In his closet hung a black trench coat that he had never worn, aside from trying it on. To him it was the symbol of that next step, of becoming a real detective. With great care and near reverence he guided the coat off the hanger one shoulder at a time and slid his arms into the proper holes, feeling the cool silk lining against the skin of his hand and wrist as it whispered by. A few minor adjustments to make sure his suit jacket found its way into the coat's shoulders and he was ready to look in the full length mirror. His eyes searched his reflection from head to toe and back before meeting their own image as he stared at himself eye to eye. "You're ready. The future begins today."

The station looked somehow different that day. He climbed the stairs as he had done for five years, but with a spring in his step. Walking past the briefing room he had sat in at the beginning of every shift it felt like he was a college student visiting his former high school. He heard an occasional

"Good luck" Or "Nice job" but no sincere hand shakes or pats on the back. What good would it have done to build a relationship with any of them anyways, he would just have had to leave them behind he thought. He had a fresh start with a new group of people and perhaps he would make friends now that he was with others that truly were his peers.

He gratefully handed in those old uniforms and made his way to the second floor, where the real police work was done. Inside the room where just days ago he was taking a test, he found a seat near the front and excitedly awaited his first briefing as a detective. Several other men and women had made their way around the tables and had begun to take seats. The conversations that blurred together into one cloud of noise continued at full force and gave Bill a sense of separation because he was not part of any of them, nor was he invited to be. He looked around and did not see anyone else that was wearing a uniform prior to that morning. Was he the only one that made it?

Lt. Paul Ferguson walked in and placed a folder on the temporary podium at the front of the room. Clearing his throat, he opened the folder and called for everyone to quiet down. "I won't keep you long" he continued. "There are a few highlights we should go over before you get on your way. Cooper and Gaines, nice job on wrapping up your latest case." There was a pause for a brief round of applause and the two nodded in acknowledgement. "We are still getting a lot of complaints about break-ins in district six so keep an eye out. Oh, and we have one new detective joining us today." It sounded like an after thought and it didn't help that the Lt. had to look through his papers to find Bill's name. "Bill Edwards. Everyone please be sure to welcome him and help make his transition a comfortable one. I guess that's it, get to work."

Bill sat and waited for everyone to stop by and say hello, welcome him, but no one did. Instead the conversations started back up and the group filed out through the door at the back of the room. When it was clear that he could sit there all day without anyone approaching, he stood and turned towards the door.

"Edwards, hang on a minute." Ferguson was finishing a conversation with one of the detectives and gathering his papers, then he turned his attention to

Bill. "Don't take it personally, they never actually welcome anyone. I always ask, but they never do. Anyway, you are going to be working with Detective Simeon Jackson." The Lt. gestured towards a middle aged man sitting towards the back and the only other person in the room not talking to anyone. "Jackson will be showing you the ropes for a while and teaching you everything you need to know to be a great cop."

Bill tried to speak but nothing came out. He couldn't believe it. He was training all over again. This was a nightmare. Worse yet, a reoccurring nightmare. Ferguson guided him over to Jackson by the arm.

"Detective Jackson, let me introduce to you, your new student, Bill Edwards."

Jackson stood up, all five foot seven of him and extended a hand. With a warm smile he added "Bill, it's nice to be working with you."

"Same here" Bill managed to reply. He felt his heart all the way down in his shoes it had sunk so hard and fast. When would he be treated like a grown up, capable of just doing his job and being left alone? As those last words reverberated around in his mind, he was reminded of what was said at his detective interview. Why did it always come back to him wanting to be alone? Perhaps that was something he needed to work on. Still, he didn't need to have some middle aged man telling him what to do and treating him like a kid. Couldn't he just have a partner, an equal?

These thoughts made it difficult for him to look Jackson in the eye. When he did manage a glance in his direction, he got the feeling the detective was analyzing him, creating a psychological profile in his mind to use against him later. Ferguson was babbling about something Bill was not interested in and finally left them alone. Bill waited to see if Jackson would give a speech, play the getting to know each other game, or just welcome him to the squad by introducing him to the others who had long since left the room. As it turned out he did none of them, but simply said "Let's get started" and walked away.

Now here it was, six months later and Bill felt like a flunky. He always did the menial tasks no one else wanted to do. He spent little if any time at actual crime scenes, spoke to few possible witnesses and had yet to chase a bad guy. The worst part was, this was an open-ended training situation. Before he at least knew how long he had to deal with his circumstances before he would either move on or fail. This was different. It was up to Jackson's discretion whether he was ready to move on. He didn't know how he could ever prove that to him when he wasn't allowed to do anything of consequence.

Turning off the alarm, after hitting the snooze button for the third time, Edwards made a slow and deliberate attempt to open his eyes. They burned as if sometime during the night someone had glued them to his eyelids. He could actually feel the swollen red veins as the morning sun seemed to dry up what little moisture was there to begin with. It might have felt worse if he had taken sandpaper and rubbed his eyes, but not by much. Suddenly Jackson's words from the night before echoed in his mind, "I want you fresh for tomorrow."

With a choice word or two muttered under his breath he kicked off his covers and rubbed his eyes, hoping to induce the return of moisture and stop the burning. Looking at the clock he quickly figured out that he had been able to manage perhaps three hours of sleep. After taking a moment to marvel that he had figured out a mathematical problem in his current state he realized he had precious few minutes to wake up, clean up and get to the squad looking fresh and ready for whatever the day held for him. Knowing a shower would help immeasurably; he quickly turned on the water and jumped in. He scrubbed with a vigorous fury to both save time and awaken his senses. Moments later he jumped out and brushed his teeth while dripping all over the floor. Turning quickly his foot slipped on the now wet floor and he almost went down, catching himself on the sink. He toweled off quickly and used his foot on the towel to dry the floor, then ran into his bedroom to dress.

Wearing a clean suit and his now slightly worn trench coat, he ran out the front door of his townhouse, running a comb through his wet hair. Appearance was a source of pride for him, and he tried hard to look his best at all times. He jumped in the front seat of his department issued sedan and drove off with a screech from his tires, not twenty minutes after waking up. A true accomplishment he thought to himself with pride. As he drove along the city streets fatigue weighed him down in his seat, the adrenaline fading. These late nights of partying were getting harder to recover from. He immediately began searching for someplace he could get a free cup of strong coffee. That and a day of serious police work would be enough to get him through.

Chapter Seven

The morning sun was making its way over the skyline and beginning to warm the air. Long shadows stretched across the police station parking lot around seven o'clock when Edwards pulled in and stopped in one of the spaces reserved for detectives. After his obligatory look in the mirror he stepped out of the car and looking across the lot noticed that Jackson still sat in his. Something seemed odd and caused Bill to pause for a moment. Jackson gave the appearance of sleeping as he sat with his head down and eyes closed. This seemed odd to Bill and he was tempted to do something, though he didn't know what, but just then his head lifted up and his eyes opened.

Edwards decided to hang back for a second and see what would happen next. Jackson left his car and moved toward the station as if nothing had happened and Bill began to doubt himself. Suddenly the idea came to Bill that this would be a good opportunity to check out Jackson's front seat. He started to walk that way but moved too soon, for he caught Jackson's eye, who changed direction and cut him off before he made it very far. Disappointed, he knew the mystery would not be solved, so he resigned himself to joining Jackson and entering the station together.

"So what do we have planned for today?" Edwards began, eager to know why he needed to be fresh. Thoughts of great excitement played on his mind as he waited for the reply.

"That depends" was Jackson's response.

"On what?"

"What we hear from the evidence technician, the autopsy results, any new leads that might have developed overnight. There's no telling where the day could take us. How's that for exciting?"

"Oh yeah, thrilling." Edwards hopes were once again dashed. It looked to be another boring day of phone calls and research.

The station was alive with activity. It was time for the midnight patrol shift to come off duty and the day shift to begin. This led to many lingering uniformed officers standing around. Some relaxed, having finished their shift and in no hurry to be anywhere. They might be going to work out before heading home. Others liked to go for breakfast, which to them might be considered dinner. Either way, it was too early in the morning to go out drinking.

Then there were the ones just starting their shift who were no more anxious to get to work. They stood around drinking coffee, talking to each other and stalling as long as they could before one by one making their way out to make the streets safer.

There was a sitting area for people waiting to see an officer, bailing out a loved one, or any number of reasons that average and not so average citizens would need to sit at the police station. A table with coffee and donuts was along the wall and always a hub of activity. Across from the sitting area was a long reception desk, the kind that forced you to look up at whoever was behind it like a child speaking to their parent. This gave the person behind the desk a false sense of power that worked pretty well on most people. Something in the human psyche makes most people feel inferior if they have to look up to speak to someone. Take Napoleon for example. They even named a complex after him. Would history have taken a different turn if Napoleon were six feet tall? What if Abraham Lincoln were five feet tall?

Jackson and Edwards entered the station and through the crowd saw Dan Besson, the evidence technician. To those who knew him, Dan was a brainy, loner type. His social skills were developed from years of looking for DNA samples on inanimate objects, often staring at a piece of furniture for hours at a time, going over every fiber. This led to him becoming somewhat of a recluse. He was never what would be called a people person to begin with and his job made him even less so. An extremely patient man, he paid great attention to detail and thrived on the endless search for evidence no one else could see. Many nights he didn't bother going home, but would hunker down and work all night. He kept a small army cot in his office and would take brief naps when his eyes simply refused to stay open. At times the work came in at a furious pace and all needed to be done yesterday. He didn't mind though, it gave him a sense of purpose and meaning. Lives hung in the balance and he was the one that could save them, the uncrowned champion that no one ever knew about. His name would not be the one in the news when a criminal was brought to justice. Families would not send him thank you cards for giving them closure or making them feel safe again. Those honors were reserved for the detectives, the public face of the police department.

Dan had spent the night in his lab carefully analyzing the towel taken from the motel bathroom, followed by the chair. He went over the fibers of the towel under a microscope painstakingly separating each strand one by one looking for a hair, flake of skin, dried blood or anything that might prove worthwhile. Unfortunately there was nothing to find. If the towel had been used, the only sign of it was the wrinkles.

The chair had been a different story. Although it took most of the night to check the various surfaces and fabrics, in the end it paid off. He decided to reward himself with a nap while he waited for the day shift to arrive. It was the commotion and noise of that very event that had awoken him and he was now pouring himself a cup of lousy tasting but much needed coffee when he saw the detectives enter.

With a look and slight raise of his coffee cup he called Jackson over to a vacant corner of the room. Edwards saw this and was expecting Jackson to send him on up to his desk while he talked to Besson. He anticipated another day that would feel more like a "Bring Your Child to Work" day than a partnership between fellow police officers trying to investigate a homicide. It was to his utter astonishment that Jackson tapped him on the arm and told him to come along. He had already begun to walk away and turned back almost stunned.

"Really, you want me to come too?" he asked, childlike.

"It's your case too isn't it? You need to hear this" Jackson said, knowing he had not only made his day, but had closed the gap between them just a little more. Bringing along a new detective was all about incremental steps carefully planned and used at points of greatest effect. Jackson was a master of knowing when someone needed to be broken down or built up.

He could stroke an ego or put someone in their place with the precision of a surgeon.

"Morning Dan, looks like you had a long night. Do you have something for us?" Jackson asked as they reached him.

"Sure do. It took some time, but I definitely found something" Dan replied and his face brightened visibly. He enjoyed these moments, getting to reveal what he had worked so hard on to the only people that might actually appreciate it.

Edwards watched Dan closely. On the surface he wanted to look interested and he was, but deep down he was watching to see if Dan would give any indication that he felt Edwards didn't belong there. Maybe it would be a questioning look or he would direct everything towards Jackson as if he was not even there, but Edwards saw no such sign. Later it would occur to him that Jackson was well respected, and perhaps others based how they treated him on how Jackson treated him. If Jackson thought he belonged in a conversation, it would not be questioned. At that very moment however, he just enjoyed feeling good about himself.

"I looked over the towel, but didn't find anything we can use. Between that and the other stuff in the room I'd say this guy is very thorough. However, he did make one mistake."

Edwards noticed the way Besson kept referring to the killer as a male and waited for Jackson to reprimand him, but knew he wouldn't. He reserved that pleasure for him alone. "What was it?" Jackson asked instead, a glimmer of hope detectable in his voice.

"Well I remembered you saying you thought there was a good chance he slept in the chair. That intrigued me, got me to thinking. After all, when we sleep, we let our guard down. We do things involuntarily. Accidents happen. This is very helpful in my profession. So I saved the chair for last, building up to the grand finale as it were."

"And?!" Edwards blurted out, his patience worn thin. He regretted it immediately, feeling he had just taken a step backwards and felt Jackson give him a look, though he didn't see it. It occurred to him that this was a big deal to Besson and he wanted to tell it his way.

"And...I found a sharp fabric tack sticking out near the top of the chair back. It sits right about where someone's face would be if they sat in the chair in a relaxed state. I analyzed it and found some tissue samples meaning..."

"Meaning we might have a sample of the killers DNA" Jackson finished for him. "Did you run any tests on it yet?" He asked as his enthusiasm built.

"Some. You are dealing with a Caucasian male, if indeed it belongs to the killer, and I'd say it probably does because it was fresh and obviously not the victim's."

"Thanks Dan, good work, let me know if you come up with anything else." Both Dan and Jackson were smiling now.

"Sure thing" Dan said and headed back to the lab.

Jackson and Edwards climbed the stairs to the detective squad with an added spring in their step, anxious now to see where the day might lead them. Jackson's smile continued but a thought came to Edwards that gave him a perplexed look.

"Okay, I don't get it. I mean I know we aren't supposed to make assumptions about the killer until you have the evidence to support it, but really, didn't you kinda figure it was a man to begin with?" Edwards was more concerned about learning than looking ignorant. This was a true sign of progress.

"Maybe, but now we know for sure" Jackson said as they reached their desks and began to settle in.

"Alright, so we confirmed what we both already suspected, fine, but how does this really help us?"

"It not only narrows our search with a definitive description which eliminates being open to certain possibilities that no longer fit, but it will also help us make an unshakable case when we do arrest him."

Edwards found it refreshing to be able to now use the various male pronouns, but he was still not convinced that they had made real progress and it showed on his face. Jackson continued "Do you know what the most frustrating part of our job is?"

"Research, paperwork, red tape..."

"Funny, but no. Sure it is difficult to catch criminals and there are so many that never get caught and we have to learn to live with it and move on, but the most frustrating thing is when we do catch them and watch them walk away because we couldn't prove they were guilty. We know they're guilty, the judge knows, the jury probably knows too, but if we can't eliminate that doubt, they walk. When you spend as much time and effort as we do to catch them only to see them go unpunished and probably do it again, nothing is more frustrating, believe me. This DNA will put someone at the scene of the murder, the night of the murder and that will be awfully hard to explain away."

"Okay, I see your point" and he did. Lesson learned. "Now all we have to do is catch him" he added.

"Exactly" Jackson found a note taped to his computer screen with a phone number on it followed by just one word, 'Call'. It had apparently been left by one of the detectives on the night shift. Knowing there was only one way to find out what it was about he reached for his phone.

"What do you have there?" Edwards asked seeing him staring at the paper inquisitively.

"Let's find out" Jackson said as he dialed the number and waited for a response. He picked up a pen and notepad so he would be ready to jot down any pertinent information and listened as the phone rang several times.

"State Police, Mackenzie speaking" said the rough voice on the other end of the line.

"This is Detective Jackson, I got a message to call you but frankly I don't know what it's about."

"Jackson huh, oh yeah, homicide right? I saw the notice about your motel victim. You say it was a strangler, drifter type as far as you can tell, correct?"

"We don't have the autopsy results to confirm that yet, but it looks like a pretty solid conclusion. Why, have you got something similar?"

"Not sure, could be I guess. Too early to say if there's any connection of course but last night a body was found in the john at a rest stop off the highway just outside of town. Looks like he was strangled. The car is still here. Nothing of value seems to have been taken, I mean the guy still has his wallet for crying out loud, so robbery seems to be out. The killer either had their own car or walked. As I say, no way to know for sure, but…"

"I understand. Probably worth checking out though. Where is this rest stop?" He wrote down the directions as Edwards anxiously looked on and thanked the officer as he hung up.

"So what is it?" Edwards inquired.

"We just might have that next victim. You ready to do some real police work?"

"You know I am."

Jackson filled Edwards in on the details on their way down the stairs. As they approached the parking lot an idea came to Edwards and he offered a suggestion. "We really don't need to take both cars do we?" He might get the chance to see that front seat and possibly solve two mysteries today, he thought.

"Good idea. We'll take yours, I'll navigate."

"Ummm, Actually I was thinking…" but Jackson was out the door and headed to the passenger side of Edwards car. Not able to come up with a reason to change his mind he reluctantly unlocked the doors and with a heavy sigh, looked over towards Jackson's car, just a few spaces away. It might as well have been miles. Why was it so difficult to just look in that car, he wondered to himself. Then he remembered where they were headed and the excitement returned. He jumped in the car and drove away with a squeal of the tires. Jackson just shook his head and marveled at his youth.

****

A short time later, Edwards' car was skidding to a stop and creating his trademark dust cloud. Jackson did not hesitate, but immediately made his way towards the men's room. Yellow police tape blocked off the entrance all the way out to and including the sedan that was parked nearby. A patrol officer stood at the door and stepped forward as they approached. "You Jackson?" the officer asked.

"Yes and this is Edwards" he replied as they both showed their identification.

"There's a detective inside waiting for you. You want me to stick around awhile?"

"If you've got time that would be great" Jackson said as he ducked under the tape and went through the doorway followed by Edwards.

The usual stench of the room itself, accompanied by the now decaying corpse was quick to hit them as they entered. Edwards' eyes were drawn directly to the victim on the floor. It was the first time he had actually been allowed on a murder scene and it was not what he thought it would be like. He was shaken by the way the body lay on the ground haphazardly, its eyes staring in wonder. To keep his composure he turned and looked around the room, trying to find something else to focus on.

Jackson had immediately begun to take in the whole scene. There was graffiti on the mirrors, the sinks were rusted and leaking, the garbage cans were overflowing with paper towels. Though it didn't look like the room had been cleaned in some time, it also looked unlikely that they would find much evidence either. Fingerprints were out because there was bound to be countless sets that would prove nothing. If there was any evidence to be found, it would be on the victim. All of this took only a moment. He then extended his hand and introduced himself. "Detective Jackson. Has anyone worked the room yet?"

"Fitzgerald, nice to meet you. Not the room per se, but we did a little background check on the victim here. Ralph Nemmers, salesman. The car is company owned and used by the victim. He was on the road for business. He had his wallet, watch and car keys on him. Briefcase and luggage in the car. Certainly doesn't look like robbery. Anyway, we stopped there because we were told it might relate to something you were working on, that true?"

"It might."

"Well I've got enough on my plate as it is. As far as I'm concerned, if you want it it's yours."

"I definitely want to see if there is a connection, so I guess we'll take it. I appreciate you preserving the scene."

Fitzgerald gave a nod and left the room, leaving Jackson and Edwards alone with the victim and an eerie silence fell upon them. Jackson looked over at the young detective and could see that he was doing his best to hide his discomfort. This was one of the defining moments that would either advance him or destroy him, a moment when reality was so real it was almost surreal. It was hard to have delusions about the homicide business when you are engulfed by the sights and smells of a dead body, a life ended at the hands of another, and that's what it did, engulf. The body projected itself to every corner of the room and played tricks with the minds of those around it. Suddenly everything that could be seen, heard, touched or smelled seemed to have some relation to the lifeless form that lay there motionless. With a sympathetic voice Jackson broke the silence "It's not the same in real life is it?" When Edwards could manage no verbal response, but merely a nod, he knew he could use a moment to collect himself before continuing. This was a fragile moment and Jackson handled it masterfully. "Let's get to work. We need to call the photographer and let him know this will be our case. I want the whole scene captured before we move anything. Why don't you step outside and see if you can get him out here. I'll give Dan a call so he can start working the scene as well. Hopefully he's awake."

Edwards was happy to step out and breathe some fresh air. He felt like he had been holding his breath the whole time he had been in that room. It took him a moment to regain his composure before calling the station. He was shaken, but proud of himself for not vomiting.

Inside Jackson listened at the window for a moment and was also pleased that the contents of Bill's stomach remained where they were. He just might make it, he thought to himself. Taking his cell phone from his coat pocket, he dialed Dan Besson at the lab.

"Dan, this is Jackson. You get any sleep since I saw you last?"

"A little."

"Good. Now that you are all rested up I have a new scene for you to work."

"Wonderful. What have you got?"

"A rest stop men's room. Doesn't look too promising, but it is only a few hours old. If you have a pen I'll give you directions." He did so. "The sooner you can get here the better." Jackson was about to hang up.

"Got it. Hang on a second, I was actually about to call you. The autopsy results are in. No rape and no tissue under the nails. The only defensive wounds are marks on the hands similar to rug burns which are consistent with your blanket theory. Seems your M.O. fits perfectly. The killer would have been able to pin down the victim, completely trapping her. She wouldn't have laid a hand on him."

"Thank goodness for that tissue sample you found on the chair. Again, nice work. So have they confirmed the cause of death?"

"Strangulation, as you said."

"Okay Dan, thanks for the update. Good job. I'll see you when you get here."

About that same time Edwards returned. "Photographer is on the way." Jackson looked at him and noticed that some of the color had returned to his face. He appeared ready to give it another try.

"Good, I got a hold of Dan and he's coming out as well." Jackson stood in the center of the room and briefly told him about the autopsy results, wanting to get Edwards working while he seemed strong enough.

As Edwards listened to what he said, he forgot about his fears of sharing the room with a corpse. A feeling of respect for Jackson grew to a new level, not just because for the first time he was experiencing the harsh realities of what Jackson and other detectives had to face so many times, but because he was beginning to realize just how well Jackson did his job. He saw how the results of the autopsy fit exactly with what Jackson had predicted from the beginning, beyond the cause of death to every detail of how the killing took place. He had heard rumors around the station about Jackson. People said he was able to somehow relive criminal acts by merely being in the place that they happened, like some sort of psychic or magical power. Of course he just laughed them off, but now he wondered, having seen evidence for himself. Magic was out of the question and psychic powers, well that was stretching it, but there was certainly something. He decided to ask. "I'm curious about something."

Jackson saw that he was looking stronger by the moment and no longer seemed too concerned about being in the room. He knew they had time before the others would arrive, so he played along. "What might that be?"

"I've heard certain rumors about you which I never gave much thought, but now I at least see where they come from. I need to know the truth."

"Alright, I'll do my best." Jackson wasn't sure where this was going. He had a colorful past to say the least and there could be any number of stories circulating about him.

"The way you figured out how that girl was killed, I mean every detail, how could you have known? Are you... I don't know, psychic or something?"

"Is that what they told you?" Jackson said through his laughter, relieved it wasn't something worse.

"Yeah, that or magic. They say you can see the crime happen in your mind by standing at the scene. Is that true?"

"Yes and no. Listen, I don't have psychic or magic powers I assure you."

"Then what is it?"

"I guess you could say I have an aptitude for it." Edwards gave him a puzzled look. "What I mean is that I have taken my education, my experience and whatever natural ability I have and over the years, developed it to the point that I can usually get a pretty good idea of what took place, not by drawing psychic energy or anything, but simply by looking at the clues and knowing how people think. There is a great deal of information that can be drawn from a crime scene if you just look at it in a practical way. All I do is clear my head and take in a scene until I begin to get a mental picture of what likely took place. I have been fortunate enough to be correct a few times. Disappointed?"

"Relieved. I didn't want to be working with a freak." They both laughed now. "Besides, that means you might be able to teach me to do it as well."

"True. Now you're sounding like someone who wants to become a real detective, not a movie star." And he was. Edwards had taken a big step and was ready to learn all he could from this man. "So let's get started with our preliminary observations while we wait. I want you to look around the room and tell me what we can learn."

Edwards looked down at the body and around the immediate vicinity. "It doesn't look like there was a big struggle. In fact it seems very controlled."

"Interesting word. Why did you use it?"

"The mirrors aren't broken, or anything else for that matter. The victim's clothes are intact. His shirt isn't even un-tucked. It just looks to me like the killer was very much in control."

"Very good. What else do you see?"

Edwards' attention was drawn back to the body. He looked at it with a puzzled expression, walking around to see it from different angles. "Something about the location of the body bothers me, but I can't put my finger on it."

"You're on to something. Go with that thought. Look around him and think it through."

He took a few moments, crouching down and standing again. "Judging from the proximity to the sink, unless the body was moved, I get the feeling he was attacked from behind."

"Excellent. What can we learn from that?"

Edwards bent down and looked closely at the victim's neck before continuing. "Strangulation seems likely, but I don't think the killer used his hands this time."

"I agree. You're doing very well. Now tell me why you think that."

"Strength. He would not have had the advantage by merely using his hands. The victim seems capable of putting up too much of a fight. To control him, the killer would need something that could not be easily removed from around the victim's neck."

"Right."

"I know there are similarities to our other scene, but there are some big differences as well. Do you think they are connected?"

"What are the differences you see?"

"This victim is a man, the other a woman. The first one was strangled with bare hands, very personal, while this one seemed to use a device of some kind. Lastly, and if I remember anything about what you were thinking this is the most crucial, the first victim had the killer on top and looking the victim in the eye, whereas this time it was from behind."

"You're almost there. All of that is correct, but you missed out on one thing. I said before that I do what I do because I take in all the information the scene has to offer."

"I don't get it. What do you mean?"

"If I stand here, similar to where the victim most likely was when the attack came, and you stand behind me where the killer likely stood, what do you see?"

Edwards stood for a moment trying to figure out what he had not seen. His eyes went from the floor up until he was looking straight ahead, and there it became clear. "I can see myself in the mirror."

"And more importantly?"

"I can see your eyes. The killer looked the victim in the eye while he choked the life out of him."

"Just like the first victim. I think we have a pattern."

Chapter Eight

Jill Hanson's nerves were just about shot. She was a secretary, or administrative assistant as they preferred to be called these days, and her boss was minutes away from leaving for an out of town business trip and that meant two things for her. First, he wanted several things done before he left, which often meant pushing the phrase multi- tasking to its very limits, making her very tense and wondering if this job was really worth the measly paycheck she received every two weeks. Second, once he went through that door, the palpable tension in the room would escape in a vacuum right behind him. The relief would cause instant relaxation and free her from the bonds of stress. Coming to work while he was gone would be just short of a pleasant experience. In fact, she would have very little to do for the next three days. If not for his periodic phone calls to just "check in" she probably wouldn't need to come in at all.

He leaned out of his office and yelled about another report he needed to take with him. She was reminded of a bumper sticker she once read that said *Lack of preparation on your part does not constitute an emergency on mine!* How she longed to say that to him. Did he not plan this or any other trip ahead of time? Shouldn't he know what reports he would need prior to the last minute? No, of course not. He was one of those people who thinks better in a crisis, so they create one to get the blood flowing to the brain. It was all well and good for him, but it meant taking it out on her and that she did not like. Just hang in there a few more minutes she told herself. Then he'll be gone and so will you. Out poked his head again, this time she saw he had his jacket on which was a sign that he was getting close to leaving. "You got it for me?" he asked anxiously.

"Yes sir, it's coming off the printer now."

A moment later his office door closed and he came towards her at a frantic pace, pulling behind him a suitcase on wheels with his briefcase bungeed to the top. Without slowing down or uttering a word he thrust out his hand as he passed her desk fully trusting that the report would be placed in it. Not missing a beat she handed it to him and watched as he went straight out the door. As it slammed closed she heard an almost inaudible sentence that contained the words "…in a few days." Then he was gone.

The feeling of relief that swept over her was like walking into an air conditioned building on a hot summer day. She could literally feel the stress melt away, both physically and mentally as the pressure drained from her body. She sat back in her chair and just let out a long, cleansing breath. It would take him a few moments to load his things in the car and drive out of the parking lot, then she would truly be free. She was supposed to work another two hours, but she had done enough. He would be too focused on getting on the plane for her to cross his mind again. Knowing his itinerary was to her advantage as well. He never called until after the first meeting let out, which meant she wouldn't need to be back at her desk until at least ten in the morning. Tonight she would go out, have a few drinks with a friend and just enjoy herself.

She had sat there, sunk into her chair for a couple of minutes and decided it had been long enough. She walked around her desk and over to the window where she had a clear view of the parking lot, he was gone indeed. A smile crept onto her face as she leisurely gathered her things, shut down her computer and turned off her radio.

The smile remained as she shut the door behind her and crossed the parking lot to her own car, a tiny hatchback that was past its prime. It wasn't pretty and it made plenty of noise, but it was rust free and hadn't failed her yet. The price was right and on her salary a car payment was not something she wanted to deal with. The door squeaked as she opened it, followed by another squeak from the frame as she sat down behind the wheel. She was used to these noises of course, but even if she weren't, they wouldn't have bothered her. She was too excited about seeing her friend and going out. On top of that, she was going to get a jump on traffic which would give her time to kick back and relax when she got home.

The traffic was lighter and she was thrilled to be driving the speed limit on her way home from work. Every song on the radio seemed like it was played just for her and she sang along with all she had. She always felt silly singing when the traffic was slow. It always felt like people were watching her and that she was the only person in the world that sang in the car, but without traffic she was free to cut loose and enjoy. Thirty minutes and seven songs later she pulled into her driveway.

She crossed the lawn to the mailbox and removed a small stack of letters and ads, none of which had her actual name on them, just occupant. She continued up the sidewalk to her front door and let herself in. Her footsteps echoed as she crossed the entryway and followed the hallway to the kitchen where she promptly dropped the mail in the garbage before throwing her coat over the back of a chair.

Three years earlier she had been away at college, studying business and was well on her way to getting her degree. While sitting in an afternoon class trying to pay attention to a lecture that was putting her to sleep, an aid came in the room and quietly asked to speak to her in the hallway. She left her books and followed the aid out the door and was told there was an urgent phone call for her in the dean's office. Her heart raced as she first walked then ran to the office. When she arrived the secretary told her in a soft tone to go on in where the dean was waiting. She entered to find him nodding and speaking on the phone in a hushed voice. He saw her and told the person on the line that she was there now and with a sympathetic smile, handed her the phone.

"Jill, this is Doctor Lucas. I'm afraid I have some bad news for you. Your parents were in a car accident earlier this morning."

"Oh no. Are they okay?" she asked, almost in tears.

"They didn't make it. I'm so sorry."

If anything further was said, she didn't know it. The phone had slipped out of her hand and she collapsed. When she came to, she was lying on a couch, the dean and his secretary looking down at her with worried expressions on their faces. The secretary bent down and asked "How are you feeling dear?"

"What happened?" Jill asked, unable to think clearly. She had thoughts swirling around in her head, but she couldn't seem to slow them down enough to know what they were.

"You passed out" the dean said a little quicker than he intended. "From the phone call" he added.

"What phone call?"

"You really don't remember?" The dean was having trouble understanding.

"Dear, you had a phone call about your parents. Do you remember that?" The secretary saw that a softer approach was needed and took over.

"My parents. Yes, I remember something about an accident or something. I just feel so dizzy."

"Yes, they were in an accident. I'm afraid they were both killed."

"But that can't be..." Jill tried to stand up in a panic. She wanted, needed to leave. She had to see her parents and see that this was all a mistake. The secretary placed a firm but caring hand on her and kept her on the couch.

"You need to rest a little more. I know this is difficult, but it is true."

Jill burst into tears. As hard as she tried to tell herself it was just a mix up of some kind, part of her began to except it as truth and that part grew until it became all consuming. She fell back to the couch and curled into a ball, crying so hard she shook but didn't make a sound.

She would stay that way for an hour. Eventually they located her roommate and asked her to come and walk Jill back to their room. Not sure what to say to her, she just helped Jill pack some things for her trip home. Going through the motions of packing put Jill in a trance of sorts and kept her occupied for the time being.

"I'm really sorry Jill." Her roommate couldn't stand the silence anymore. With a dazed look Jill nodded in reply and continued to gather her things and put them in an overnight bag. "The dean arranged a flight for you and the taxi should be here soon to take you to the airport." No response. "I know this is a stupid question, but are you alright? Maybe you should wait a little longer before you go, give yourself a chance to wrap your mind around what has happened."

"No, I need to go now" Jill said sharply, then continued in a softer voice

"I'm okay, really. I'm just a little tired. Right now I just need to go home."

One plane and two taxi rides later and she found herself walking up to the emergency room counter at the hospital near her home. "My name is Jill Hanson. I'm here about my parents." She was utterly exhausted. The emotions, the thoughts racing out of control and the trip itself had finally worn her out and she found it hard to keep standing.

"If you'll just have a seat I'll let the doctor know you're here."

She found her way to the nearest open chair and collapsed. Without realizing it she had dozed off and was awoken by the sound of her name being called. Through blurry eyes she saw the nurse at the counter pointing at her and a doctor in a white lab coat came to stand in front of her. She straightened up and waited for him to speak.

"Jill? I spoke with you on the phone this afternoon. I'm Dr. Lucas. You've had a very long day and I'm sure you are exhausted. If you would like to follow me to my office we can talk a little more privately."

She stood and followed him through a set of automatic doors and down a hallway. He made his way around his desk and offered her a seat across from him. When she had settled in he began "First off I want to tell you how sorry I, we all are, for your loss. I know that sounds pretty empty right now. I want to assure you that though the accident was indeed fatal, it appears that they both went quickly and did not suffer long." A tear dripped down Jill's face as she listened, but she kept her composure.

"Can I see them?"

"I don't think that is a good idea. I know that closure is important and it might not feel real to you unless you see them for yourself, but I don't think you should see them." Seeing she was about to protest he said what he hoped he wouldn't have to. "Jill, they were mangled severely. They aren't recognizable. Now before you start to tell yourself that it means there could be a mistake, believe me there isn't. I don't wish to get into this too much, but we have many ways to identify them and we are quite sure. What we need to concentrate on right now is you. We have people you can talk to that can help you deal with your grief if you would like."

"No, thank you, but I don't need anything like that."

"It doesn't have to be tonight, whenever you need. Or if you prefer we also have groups that meet every week just to talk."

"I'll think about it."

"Okay, you just let us know, anytime. Now the other thing is, and again it doesn't have to be tonight, but we will have to make arrangements to have the bodies, forgive me, your parents moved to a funeral home. I'm sure this is not something you had planned for and we can help you figure it all out, in the morning if you prefer."

"That would be fine."

"One last thing, did your parents have a lawyer or someone in charge of their wills?"

"Yes, the information is at home. I'll take care of it. Thank you for your help."

"Don't mention it. If there is anything else you need, let us know and we'll do our best. Once again I'm so sorry."

She was already tired of those words. Not only did they seem empty to her, but in some surreal way it was like everyone was saying that it was their fault, or like they had done something small to her that could be forgiven or forgotten. Sorry, what did sorry have to do with it. Unless you were the one responsible for the accident, sorry didn't seem like the appropriate word. She knew deep down that people were just saying the only thing they knew, but with each time it irritated her more and more. She was not required to think rationally right now anyway.

She left the hospital that night feeling incomplete for not having actually seen her parents. The last time she had seen them they were very much alive, and that was only a few weeks ago. How could she make herself believe they were dead if she couldn't see for herself? Eventually she would be grateful to the doctor for not allowing her to see them. The memories and images in her mind would always be of them smiling and laughing, their eyes full of love for her and for each other. It would not be tarnished by visions of their mangled bodies, faces unrecognizable. But for a while there would be one thing that would elude her and make acceptance just beyond her reach and that was, closure.

She found it impossible to return to school after that. She needed to be home, a home that was now devoid of life and love, but home just the same.

She took comfort in the small things, a blanket her mother used for Sunday afternoon naps, a stack of newspapers read and unread by her father's recliner. Her parents were there with her in that house through her memories and perhaps something else. She could feel their presence in a way she could not quite put her finger on. Perhaps they were watching over her, finishing the job of raising her that was denied them in a conventional sense.

The house was hers now. The money she inherited was spent on funeral expenses, paying the last of the mortgage and supporting her until she could find work. Young, without a degree and no real work experience gave her few options and she found herself taking the secretary job when she got desperate. She planned to go back to school one day to finish her degree. With no mortgage or car payment, she did manage to put away a little money and was getting close to having enough to do just that.

It had been a lonely three years. She had her things sent to her from school and cut her ties there completely, including her friends. It was too painful to remember that time in her life. Withdrawn for many months she didn't speak to anyone for a long time. When the day came that she woke up and felt that glimmer inside, that ever so small hope that reminded her that though her parents were no longer alive, she was, she took inventory of her life. Lying around for so long had changed her physically, putting on weight and weakening her muscles. She decided her first step was to join a gym. That is where she met Kate.

Kate was her best and only close friend. She was popular in high school, but with average grades and parents that could not afford to send her to college, she went straight into the work force. Most of her friends went away to college and didn't look back. When she saw Jill working out on the machine next to her she decided to say hello. They became instant friends.

Kate was more outgoing and over time built up many friendships and always had a boyfriend, but Jill was not ready for all of that. It took a lot for her to allow herself to care about someone again. So for the last year Kate was enough for her.

She picked up the remote and turned on the television in the living room. The sounds of her favorite soap opera filled the air as she took a water bottle from the fridge and made her way back to the couch. Her father's recliner still sat where it always had, the newspapers stacked by its side. She never sat in it, nor would she allow anyone else to. It seemed creepy to everyone else, but Jill felt her father still sat there, perhaps not literally, but in her mind. It would always be his chair and no one else's. She was on the verge of drifting off to sleep when the phone rang and made her jump.

"Hello?"

"Hey Jill, its Kate. So I see you bailed early. Your boss must be flying away."

"As we speak. He's gone for three days and I couldn't be more thrilled."

"We still going out tonight?"

"Absolutely, I need to do some drinking. Meet me at Mickey's at around eight."

"Okay, but I can't be out too late. Not all of us get to go in late tomorrow. I'll see you at eight."

She hung up the phone, took a long drink of water and settled in to watch her show. However, it was not long before she was once again drifting off to sleep. The drama on the TV was building and a big secret was about to be revealed, but she was already out.

****

Trevor Simmons had reached the point where he was ready to stop driving and find a place to stay for the night. After many years of traveling he was very familiar with just how far he could drive and when it was time to stop. He had seen several roadside signs for motels and hotels and each one began to look more appealing. It was time.

He had entered what could be loosely described as a small town and saw a motel up on his right. Pulling into the circle drive he could tell by the parking lot that there were plenty of vacancies. He couldn't imagine a time or reason there ever wouldn't be. Still, it was a clean looking place and should suit his needs. It was a one story, ranch style building with well kept lawns and hedges. Someone seemed to take pride in its appearance. He stopped his car by the entrance and walked through the first of the glass double doors. Along the wall was a rack of brightly colored brochures depicting people of various ages having every kind of fun. The words 'Local Interests' appeared in big block letters across the top of the rack. Upon closer inspection Trevor laughed to himself as he noticed that all of the attractions were at least fifty miles away from where he now stood. Apparently "Local" has a different meaning here than where he comes from. The smile faded when he was reminded that this meant that once again he found himself alone in the middle of nowhere.

Past the second door was a cramped but functional lobby complete with a small end table that held a heavily stained coffee maker. A young girl, who seemed to have fallen asleep poring over her textbook, sat at the front desk. The sound of the door closing behind him caused her to wake with a start, knocking her book to the floor in front of the counter. An exclamation slipped past her lips to which she was quick to apologize when she saw there was a customer standing in front of her.

"No problem" Trevor replied bending down to retrieve the book. She took the opportunity to wipe the drool from the corner of her mouth before he straightened up. He glanced at the cover before handing the book back to her. "Astronomy huh? You into star gazing?"

"What? Oh yeah, well I thought I would be. I mean it seemed cool, so I took the class figuring it might be easy. Turns out it wasn't so cool or easy. All we do is memorize these different consta...consta...star patterns, you know? We haven't even used a telescope yet."

"That's too bad. There's so much to see up there. Say, do you have any rooms available?"

"You're kidding right? We're practically empty, as always. I can even give you the deluxe if you like?"

"Just what makes it a deluxe?"

"Bigger bed, tub and shower. I won't charge you extra or anything 'cause you seem like a nice guy. Besides, it's not like anyone's using it anyway. Though if the president or Elvis stops by, I may have to ask you to move."

"The deluxe it is, and I won't unpack too much just in case." He smiled and actually enjoyed the moment. Sure she was just a young girl, probably as lonely as he was, but still, talking to her so easily gave him hope. He paid for one night with his company credit card and was handed a key, not keycard, but an actual metal key with a four inch piece of plastic hanging from it. The number eight was handwritten on the plastic in black marker.

It didn't take him long to pull his car to the space nearest the room with the corresponding number, this time in brass and nailed firmly to the door. He decided to open up the room and let some air in while he retrieved his luggage, knowing these places usually were musty at best and sometimes far worse. The air that greeted him was on the upper scale of musty and he was pleasantly surprised, but thankful for his decision.

Within moments he was making himself at home in the deluxe suite. The door now closed, he opened the window just enough to maintain a flow of outside air. As he sat down on the edge of the bed he wondered briefly if he had ever stayed there before. He could no longer remember where he had stayed and where he hadn't as over the years they all began to meld together into one generic interpretation of a cheap, roadside motel in his mind.

The cable TV listing didn't seem the least bit appealing and it was too early for bed. An add lay on the table for the local pizza place that offered delivery to the motel, but tempting as small town, cardboard pizza sounded, he considered his other options. Room service was certainly out of the question. Maybe he would drive into town, if there was one, and see if there was a better alternative.

****

Jill awoke with an involuntary stretch before quickly checking her watch to see how long she had slept. She relaxed when she saw that she had plenty of time to get ready and still meet Kate. She needed that nap and now felt refreshed and ready to have fun. Swinging her feet to the floor she stretched again and found her way to the bedroom where she removed her conservative work clothes and put on a robe before sitting in front of the vanity mirror. She brushed her hair and added enough makeup to be noticeable, yet still understated.

After a few sprays of perfume she found a pair of tight jeans and a low cut top. She hung the robe on the closet door and reached in for a pair of leather boots. One quick glance to check her ensemble and she was ready to go. Mickey's was only ten minutes away and she had plenty of time.

She grabbed her car keys and went out the door, locking it behind her. Making sure she had her cell phone, and that it was on, she made it to the car and was on her way.

A smile was on her face and try as she might, it wouldn't go away. She looked forward to these nights, probably more than she should, but it was a chance to get out of the house and talk with someone who not only didn't talk down to her, but actually cared about what she said.

Mickey's was a local bar that she had been passing for years and one day she decided to go in. Though she only drank occasionally and even then it was a social thing and never to get drunk, she had the sudden urge to be around other people. This was before she met Kate. She would go there when she felt particularly lonely and the bartender was always kind enough to talk to her when he wasn't too busy. After she became friends with Kate, they started meeting there and made it their place. It was a good place to unwind and not be bothered by people. There was a dance floor that rarely saw use and though there was always sports on the TV, the screen was too small to compete with actual sports bars. These days if someone wanted to watch sports, there were any number of places with screens on every wall, some taking up the whole wall. She had even heard of places that had screens in the bathrooms. So Mickey's was just a local hang out for a select crowd.

The only problem Jill had with Kate was her boyfriend. He was very demanding, especially of her time, and would often manipulate her into being with him instead of Jill. She really hoped that wouldn't happen this time because she really wanted to talk to someone. Though the work week was not over, it felt like it had already been six days long and full of stress. She could not keep bottled up and sit in silence, not tonight.

Pulling into the parking lot she could tell by the number of cars that it was going to be a small crowd. It was a weeknight after all, and not every-one's boss was out of town. She parked and walked along the nondescript brick wall that ran the full length of the building. Mickey's sure wasn't much to look at, but it kept out the flashier crowd and that's how they liked it.

She could already hear the jukebox inside, playing classic rock. Inside she saw that it was almost empty and the music seemed particularly loud. It occurred to her that the music always seemed louder, the emptier the room was. Perhaps people's bodies were better at absorbing sound than hard floors and wooden furniture. She looked around the room before finding a seat at the bar. Checking her watch she saw that it was just past eight and once again, Kate was late.

"Hi Jill, what can I get you tonight?" the bartender asked.

"I'll have a beer, thanks."

"Kate going to be joining you tonight?"

"She's supposed to, but you know her."

"I hear you. I hope she shows for you. Let me know if you need anything." He placed a square napkin in front of her and set her beer on it before walking away. She reached down a few feet to where a basket of pretzels sat and slid it down in front of her. She hadn't really eaten since lunch and didn't want to drink on a completely empty stomach. After nervously checking her watch every few minutes she ordered a second beer and saw that Kate was now twenty minutes late. It seemed odd to her that she could sit and relax on that very barstool for hours when she knew she would be alone, but when she was expecting someone, every minute made her more anxious. She had come to not worry for Kate's safety at times like this, but knew that most likely she had been detained by her boyfriend. What did she see in him anyway? He didn't respect her, and especially didn't like her friends.

Another glance at her watch told her it was eight thirty and the tension was building. The bartender seemed to be spending much of his time through the door behind the bar, which she assumed was some sort of office, and she felt very alone. Just then she noticed the door open and she spun her head to see if it was Kate. Instead she saw a man she had never seen before. He was somewhat attractive and though he looked a little road weary, it was nothing a few more beers wouldn't take care of. As he sat down just two stools away from her she jokingly thought to herself that she might not mind if Kate didn't show up, at least not yet.

****

Knowing she was already late, Kate was taking side streets and short cuts to get there as fast as she could, when suddenly she heard a strange sound coming from somewhere on her car. She thought about just driving on and worrying about it later, but when it got louder she knew she had to stop and take a look. She pulled over to the curb and put the car in park before getting out and walking around the outside of the car. She let out a few choice expletives as she saw that her front tire was torn to shreds. Walking around to the back she popped open the trunk to check the spare, only to find it was flat. She closed the trunk and leaned up against the car to think. Looking around she noticed she wasn't quite sure where she was. It was some kind of warehouse district that looked abandoned at that moment. There was very little light and she felt small and alone, not to mention vulnerable. With a few quick steps she jumped back in her car and locked the door. Her hand reached for her purse on the passenger seat and found her cell phone inside. She dialed Jill's number first.

The ring tone on Jill's phone worked well under most circumstances. It was a loud rock song that stood out effectively in most environments. However, in a bar where music was already playing a little too loud, it did little more than blend in, making it nearly impossible to be heard. Normally she would have switched it to vibrate or set it on the bar where she could see it, but on this night she forgot. From the depths of her purse it called out to her in vain, but she was paying more attention to the ever more attractive stranger sitting just a few short feet away. She wondered how she could start a conversation with him without coming across as sounding desperate, though in a way, she was.

As Jill's phone went to voicemail for the third time, Kate's anger grew. She left a message and decided she needed to try something else. She knew that if she called her boyfriend he would give her a hard time. Even if he came to help her, he would likely not just let her drive away. "Jill is going to kill me" she said, resigned to the only thing she could think to do. She dialed his number and hoped for the best.

"Yeah" he answered, sounding less than happy to be getting a call from anyone.

"Babe, it's me." She tried to sound as upbeat as possible.

"I thought you were out with your stupid friend tonight."

"I'm supposed to be, and she's not stupid. I was on my way when I got a flat tire."

"So change it, you know how."

"The spare is flat. This place is really creepy, will you come get me?"

"Alright, but you owe me" he said after a long pause.

"Uugh, alright fine, but not tonight. I promised Jill and I'm already really late." There was nothing but silence on the other end, but she knew he was still there. "I'm serious Babe, I just need you to pick me up" Kate pleaded. She held out little hope, but at least she would get out of this area, even if it meant ditching Jill.

"Fine, but then you really owe me." He hung up the phone before she could say another word.

Though her agitation with Kate grew, it became less important as she became more intrigued by the man she was now determined to meet. "Can I have another beer and would you mind refilling the pretzels please?" She said it a little louder than she needed to, hoping that he might look over at her and make it easier for her to introduce herself. It worked better than she expected.

"Hello, my name is Michael, well Mike" he said with a smile that was warm enough to melt the rest of her tension away and put her at ease.

"I'm Jill, nice to meet you. Would you like to join me?" she asked, indicating the open stool between them. She was surprised by her own boldness, but decided to just go with it.

"I'd love to. I didn't realize you were alone or I would have introduced myself sooner."

"Well I wasn't supposed to be, but I think my friend has once again stood me up for her boyfriend. She has a habit of doing that."

"I'd tell you I was sorry, but I'd be lying."

"What do you mean?" Jill asked, confused.

"Well if she had shown up, I doubt you would even give me the time of day. You probably wouldn't have even noticed I was sitting here. But this way, I get to actually sit next to you and enjoy the pleasure of your company. So, selfish as it may seem, I'm afraid I just can't be sorry for my good fortune."

"Well thank you" she said as her face began to turn bright red. She wasn't used to being talked to like that. Maybe instead of yelling at Kate when she saw her, she would thank her instead.

Kate stood next to her car, having a cigarette and looking at her watch repeatedly. She was now in a bad mood, and she hoped that if she stayed that way, her boyfriend would want to spend as little time with her as possible, allowing her to get to Mickey's where she was sure Jill was fuming. She hoped Jill would forgive her. After all, it wasn't her fault this time. She didn't want to get a flat tire and stand around in the middle of nowhere.

After waiting inside the car for a while she felt safe enough to get out for a smoke. She hadn't seen or heard another car or person since she stopped which both comforted her and made her uneasy at the same time, which didn't make sense to her, but that's how she felt. Off in the distance she could hear the sound of tires screeching, a little louder around each turn that brought the car closer to where she stood. Her heart was again faced with the duality of uncertainty. She wanted to be excited and relieved that he was finally there to pick her up, and she was, but then she wondered what she would do if it wasn't him. What if someone else, someone deranged were to suddenly come around the corner and pull up along side her? Instinctively her hand searched for the door handle and prepared to open the door, should she need to dive inside. Images of a drive-by shooting straight out of an action movie raced through her mind, her pulse quickened with fear and excitement. It got to the point that she was disappointed to see her boyfriend pull up next to her and screech to a halt.

The overhauled hot rod that he had spent years working on in his spare time at work rumbled as he revved the engine. The rough surface of grey undercoating always felt strange to her. It wasn't the smooth, glossy feel she was used to with any other car. Behind the wheel sat her boyfriend, still wearing dark blue coveralls as if he had come straight from working on someone's car, his grease stained hands gripped the wheel. He revved the engine again as if to tell her to hurry.

She reached in her car to get her purse, locked the door and with a final drag on her cigarette, she let it fall to the ground and crushed it with her shoe. Running in heels was not easy, but taking tiny, deliberate steps, she hurriedly made her way around the back of his car, feeling the warm exhaust on her bare legs as she passed the tailpipe. She reached the passenger door and flung it open before hopping in the car. The momentum of the car taking off closed the door before she had a chance to do so herself. Though it was rude for him to take off before she was secured, she couldn't help but feel the thrill of the big block engine as it roared to life and pinned her to the seat. Knowing that his hands had helped build such power excited her greatly.

"Thank you so much babe. If you can just drop me off at Mickey's that would be great." She was greeted with silence. "I can have Jill drop me off later, so if you could get my tire fixed..." he glared at her causing her to stop mid sentence. "Please, I promise I'll make it up to you."

"I don't know, that seems like a pretty big hassle. I mean I was supposed to hang out with the guys tonight and I haven't even cleaned up from work. If I have to do all that running around for you, changing tires and driving you to see your idiot, loser friend, how am I supposed to do that?"

"She's not a loser! Her parents died, alright? She just needs to meet people and socialize a little."

"Well tonight would be a great opportunity for her to do just that. Now here's what I'm thinking. We go back to your place and mess around for a while. Then I'll take you to see your friend."

"I'm so late already. By the time I get there she will have gone home and won't speak to me for days."

"Good. That will give us that much more time to be together." He leaned in and kissed her as the car came to a stop at a red light. With a softer voice he added "You know you want to. Come on." She tried to respond but her words were smothered before they could reach the air as he leaned in and kissed her passionately. Before long she ceased fighting it and responded in kind. As the lights completed a full cycle and made it back to green, he knew he had won her over. Confidently he leaned back in the driver's seat and hit the accelerator. "That's more like it" he said with arrogance. He drove straight to Kate's apartment where they both knew they would be until morning. Jill would just have to be angry for a while.

Forty five minutes later, and anything but angry, Jill and Mike were deeply engaged in conversation. He continued to be charming and she lapped it up like a starving kitten that was given a bowl of fresh milk. As she had predicted, he grew more attractive as the night went on, but she no longer believed that alcohol had anything to do with it. It had been so long, certainly before her parents died, since someone had paid so much attention to her, and since she allowed them to. The way Mike looked at her gave her the feeling that the rest of the bar and all of its occupants had faded away, leaving just the two of them in their own little world. It was in the way that he looked her directly in the eye and the words he spoke. She found herself calmed by his voice. She also sensed that although he appeared to find her attractive, he was respectful enough to keep his eyes away from her low cut shirt, but she wouldn't mind if he glanced down now and then. He seemed to be really interested in her as a person. One thing she knew for certain was that she did not want this night to end.

"Well, I guess I should be going." Reality landed on her with the full weight of the world as his words felt like a slap to the face. The sounds of the bar and all its occupants came rushing back to her ears as she tried to comprehend what he said. Did he say get going? No, she couldn't allow that, not now, not so soon. Her mind scrambled for the right words but impatience won over and she sputtered "No, why, I mean, are you sure you have to go?"

"I'm just passing through and have to find a place to crash for the night. By the way, do you know where there's a cheap motel around here?"

"Umm, yes, I mean no." She took a deep breath and tried to speak without stammering. "Sorry, what I am trying to say is, I would really like you to stay a little longer. I'll tell you where one is in a little bit, okay?"

"Sounds a little like I'm being kidnapped or something" he said and they both laughed. "That would be great, but it needs to be fairly close because I'm on foot. Will that be a problem?"

"No, not at all. In fact I could drive you." The next suggestion came out without her thinking it through. "Or maybe…you could just stay at my place. I have plenty of room." She didn't intend to offer, not so soon anyway, but now that it was out there she wasn't sorry, especially if it would keep him from walking out the door and out of her life. It would just be for the night, but one she would remember the rest of her life.

"Really? Are you sure about that? We did just meet, but I'm fine with it if you are. You trust me that much?"

"I guess so. I just don't want you to go, okay? There, I said it."

"I'm honored and I accept your gracious invitation and I promise to be a perfect gentleman. I'll even sleep on the couch or a chair if you want."

"I don't think that will be necessary" she said with a twinkle in her eye.

"It wouldn't be the first time, I assure you" he replied with a twinkle in his.

Chapter Nine

Jackson sat at his desk and compared his notes from the motel case with the ones from the rest stop men's room. He already had a general sense of what matched up and what didn't. It seemed pretty obvious to him that it was more likely the same killer, than not. He was preparing to transfer his notes to email and send them to Bill Davis to get his opinion when Lt. Ferguson approached him.

"Simeon, can I have a word with you in my office."

"Sure." Jackson looked over at Edwards and wondered if he was hurt that he was not invited. Edwards' expression was more one of concern than jealousy.

Jackson followed the Lt. across the squad and into his cramped office, closing the door behind him. The walls were mostly glass and did not reach the ceiling, but did an effective job of keeping sound both in and out as long as voices weren't raised.

"Have a seat."

"What's up Lt.?" Jackson asked as he sat down.

"I've been informed that you took over a case from outside our normal jurisdiction."

"Yes, that's correct."

"You think this is related to your other homicide, the one from the motel?"

"There's a strong possibility it is."

"Have you run that past Davis yet?"

"I was getting my report ready to send to him when you called me in."

"I know what kind of detective you are, and I don't doubt your instincts, so if you think there is a connection, I believe you. However, I know I don't have to tell you that if we are looking at a serial killer here, or even the hint of one, the media will be all over it. We have got to keep a tight lid on this. The media can be a great asset as long as we control them, but if the roles are reversed, we could have problems."

"I understand completely."

"I know you do, but what about your protégé? Can Edwards handle this with a level head if it turns into something? He seems like he would enjoy the spotlight."

"I'm working on that. I will talk to him about this though and make sure he keeps it under control."

"Good. I'll leave that to you. So what kind of guy do you think we are dealing with here? Is it going to give me ulcers?"

"It might. This guy is good. He knows exactly what he's doing. Likes to kill by strangulation and seems to insist on looking the victim in the eye at the time of death."

"And what are we doing to stop him?"

"We have a DNA sample."

"How about a pattern of some kind?"

"That's the tricky part. His pattern, if you can call it that, shows us that his victims and where he kills them will be random, at least to us. He's likely a drifter that doesn't know his victims, making him difficult to predict. I am sure that he will keep killing though."

"How so?"

"I truly believe that he needs to. Whatever he gets out of it seems to bring him great pleasure."

"There goes my ulcer. Use what resources you need and catch this guy, quickly. We don't need a panic on our hands. We don't need a body count either."

"I'll do my best, I can promise you that."

"As always, but Simeon, keep the reigns tight on that kid Edwards."

With a knowing nod and smile, Jackson headed back to his desk. The Lt. was right, the media could be a great help when used properly. Many false confessions had been ruled out based on what the media had been told and what was kept quiet. Somehow the words 'serial killer' had a way of turning everything into a circus. The media would swarm, the lunatics would surface and panic would spread. The mere mention of a pattern between two unsolved homicides could get people frothing at the mouth.

Edwards could prove tricky as well. Few things were better for a career than the media spotlight and public opinion. If word was spread of a dangerous killer on the loose, people would want results. The detective standing before the cameras announcing the successful capture of such a criminal would have great power. Edwards was just starting to come along but delusions of grandeur would have a mighty strong pull. It was obvious that he didn't like being "Trained", and this would be a great way to propel him forward.

Tracking a serial killer was a great training ground in many ways. It was an accelerated environment of information and action. It was a true trial by fire. Jackson hoped Edwards was strong enough to survive it.

"Everything okay?" Edwards asked as he arrived back at his desk.

"Yeah, fine. He just wanted to know where we were on the case. He found out about the second victim."

"Oh." The hurt expression had returned to Edwards, but he didn't say anything.

Jackson sat down and typed up his findings and sent the email to Bill Davis for his psychological comparison. It was nearing the end of the day and he was feeling tired. It had been a long couple of days and he was ready to go home and let his mind clear. Another thing he had learned over the years was the need to let your mind relax. Too many thoughts pulling in different directions made making sense of any of them difficult. One day he would pass that on to Edwards, but he wanted him to start thinking, before he taught him to stop.

"I'm going to take off, I'll catch you in the morning" he said as he pulled his coat off the back of his chair.

"Oh, okay. I've got a couple things to finish up first. I'll see you in the morning" Edwards replied.

Watching to see that he had left the squad, Edwards quickly turned to Palmer. "Alright, he's gone. Now will you please tell me?"

"You're still on that? And you call yourself a detective."

"Come on, just tell me."

"Sorry, I'm out of here. Why didn't you walk out with him? You could of kept him talking long enough to sneak a peek."

"Darn it! You're right, I should have."

Palmer laughed and shook his head as he walked away, leaving Edwards angry with himself. Though he denied it, he did find pleasure in watching young rookies squirm. At his age, with all he had seen, it was the only fun he had left.

Jackson arrived at home a short while later. He flipped the switch to turn on the entryway light and hung his coat up in the closet. Typing in the code, he opened the lockbox on the shelf above and placed his gun inside, securing it for the night. He made his way to the kitchen and turned on a small am/fm radio that sat on the counter. The jazz stylings of Charlie "Bird" Parker filled the otherwise silent apartment with rolling alto sax notes, played with lightning speed and precision.

He pulled open the freezer to check out his dinner options from the array of frozen dinners he purchased earlier in the week. He ran his finger along the stack of colored boxes, glancing at the contents, before settling on a pizza. Removing it carefully so as not to have anything fall out on him he set it on the counter and checked the instructions before setting the preheat temperature on the oven. He took a can of cola from the fridge and headed for the couch to wait for the oven to be ready.

Still sitting on the table were the files he had been looking through and for a moment he considered starting up again, but then decided to follow his plan for clearing his head. He sat back and took a long drink, ignoring the burning sensation of the cold bubbles pouring down his throat as he gulped. The music and the soft cushions had almost put him to sleep when the oven beeped to let him know it was time to cook his pizza. He returned to the kitchen, but decided to turn off the oven and put the pizza back in the freezer. His fatigue outweighed his hunger and thoughts of lying back on the couch sounded more and more like paradise.

The thoughts in his head, swirling like that machine that makes cotton candy by whipping the ingredients round and round until they turn light as air, one by one began to dissolve as he sank deeper into the couch cushions. One thought still lingered after the rest had been put aside and that was about his young protégé. As he thought about the young detective, so anxious to make a name for himself and be recognized as a peer, he was reminded of the time when he first became a detective. The circumstances were far different.

With his marriage behind him and a beautiful daughter to protect, Simeon Jackson was ready to dedicate himself fully to his career, the career of fighting crime. The next logical step was to become a detective and fight the worst of the worst. Jackson had been well respected in the department. He was intelligent, got along well with others and was a quick learner. Having nothing to hold him back made him that much better. When it came time to take the test, people were lining up to recommend him. His peculiar insights and abilities were already showing on crime scenes and they would be a welcome addition to a squad that was struggling to keep up with its case load.

In the back of his mind, he still felt like he could make a difference and make the city, if not the world, a safer place for his daughter to grow up in. He eagerly took on this latest step in his career and jumped right in. Day after day he saw what the world was coming to, a place immersed in every kind of evil. As good as he was, the crimes happened faster than they could be solved and he felt like he was drowning in darkness. This led to depression and eventually his anger again reared its ugly head.

He was alone. He became so unrecognizable to his ex-wife that she would not allow him to see his daughter. Frustration took over and when the rules didn't work, he broke them. Teetering on the edge of the abyss, a case came to him that would change his life forever.

Several anonymous tips were coming in about a man that was allegedly raping and abusing small children, children about the same age as his daughter Judy. With each report he pictured it being Judy that was treated so awfully and his anger grew. There was no evidence to go on and no witnesses were willing to step forward. In speaking with one of the callers Jackson learned that this man threatened the children in such a way that it was unlikely any of them would be brave enough to go on record. He could hear the sincerity in the person's voice and knew they were telling the truth about the crimes, but he was helpless to act. He could not blame these young victims for being afraid, but he desperately needed one of them to come forward.

One night while working late, he got his wish. The rest of the detectives on his shift had all gone out for beers or went home. It was late and his head began to hurt as he pored over the little information he had been given on the case, trying to come up with a way to catch the man in the act. He heard a sound near the doorway to the squad and as he looked up he felt the most peculiar sensation. Standing there, perfectly still, was a young girl that he thought was Judy. She was about the same size and age, had the same hair and even similar features. It was obvious, even from a distance that the girl had been crying recently. Then he noticed a woman that he did not know standing behind her. It was then that he realized that this was not his daughter at all.

"Can I help you?" he asked as he stood up so they could see him clearly.

"Go ahead dear, it's alright" the woman said to the child. They walked over to his desk. As she came closer he could tell that she had been beaten and probably worse. There were bruises on her face and neck. "My name is Elizabeth and this is my daughter Amanda" the woman said.

"I'm Detective Jackson. Why don't we move to the conference room so we can talk?" He led them to one of the interview rooms with a table and chairs in the center. "Why don't you have a seat? I'm going to ask a female youth officer to join us. Can I get either of you a glass of water while we wait?"

"No thank you" the woman answered. The girl began to nod her head.

"Alright Amanda, I'll be right back with that. You just relax, okay?" She nodded again.

Jackson returned to his desk and called downstairs to request the officer. It was not only for legal reasons, but he wanted the girl to feel as comfortable as possible. If this was what he thought it was, the last thing she needed was to be in a room with a man she did not know. He got the glass of water and was grateful to see the other officer had made an effort to join them quickly. "Thanks for getting here so fast" he whispered before they went in.

"Here's your water. Amanda, this is Officer Diane. I've asked her to join us, I hope that's okay." The girl took a sip of her water and again nodded without speaking.

"Now, why don't you tell me why you are here tonight?" This was met with silence. "I know you're scared and that's alright. It looks like someone hurt you, is that why you are here?" She glanced over to her mother for approval.

"It's okay Amanda. They want to help you. Go ahead and tell them everything you told me." Amanda took another drink of her water as a solitary tear ran down the length of her cheek. Then she broke her silence for the first time.

"It happened when I was coming home from school. I was trying to remember if I brought my spelling book home, so I started to check my bag. When I looked up, there was a man standing there by my front steps. I was scared and just kind of stood there."

"Have you ever seen this man before today?"

"Yes, he hangs around in the neighborhood. Everybody's scared of him and we try to stay away from him. People say he does mean things to kids. I started to back away but he spoke to me and I froze. He told me he knew who I was. He said he knows my mom and that this is where I live. I guess he could tell I was scared because then he started to use a nicer voice. He told me he had just bought a brand new TV and that he had some movies I might like in his apartment. He wanted me to come up there with him." The tears welled up in her eyes and she was overcome with emotion. It took her a few moments to compose herself.

"Are you okay?" Jackson asked. "Do we need to stop for a minute?"

"No, I'm okay" she said through the tears. "I want to finish and go home."

"Alright, what did you say when he wanted you to go up to his apartment?"

"I tried to tell him that I had homework to do and that I would get in trouble if I didn't do it right away. He had an evil look on his face and said he would go talk to my mother for me. I didn't want him in my home and I could tell by the way he looked that he would hurt my mom, so I said I would come up for a few minutes." Now it was her mothers turn to cry as she realized her daughter was trying to protect her, when it should have been the other way around.

"Did anyone see the two of you talking or you going with him?"

"No, I don't think so. Like I said, everyone tries to avoid him, so if he's around, no one else is. I wish I wasn't looking for that stupid book. I never would have gotten that close to him."

"It's not your fault. You shouldn't be afraid to go to your own home. I know this won't be easy, but can you tell me what happened next?"

"I followed him across the street and down the block to his apartment building. He was being nice again and I tried to tell myself that it was going to be okay. I would see his TV and then get out of there. He opened the door and took me upstairs. Once he let me inside his apartment everything changed. I looked around and the place was so dirty. I didn't see even an old TV, so I turned to ask him where the new one was and he looked so mean. He told me to shut up and then he hit me. I fell down and hit my head on something and that made me feel dizzy." The tears returned but she tried to keep going. "He climbed on top of me and hit me over and over..." She could no longer speak.

"Okay, that's enough for now, we can stop. Amanda, thank you. You are a very brave girl and I am so sorry this happened to you. Right now I would like you and your mother to go with Officer Diane to the hospital so they can check you. She will ask you some questions a little later. Amanda, I promise you, this man will never hurt you or anyone else ever again. If you can just tell me his address I will make sure of that."

Amanda looked deep into his eyes to see if there was truth in them. Satisfied that he meant what he said, she felt better for the first time since the attack. She told him the address and left with the other officer and her mom.

Holding the address in his hand, he tried to decide what to do. Glancing at his watch he decided that his fellow detectives were likely on their third beer and in no shape to go with him. It was never a good idea to go alone to arrest someone. To begin with it wasn't safe. But beyond the physical dangers were those regarding witnesses to make sure that proper procedures were followed to prevent law suits and legal technicalities that might destroy a case in court. However, he was full of adrenaline and this could not wait until morning. He went alone.

As he drove down the block where Amanda and her mother lived, his heart broke. Long ago this was probably a nice neighborhood. Now the gutters were full of garbage, there was little light, windows were boarded up and it wasn't safe after the sun went down. He drove past what he thought was their house and pictured Amanda coming home and finding the scary man standing by her front steps. He continued on and pulled up in front of a broken down apartment building with the correct address. The walls were covered with graffiti as gangs and artists tried to out do each other, leaving nothing more than layers of indistinguishable paint patterns.

He wasn't surprised to find the entranceway unlocked. Either it was honor among thieves or there was nothing to steal. Even more likely was the building owner didn't care enough to offer even the most basic security. The smell in the stairwell caused Jackson to stop breathing through his nose for fear he would vomit, though from what he could tell, he wouldn't be the first one to do so. He climbed the staircase to the right level and when he found the right apartment, took a moment to catch his breath. The state of mind he was in could only be described as dangerous. Thinking of that poor girl and what she went through. Sometimes in his thoughts her face was replaced by Judy's as he pictured this man on top of her. Waiting was no longer helping as he became like a keg of dynamite with a very short fuse he hoped wouldn't be lit.

He knocked on the door and listened to hear if the occupant would try escaping some other way, fully expecting to have to break his way in. To his amazement the door opened. Fighting his every urge to just leap through the doorway and attack this vile creature that should not be considered human took all of his strength.

Standing before him was a man that stood well over six feet tall and well built. He looked down at Jackson with an expression that showed utter disregard for anything that was to follow. Slowly and deliberately Jackson removed his badge from his pocket and calmly proceeded to tell the man he was under arrest.

With a smirk and a contemptuous laugh, he sized Jackson up and said "Yeah right little man. You'd better run along and come back when you have some help." The fuse had been lit and the explosion quickly followed. Jackson sprang forward in a rage, unleashing a fury of punches that beat the man almost beyond recognition. Expelling the rest of his energy, he half carried, half dragged the man down the stairs and to his car before placing him in the backseat and driving him to the station.

When he arrived at the station, he noticed one of the day shift detectives crossing the parking lot. Apparently he had opted to work out in the station gym instead of joining the others for drinks. Had Jackson been aware of this he would have asked for help making the arrest and perhaps could have avoided the confrontation that now jeopardized his future.

"Mercer, you got a second?" Jackson called from the car.

"Sure, what's up?" he asked, walking over. He looked in the backseat and saw the man still unconscious. "Whoa, what happened to him?"

"This is the guy that's been raping those kids. I went to pick him up and got a little upset."

"A little? Geez! You didn't go alone did you?"

"There wasn't anyone else around. There was no way I could let this guy have another night on the streets doing who knows what."

"Yeah, but you know better than to go alone, especially now. I mean the guy is seriously messed up."

"Can you help me get him inside at least?"

"Yeah, I guess. We'll have to clean him up and hope for the best. If this goes bad you can say goodbye to your badge, not to mention the case. This guy could end up right back on the streets and with a lawsuit on top of it."

"I know, I know. I messed up."

Jackson parked the car, and with Mercer's help, managed to bring the suspect inside to the lock up area. Once they had secured him, they proceeded to do their best to wash off the blood, control the swelling and bandage the cuts before putting him to bed for the night. They hoped it wasn't as bad as it looked.

Jackson thanked Mercer and returned to his desk to file his report. As he did so, he cursed himself for losing control the way he had. It was the worst incident since high school, but with far more serious implications. If this man did indeed go free, he would never forgive himself. He felt a fear in the pit of his stomach the likes of which he had never felt before.

The next day when the man awoke, there were no serious problems. The wounds were superficial and aside from a headache that may have resulted from a minor concussion, he was feeling alright. He was afraid to say anything at first, figuring that all cops stick together and any accusations he made would merely result in further beatings.

With no money to speak of, he was forced to settle for a public defender. That was hit or miss at best. Some public defenders were young go-getters, trying to prove themselves and build the foundation for their careers, with aspirations of going into private practice and making the big bucks. Others had long ago decided that they had gone as far as they were going in their careers and became comfortable with the system and how it really works. This second type could usually be reasoned with. It was to their advantage to have a working relationship with the police and would often try to work things out to be mutually beneficial. Whatever concessions were made could either help their current case move faster or lay the ground work for getting what they need in future ones.

Harvey O'Brian was just such a lawyer. He was in his fifties and had been around the system a long time. He was a good lawyer that started out feeling noble about serving the public, representing the under privileged. Somewhere along the way he found himself no more than a pawn in someone else's game and just did his best to play his part. He knew all the detectives by name and had a working relationship with most of them. He was appointed to represent the man Jackson had arrested, and after talking to him, asked Jackson to stop by and talk.

"Thanks for coming by Jackson. I understand you were the arresting officer on my alleged child rape case."

"Yes I was." Jackson sat in the lawyer's office that was filled with files and boxes, wondering how he could keep track of anything. The one file that mattered to him was on the desk before O'Brian who was looking through it as he spoke.

"I stopped in to see him this morning. He's in pretty bad shape.

Somebody sure put a beating on him. You know anything about that?"

"He was pretty messed up when I got there. The guy's a real lowlife. He probably messed with the wrong guy. He lives in a broken down apartment in a bad neighborhood. Who knows what goes on there?"

"And you went alone? That seems odd."

"Listen Harv, all I know is this guy is a sick child molester. He deserved what he got and worse. He needs to be put away where he can't hurt anyone ever again. Now I'm not saying I know how he got hurt or by who, but I'm asking you to forget the bruises, as a favor."

"That's a pretty big favor. I am the guy's lawyer after all. That still means something to me you know?"

"I know. You're a good lawyer and a good guy. I've known you for a long time. I'm just saying that maybe this time you be a better guy than a lawyer. There's a little girl that looks as bad as he does, willing to testify that he's responsible for making her that way."

"I can't promise you anything" he said after a long pause. "If it were under different circumstances, I would be offended that you would even ask such a thing."

"If it were different circumstances, I never would."

"I'm no fan of anyone who 'allegedly' hurts kids. Even still, if I try to keep this out of the trial, you will owe me, big. I'm not losing my job over this, and even at my age, I still have a reputation to protect."

"Whatever you want, I promise." Jackson stood and shook O'Brian's hand and held it for a moment before adding "Thanks Harv, I won't forget it."

"I know you won't. I won't let you."

Jackson left and for the first time since he showed up at that apartment, felt like maybe it would all be okay.

The man sat in the courtroom and tried to keep up with what was happening. The way he figured it, the whole case against him rested on the girl's testimony. Without her there was no solid evidence since even he was smart enough not to leave DNA behind, so he would go free. How he wished he could have had just one more conversation with her before she took the stand. After he was finished, she would never tell on him.

However, since she obviously didn't visit him in his jail cell, that conversation had not taken place. Perhaps if he glared at her she would get scared and stay quiet. That would destroy their case against him.

If that didn't work, he had one final card to play. He would accuse that cop of police brutality and have the whole thing thrown out. He wondered why his lawyer had never talked to him about the cuts and bruises on his face, but figured maybe it was obvious what happened and didn't need to be discussed. Intelligence was not his strongest attribute and not knowing the law he decided to trust the lawyer. It was the lawyer's job to win the case for him wasn't it? He was probably saving the whole brutality thing until the end for effect. That way it would be prominently on the minds of the jurors as they went into deliberations, he reasoned.

With that issue resolved in his mind, he started to doze off until they called the little girl to the stand. He did his best to work up the most intimidating expression he could muster, though he risked having the jury see it as well. She walked past him and up to the stand, never once glancing in his direction. She was sworn in and the questions began.

He listened as she told the story and refused to look in his direction as if he were not there. Someone had coached her well, he figured. He turned his attention to the jury to see if he could tell how they were reacting to her testimony. They appeared to be listening intently, hanging on her every word. When the little girls voice broke at one point, several of the jurors were visible moved, some to tears. She had won them over, of that he was sure. When his lawyer cross examined her and failed to shake her testimony he knew he had only one shot left.

The prosecution finished their arguments and the judge called for a one hour lunch break. He stood as the judge left the courtroom and the jury filed out silently. He was escorted back to a room with no windows to eat a cold, bland lunch.

After the break it was time for the defense to have their say. The little evidence that had been brought up was circumstantial but hard to argue with, the strongest being the girl's testimony, but that had already been addressed ineffectually. All that remained was the testimony of the arresting officer, Simeon Jackson.

Jackson took the stand and was sworn in before Harvey O'Brian came from behind the defense table to address the court. "Detective Jackson, you were the arresting officer in this case, correct?"

"Yes I was."

"Would you please take us through the events of that evening? Your Honor, I have a copy of the arrest report for you."

"May the record reflect that I have a copy of the arrest report" the judge said as he took the report and began to follow along with Jackson's telling of it.

"I was working late assembling the evidence which has already been discussed in the trial, trying to find a way to close the case when the little girl Amanda and her mother came to see me." He went on to discuss what transpired during that meeting up to his decision to go make the arrest.

"Am I to understand that you went alone to arrest the suspect?" O'Brian asked. He had to show that he was doing his job, and was never asked to forget that part of the arrest.

"Yes I did."

"Is that normal practice?"

"No, not really."

"So why this time?"

"There was no one else around at the time and the thought of waiting and taking the chance on this man hurting another child while I went home for the night was just too much."

"Alright, please go on."

"I went to the address given to me by Amanda and her mother and knocked on the door. When the defendant answered the door I showed him my badge and announced that he was under arrest. There was some minor resistance, but I managed to cuff him and take him in without using my weapon. Once I was back at the station I filled out my report while it was fresh on my mind and went home, feeling better knowing he was behind bars."

The man was fuming now. He couldn't wait for his lawyer to exploit the words "minor resistance" and let the truth be known. This is where it would all turn around. To his amazement the lawyer was walking back to his seat.

"I have nothing furth..." but before he could finish the sentence the man blurted out "That cop beat me Judge!"

"Counsel, control your client" the judge replied.

"But judge, that guy beat me. Don't you see the bruises on my face? He did this!"

O'Brian pulled him back to his seat, with some effort. The judge took a long look at the defendant to assess his claim. It had been weeks since the night of the arrest and most of the damage had faded or healed completely. There were no pictures from when the wounds were fresh. Still, the judge had to pursue the issue to satisfy the record and prevent a mistrial.

"What about that Detective Jackson, do you know what he's talking about?

"No your Honor. Any injuries the defendant had that night were there when I arrived." Jackson felt a wave of guilt flow over him. He had never outright lied under oath before and it sickened him to do it. The only justification was that the streets, the children, would be safer. If he had to break the rules a little for that to happen, so be it.

The man stood up again, but remained silent. He stared at the judge and waited for a response. The judge returned the look and sized up the man before looking over at Jackson. Then he looked through the arrest report again to verify what had been said. The room was silent as he began to speak.

"What this comes down to is the word of one man against another. On the one hand I have a highly decorated police detective with a record of tremendous service to this city. On the other I have a man who is accused, by a witness, of beating and raping a sweet young girl. The report states that the detective did not draw a weapon, which was also in his testimony and was not disputed. Having said that, I see an obvious size and strength advantage to the defendant over the detective. In my mind, it seems any physical confrontation that took place during the arrest was indeed minimal, probably in self defense on behalf of the detective. Even in the scale of force, the officer would have been justified in the use of some sort of weapon given the physical discrepancy. I'm inclined to deny the claims of police brutality. However, Detective Jackson, to avoid future problems,

I would strongly suggest that you do not make such arrests on your own again. I may not see things the same way if such a claim is brought before me a second time. Now, was the defense about to dismiss the witness before we were interrupted?"

"Yes your honor, the defense rests."

"Very well, I will instruct the jury to disregard the defendant's outbursts and what has transpired since and base your findings on what happened up to that point only." After this both sides were given the opportunity for a closing summation followed by the judges instructions to the jury and their eventual dismissal for deliberations.

It didn't take long. He was found guilty on all counts and sentenced to life. Even prisoners don't have a stomach for child molesters. After less than a year, one filled with rape and abuse, the man was found dead in a laundry room. He had been stabbed more than thirty times.

The case had been a real wake up call for Jackson. He could forgive himself for lying under oath, but his inability to control his temper had come dangerously close to allowing a sick and dangerous man to go free and continue hurting children. He knew it was time for a change even before the lieutenant asked to speak with him.

"Jackson, you are a great cop with a great reputation, but a lousy temper. You compromised your case, your integrity and jeopardized your career. Now I know the judge believed your story, and as a result there is nothing official I can do. But off the record and as a friend I'm telling you, you have to get some help. Next time you might just kill someone. You sure as heck might not get so lucky with the judge again and I can't risk letting cases rely on your ability to control yourself the way you are now. So here it is, you find some program, talk to a shrink, or whatever, I don't care what, but you find a way to get help. This will not happen again and if it does, I will not stand by you."

When he finished he could tell in Jackson's eyes that the message had more than gotten through. Fighting back his emotions, Jackson managed to say "You're right and I will get help. I promise you that." There was no question that he meant it. With just a firm nod and a pat on the shoulder the lieutenant dismissed him.

Jackson left the office that day determined to finally figure out how to fill the void in his life that so far had only been filled with anger and rage. He knew there was something missing and until it was filled, he would never be complete. Before long he found the answer that changed him forever.

Chapter Ten

Frustrated with himself for not solving the 'Jackson Mystery' and for caring so much in the first place, Bill Edwards eventually left the station for the night, knowing he would get nothing further once Palmer was gone. He wanted to stay and work on the case, but had to admit to himself and no one else, that without Jackson's guidance, he wasn't really sure what to do. He had gotten used to doing what he was told and had lost the ability to think on his own. Now that he could feel Jackson slowly treating him like a detective instead of a student, he would have to work on that, but not tonight. Tonight he felt like going out and cutting loose.

He made his way home as the last of the evening sun dissipated in the sky putting an edge to the night air that blew steadily. After fixing a sandwich he made his way into the bedroom to undress. He wasn't all that dirty, but he always felt better if he took a shower before going out, especially if ladies would be present. Standing before his closet, a bite of sandwich in his mouth and the remainder in his hand, he looked for just the right clothes to lay out on the bed. He wanted to look confident, handsome and important with the proper combination of comfort and style. He wanted to look casual, yet elegant. Finding just the right clothes could take time, but it was time well spent. He had long believed in the expression, 'the clothes make the man'.

Another bite of the sandwich, another piece of the outfit selected. This went on for a good twenty minutes, holding up various combinations to the mirror and ultimately putting one or both articles of clothing back in the closet before selecting something else. Finally he had just the right shirt with the right pants. That made the shoe and sock decision much easier. That only took five minutes.

With his clothing chosen and his sandwich eaten, he stepped into the steaming hot shower to dissolve all the day's stress and sending it spiraling down the drain. Leaning forward he allowed the hot water to beat down on the muscles of his back until he could feel them begin to relax. As it reached the point where he was in danger of passing from relaxed to sleepy, he reluctantly shut off the water, slid open the door, and let the room's cooler air hit him.

After drying off, he wrapped the towel around his waist and went to the kitchen to get a bottle of water. Drinking alcohol has a way of dehydrating the human body and he planned to do some serious drinking, so to help prevent a hangover in the morning, he started off his evening with a bottle of water. Already thirsty from the hot shower, it went down quickly.

He dressed very methodically, always in the exact same order. First came the underwear, followed by socks and an undershirt if applicable. Then he would put on the outer shirt if it was to be tucked, followed by the pants. If the shirt was of the type to stay untucked, it went on last. Once dressed, he could move on to hair styling and finally shoes. A few sprays of cologne and he was ready to go.

There were several clubs and bars that he frequented depending on his needs and the night of the week. Certain clubs really packed in the ladies, but usually only on the weekends. This being a weeknight, he chose a smaller bar, instead of a dance club. He had not yet reached the status of being able to go to the bars that were known to have cops hanging out. He would be treated like a rookie and that was the very thing he was trying to avoid. However, there were other bars where people were drawn to police officers, and he could become anyone he wanted. Once he flashed the badge, subtly while paying for a round of drinks, he could regale the crowd with crime stories as well as anyone. They would never know that he wasn't actually a part of the story because they weren't cops. It felt a little like lying to him, but he reasoned that if they would let him be a cop instead of a trainee, he would have his own stories to tell. Besides, it wasn't hurting anyone. It was just entertainment, pure and simple.

He walked into a local, corner bar that he had been to a few times, but not enough that people knew him. He didn't want to run the risk of having everyone already know his stories and be bored with him. He could keep people listening until they were drunk enough that it didn't matter what he was saying anymore, but if he didn't have his full arsenal of material, he could be in trouble. Looking around before finding a seat, he didn't recognize anyone and felt safe.

A few feet away from the far end of the bar was a round table surrounded by tall stools that held several attractive, young women that were talking and laughing together. Like a predator drawn to its prey, he made his way down the bar and found an empty stool as close to the group as he could find and sat down. After ordering a drink from the bartender, he made a show of laying his wallet out on the bar, revealing his gold shield. He sat and waited, hoping the question would come soon. On the verge of discouragement he paid for the drink and slowly began to withdraw the wallet when finally it came.

"Excuse me, but are you some kind of cop or something?" One of the young women asked.

"Yes, a detective actually" he replied, fighting the grin that was creeping up on his face.

"Wow, that is so cool. I've never known a real live detective before."

"Well I am one. Would you like to get to know me?" He almost winced when he realized how cheesy that sounded. That is until she responded.

"Yeah, definitely. Do you want to join me and my friends over here?"

"I'd love to." And just like that he was in. He wasn't too sure whether there was a God or not, but he silently thanked someone as he picked up his beer and slid his chair over to the table.

"Ladies, this is Detective…." the girl began.

"Edwards, Bill. You can call me Bill."

"Detective Edwards, Bill, these are my friends." She went around the table and said the name of each of them. Some nodded, others smiled or winked, but they all looked good to Bill. He ordered another round of drinks for the whole group and waited for the next inevitable question. "So Bill, tell us, what's it like to be a real live police detective?"

He did just that, or at least what he hoped it would be like soon. Actually for the first time he had begun to feel like a real detective. The stories he had shared in the past always felt like fairy tales to him with no sense of reality. Now, without realizing it, he could relate to the people in his stories in a whole new way. He could sense what they may have felt. Though he was doing his best to simply entertain the crowd, images of the dead body he had spent far too much time with crept into his thoughts and almost caused him to lose his train of thought more than once. He wasn't sure if this was a good thing or bad and decided that he would figure that out later. For now, he was going to enjoy the moment as he had always done.

As the night went on, the group grew as the laughter carried above the noise of the bar. Men and women alike were captivated by Bill's words. He was the center of attention, something he often craved and rarely achieved. The stories and alcohol flowed for the next two hours. He threw every story he had at them hoping that at least one of the women would find him interesting enough to go home with him.

It was not the weekend and one by one the crowd diminished just as it had grown. Before he knew it, there were only a few people still hanging around him and only one of them was female. "Well it's been very interesting, but I have to work in the morning, so I'm going to take off." With that she was gone, leaving Bill and two other men staring awkwardly at each other. It didn't take long for them to all conclude that the evening was indeed over.

Bill decided to walk around the block, hoping the cool night air would sober him up enough to drive home. He went over the evenings events in his head to try to figure out where he went wrong. He obviously started out okay because they invited him to join them. From there it got better and better. Perhaps he should have left when everyone was still interested. 'Leave them wanting more' someone had once said. Maybe if he had announced that he was leaving when he had everyone's attention, one of the ladies would have asked to go with him. Instead he had milked the evening for all it was worth. He found it so hard to walk away when people were still willing to listen to him.

Whatever the reason, after his walk, he would be going home alone, again. He also would have to move on to a different bar next time since he had exhausted his entertainment value with that crowd and didn't want to run into them again.

After about ten minutes he was back to his car and feeling more tired than intoxicated. It briefly occurred to him that all he had worked for the last several years could disappear if he crashed on his way home, even if he lived through it. He considered calling a cab, but unlocked his car instead. Turning once more to the God he was not convinced was listening or even sure existed, he reasoned that if he were to make it home without incident, he would consider changing this lonesome, reckless lifestyle he had somehow fallen into. It wasn't quite a promise, but he didn't hear God promise either so he figured he would just see what happened.

He started the car and rolled down the window to help him stay awake. With the radio turned up and the cold wind chilling him to the bone, he carefully pulled out into the nearly abandoned street and headed for home. The green lights were favoring him and with very little traffic, things were going his way. Before long, though he could not clearly remember how he got there, he found himself parking safely at home.

Feeling weighed down by his own body weight, he reluctantly stepped out of the car and went inside. Dropping his coat on the floor because he didn't have the strength or energy to raise it high enough to place it on the hook, he stumbled to the bedroom, eyes half closed and already beginning to burn. He fell face first to the bed and used the very last of his energy to kick off his shoes before sleep overtook him like grim death. His fading thought brought on by a glimpse at the alarm clock was that he had to be awake in just over three hours.

****

As the early morning sun pushed its way through the low lying clouds and into Kate's bedroom window she fought with herself about whether to go back to sleep or get out of bed. She stretched involuntarily and decided to sit up. Looking down at the bed she saw the shape of the body next to her, her boyfriend, and a twinge of guilt shot through her, not for what she had done with him, though she knew deep down that it was wrong, but for abandoning her friend the night before.

The guilt grew in her mind to the point that she knew it would be fruitless to try to go back to sleep. Wearily she pulled back the covers and found her fuzzy slippers on the floor. A big yawn and full body stretch later and she made it to the kitchenette in her apartment. She reached for the coffee maker like an addict for drugs and quickly began brewing a single serve of liquid caffeine. Knowing it would take a few minutes to finish, she began getting dressed. As she did, she couldn't help but think of how angry Jill must be, and justifiably so. Not that Kate hadn't tried to call, several times in fact, and she didn't get a flat on purpose. Her only real crime was that she wasn't strong enough to get that lump that now lay in her bed to drive her to Mickey's instead of home.

As she pulled on her shoes, the aroma of coffee filled her nostrils. Similar to the cartoons she had seen as a child, she was led back to the kitchen by her nose, though in cartoon land she would have scurried across the floor on nothing but her toes. Taking that first sip of coffee that was always a little too hot, but oh so good, she reasoned that maybe what her boyfriend said last night was true. Her not being there would be a good chance for Jill to talk to some other people. She might have even met some-one special. But even as she thought it, she was sure it wasn't true. Despite her efforts and all the progress she had made since Kate had met her, Jill was just not ready to be a social butterfly. She likely got upset and went home to stew in anger for the night.

Kate looked at the ladybug clock she found at a yard sale for only one dollar that now hung over the sink and seeing that she had extra time came up with a plan. She would swing by the bakery and get some doughnuts before stopping by and waking Jill. Knowing her boss was out of town, she would be leaving late for work, giving Kate plenty of time to get there. Since she probably went to bed early anyway, she wouldn't need to sleep in and would likely be happy for the visit. Then, when presented with her favorite bakery fresh doughnut in her own bed, she would not possibly be able to stay angry. It was a plan.

A smile now on her face and the guilt barely holding on, she kissed her boyfriend goodbye and went out the door. There was a ten degree difference between the shade and the places where the sun reached the ground, and neither of them was warm. She walked quickly to her car and shivered at the ice cold vinyl of the seats. She hated to put down the coffee cup that was the only thing keeping her warm, but the car was a manual and she would need both hands to drive.

It was just a few blocks to the bakery and there was a car pulling out right in front, giving her the perfect parking space. Leaving the car running, she ran in and was greeted by the smell of fresh bread and pastries. Sometimes on the weekends she would come here with Jill and get a special treat. Jill always chose two things; a chocolate chip Danish and a strawberry jelly doughnut. She was always able to convince herself that the jelly doughnut was healthy because it contained fruit, in name at least. Kate bought one of each for Jill and selected a blueberry muffin for herself, having had enough guilt for one morning.

Pulling into the driveway alongside Jill's house she was happy to see that Jill's car was still there. She hurried up the stairs to the backdoor and looked in the window that showed the kitchen. It looked like Jill had not gotten up yet. Just before knocking on the door Kate pulled her hand back and decided to keep it a surprise for the moment. She bent down and lifted the corner of the mat on the porch and was happy to find the key was still there. Feeling the dirt slide under her fingernails, she got ahold of the key and slid it into the lock. Jill rarely used the backdoor and it creaked open as the seal was broken. Grateful to feel the heat as she walked through the doorway she quickly closed the door behind her. Figuring the noise of the door might startle Jill if she heard it, Kate called out to her to let her know she was there. Inside the kitchen was a small dining table covered by a handmade table cloth that belonged to Jill's grandmother. Kate sat the bakery bag on the table and took off her coat before calling out again. "Jill you sleepyhead, I know you're mad at me but you won't be for long. Get in here!" She opened the fridge and got out a carton of orange juice. Her coffee gone, she was thirsty for something she could drink fast. In the cabinet she found two juice glasses and set them down on the table before pausing to listen for a sign that Jill was awake. When she heard nothing, she poured a glass of juice and took a drink. "Alright you lazy bum, you've asked for it. I'm coming in there." Still no response. Juice in hand, Kate slowly began to make her way towards the bedroom. "Jill honey? You're starting to scare me now." She walked around the corner and could see the half open bedroom door, the room still dark. "Please say something, even if you're mad." She reached the doorway and pushed the door open the rest of the way. She thought she could see Jill sitting in a chair, facing the other way and reached for the light switch. "Jill, is that you?" She flipped the switch, and as the room flooded with artificial light, she let out a scream that rattled her own ears. The glass of juice fell to the floor and Kate was soon to follow.

Chapter Eleven

It had been six minutes since Edwards had hit the snooze button on his alarm clock. That meant he had three more minutes until it went off again and he would actually have to get up. He closed his eyes, determined to make the most of those three minutes. It always amazed him just how important those were, or any extra minute in the early morning. He began to slip back into a state of sleep, reality slipping away. It also amazed him that he could so quickly begin dreaming again, even though it had been mere seconds before that his eyes were open and registering some amount of conscious thought. As the dream world welcomed him back like a thick, warm comforter wrapped around his shoulders he was suddenly startled by a noise that sent an electric shock to his every nerve ending. Awake now and knowing he would not recover those precious minutes, he realized it was his phone ringing. "This had better be good" he mumbled to himself. One hand reached for the phone as the other tried to rub his eyes to life.

"Hello?"

"Oh good, you're up. Meet me at Sally's" Jackson said on the other end of the line.

"When?"

"Twenty minutes."

"Fine." Edwards hung up with a sigh. His arms dropped to the bed and he sat staring for a few seconds, not yet ready to begin his day.

It was just a short drive to Sally's, a local pancake house, but with his need to shower, twenty minutes was really pushing it. As he pulled into the parking lot he was excited to see that he made it with seconds to spare. This was not the first time they had met at Sally's. Every week or so Jackson would call and they would start the day there instead of at the station. Usually

Jackson had some agenda and liked the informal setting, feeling it would be more relaxing and pleasant. Edwards wondered what was in store for him; a lecture, advice, constructive criticism, there was no way of knowing. As he parked his car, there was one thing he was sure of; whatever it was would most likely not be worth the loss of those extra three minutes of sleep.

As he closed his car door and began to make his way towards the entrance, he saw Jackson's car two spaces over from his own. This was it, nothing would stop him from seeing inside that car and finally finding out what was on the front seat, nothing that is except for being seen by Jackson. No sooner had he started walking towards the car when he caught sight of Jackson in the restaurant window, already seated at a booth. Eye contact had been made and Jackson had waived him in. Edwards hesitated for a moment, his mind scrambling quickly for an excuse to just take a quick peek, but when Jackson continued to watch him he gave up and turned back towards the restaurant. He couldn't help but chuckle at the absurdity of the whole thing.

The moment he stepped through the door he could hear the sounds of a flurry of activity. The over worked waitress looked up at the sound of the bell, positioned above the door to alert the staff that someone had entered or left. Edwards gave a silent gesture to signify that he would be joining someone else and not needing to be seated. The place was full which was not unusual, even for what Edwards considered to be an early hour of the day. Sally's was a popular place with the 'older' crowd. Early Bird Specials kept the over sixty crowd coming at the crack of dawn. Decent coffee served by a tired but pleasant waitress had them lingering for hours as they sat and talked. "Kids these days..." was how many a conversation started or ended as they watched the people going back and forth on the sidewalk. Between seven thirty and eight thirty a parade of teenagers passed by on their way to high school. The clothes, the haircuts, the skateboards, all made for lively conversation. Every afternoon found the same crowd both inside and outside of the restaurant as the kids came home from school and Sally's patrons returned for afternoon coffee and more talk.

Edwards had a fleeting thought about just coming out and asking Jackson and getting the mystery out of the way once and for all. After all, they did have two homicides to solve. As he sat down on the bench opposite Jackson and saw him face to face, the thought dissipated instantly. There was still an intimidation factor that he could neither explain nor admit to.

"Good morning" Jackson greeted him cheerfully.

"Morning" Edwards mumbled back.

It was clear to Jackson that Edwards had gotten very little sleep, most likely due to a late night of partying for which he was starting to get a reputation. Word got around, especially in the squad, and people had been talking. It was not unheard of for a young detective to get a little crazy at first. There was plenty of pressure and no one made it easier for them. It was almost a right of passage to change from a young party animal to a mature detective that took his job and his own life seriously. In order to achieve longevity in this career you have to develop some sort of coping mechanism. Many officers develop what is known as black humor, which is making jokes out of tragedy. To deal with the seriousness of the scene of a homicide, they will make jokes about the victims to keep their emotions in check. Others turn cold, emotionless, and try their best to just not care about anything. Then there are those who turn to alcohol, trying to obliterate the images from their mind by frying their own brains and losing their grip on reality. It was no wonder the divorce rate among police officers was one of the highest of any career.

Jackson considered teasing him about his late night antics, though he was concerned for him. Instead he thought he would try a different approach. If he treated him with respect, like an adult and a peer as he had wanted so bad, maybe he would try to earn it and put aside the youthful behavior that could prove to be self destructive. He chose to keep his comments to himself and get down to business.

"Thanks for meeting me here. I thought maybe we could talk a little without so much activity around us." As the words left his mouth, the sound of crashing dishes came from the kitchen, a waitress was yelling out food orders to the cook, the register was ringing up someone's total and a bus boy was clearing the table next to them. "Police activity that is" Jackson corrected himself with a chuckle.

"What did you want to talk about?"

"I thought we could go over the case, compare notes and see where we are."

"Okay, that sounds good. Where should we start?" Edwards perked up a little. Unless he was mistaken it appeared that Jackson wanted to hear his opinion.

"With ordering, I'm starving. I skipped dinner last night and now I'm feeling it." It took a minute to get the waitresses attention, but when she glanced over, Jackson signaled her that they were ready and she nodded that she understood. She dropped off the check at another table and went to the front to get a pot of coffee before coming to their table.

"Morning gentlemen would you like coffee?" she asked.

"Yes please" Jackson said turning over the cup that sat on the saucer before him.

"How 'bout you dear?" she turned to Edwards.

"Yes" he said emphatically. "Thank you" he said as he watched the dark, steaming liquid pour into his cup and caught the aroma that had an immediate effect on his senses.

"Are you ready to order or do you need a few minutes?"

"I'm ready" Jackson said. Edwards picked up the menu and quickly flipped through its pages. "I'll try the number four with bacon."

"And how did you want your eggs?"

"Scrambled will be fine, thank you."

"Any juice with that?"

"Orange please."

"And how about you hon'" she again turned to Edwards.

"Oh, just get me the pancake special with extra sausage."

"Juice?"

"No, just the coffee is fine."

"I'll put that in right away, thank you gentlemen."

She walked away and they could hear their order repeated to the cook. Edwards took a long, painful sip of coffee and waited for Jackson to start things off.

"I think it's best if we start by going over what we know for sure and then seeing where that takes us. So why don't we talk about what kind of person we are looking for?" Jackson began.

"Yeah, I've been thinking a lot about that. I mean, there are two things that stand out about the killings in my mind."

"Okay, good. What are they?"

"First, they seem completely random." Edwards was thrilled that Jackson seemed genuinely interested in what he had to say. "I would bet that the killer had just met his victims within hours of killing them."

"I think that's a good assessment. And second?"

"Though obviously strangling someone to death is an act of violence, it seems very controlled you know? At least the way our killer has done it. There's been little if any struggle involved."

"In other words, the opposite of a crime of passion."

"Exactly! It's like there was no emotion, no passion, no anything."

"Yes, but with one exception."

"What's that?"

"The need to look the victim in the eye. That tells me that he gets something from the killing, especially the moment of death."

"Right. That's got to mean something."

"What do you think it means?"

"That we are dealing with one sick freak! How do people get to the point that they find excitement by watching someone die?"

"That's a good question. I've got one for you too. One day a guy walks into his place of work and pulls out an Uzi. For no apparent reason he just starts firing, mowing people down one by one. You hear about these cases all the time. It's where the expression "Going Postal" comes from. People always ask, what makes a guy just snap like that? My question is, what was keeping him from snapping until that point and how many people out there are right on the verge of losing it right now? Could there come a point that people all over just start breaking down and going crazy all at once? Will there come a day when we have complete anarchy as everyone just snaps one after the other like dominoes?"

"Well that's a pleasant thought, thanks."

"It's an interesting thought though. What is it that allows some people to keep control even under stress, and is missing from those that lose it?"

"I don't know, but like I said, I think that is the opposite of our guy. He seems the very definition of control, almost to a fault."

"You're right. If this guy snapped, it had the opposite effect. Whatever caused him to lead this unconventional life, forced him to get ahold of himself so completely that he no longer feels anything."

"Right, that could be it. Maybe he was abused or neglected to the point that to protect himself, he cut himself off from the real world emotionally."

"That's a good hypothesis. It still doesn't narrow things down too much as far as our search, but it does give us a better idea of who we are dealing with. Now we agree that the killings appear random, but there must be some reason he picked those particular victims. What do they have in common?"

"They both took place just off the highway."

"Which is why we believe the killer maybe a drifter or hitchhiker. What else?"

"The killings took place in locations that were not heavily populated, giving him privacy."

The waitress appeared with their breakfast and placed it on the table. "There you go gentlemen. Can I get you more coffee?"

"Please" Edwards said as he began buttering his tall stack of pancakes that he would never be able to finish. Jackson started eating and waited for Edwards to get his refill before he continued.

"Yes, though there is one difference. The motel would afford the killer both privacy and plenty of time. The rest stop at that hour gave him privacy, but no guarantee of how long."

"He's getting riskier as he goes."

"Right, meaning that like a drug addict, he might need a bigger and better thrill. The other commonality is that both victims were traveling, so it would take longer for anyone to notice they were missing."

They both took a moment to mull that over as well as eat some of their breakfast. Jackson was pleased with the progress Edwards had made. It was clear that he had a good understanding of the case and was drawing the proper conclusions. Even over the course of just these last few minutes, he had taken strides towards becoming a real detective. It was exciting to draw the answers out of him and see the light in his eyes as he figured things out on his own.

Edwards had a far off look as he chewed his food. His mind was working its way through everything they had discussed. There had to be more that could be drawn from what they knew. It bothered him that no matter what they learned or surmised about the killer, none of it would help them catch him. He set his fork down, resigned to the fact that he would not make it through another pancake, and took a sip of his coffee. One final conclusion became clear to him. "I think he is likely pretty intelligent as well."

"Why do you say that?"

"For starters, he has left us no clues, except for his one mistake of falling asleep in that chair. Then there are the victims. As we said, he picked people that could disappear without immediate notice, in places where he would not get caught and then he just vanishes. Plus his method of killing has allowed him total control to the point that he has probably not sustained one defensive wound. To do all of that, he must be at least above average in intelligence, wouldn't you say?"

"Well put. Which leaves us with an intelligent, emotionless "freak" as you call him, who drifts around, possibly by hitchhiking and kills fellow travelers that he doesn't know, in remote places? Does that about sum him up?"

"I'd say so."

"This begs the question, how does any of that help us find him?"

"Actually, if you think about it, we may have something else to consider" Edwards put in after taking a moment to think. "Who's to say he's even still around? I mean if he really is a drifter attacking other travelers, isn't there a good chance that he kept on drifting? He could be in another state by now."

"That's a very real possibility. Of course we will have to keep a close eye on all stories that could be related around the country. This also means that if he hasn't left the area, there must be a reason for that too."

"I agree."

Just then, Jackson's cell phone rang. "Jackson" he answered and then listened for several seconds. "And why do you think there is a connection?" After several more seconds he said "Alright, thanks for the call. We'll be right over."

"What was that all about?"

"There's been another murder."

"And they think it's one of ours?"

"Could be, though it would be a big step from the others. The victim is a young woman, killed in her own home."

"That would be a big step. Seems kind of bold for our guy. Why do they think it's him?"

"She was strangled to death, sitting in front of a mirror."

Chapter Twelve

The day following a kill was always the most difficult. Though there were few things he actually felt, impatience was one of them. Killing was the only source of pleasure that he had. No, pleasure was probably too strong a word. It was a hint towards pleasure; a spark that gave the idea that pleasure existed and could be felt, but was not the true fulfillment of it. Pleasure would always remain outside his grasp. To stay in control of the game he had to time things out properly. Much as he hated it, there had to be time between killings. He was already helping the police too much as it is.

The very thought of the police was enough to bring a rare smile to his face. To him, their actions were like a movie he had already seen, or had even written the script for, and he knew what they were thinking before they did. By now they would suspect that he was toying with them, adding more risk to each kill, as if challenging them to catch him. They would consider themselves equally involved in the game that he created and this arrogance was laughable. They were mere pawns in his game, a game being played strictly for his enjoyment. The only reason he involved them at all was to use them to add an element of danger, giving him an added minor thrill.

This latest move was one he was quite proud of. To bring them so close to feeling like they were getting to know him, and then change directions without warning would really shake things up. Having just decided that his victims would all be killed in remote locations while traveling far from home, he went ahead and killed a girl in her own house. This was a populated area, not the middle of nowhere. The girl would be missed right away when she didn't show up for work the next day. Back to the drawing board detectives. They would stand around scratching their collective heads, their only hope being that perhaps there would be more clues at this scene or at least a witness or two. Of course they would find nothing but frustration.

The only clues left behind were the ones he wanted them to find and he was never seen by witnesses. That was the beauty of today's society. Sure there were video cameras and video phones everywhere. But people only capture that which will benefit them personally. If they can get money for filming something or get some form of person gratification, then they were quick to start recording. However, if someone needed help and there was a threat of danger involved, most people put on their blinders and went about their business. When women are being trained to defend themselves against rape, they are taught to yell 'Fire!', not help or rape. Why? Because fire means that anyone within hearing range could be at risk, whereas the other two likely only affect someone else and would be ignored by people who prefer not to get involved. It was a criminal's world. No, he could bring the police closer and closer as he chose, bring them right to the very edge so they could practically reach out and touch him, then vanish in the night leaving not so much a vapor trail to follow.

The illusion of getting caught, and he was sure it was nothing more than that, had added more of a thrill than he expected. As calculating as he is, what he felt walking out of that restroom knowing that a car or truck could have pulled in at any point had been an unexpected pleasure. Even while he was choking that salesman, he could feel a tingle in his veins listening for a knock on the door. This had changed his game plan. He made a decision on the fly which was contradictory to his very being. When he was sitting at the bar listening to that girl drone on and on, and throwing her a line of talk so sweet it hurt his teeth, he had planned to get her to come to a motel with him. But the thought felt instantly dull and he knew it would bring him disappointment, so much so that he considered even letting her live and just walking away. However, when she was bold enough to invite him to her home, the excitement returned at the very thought of it. His mind raced ahead as he seemingly saw exactly what this would do to the mindset of the detectives that were trying to profile him and his mind was made up. There was electricity in the air from the moment they left the bar. He almost hoped some nosey neighbor would look out the window to see who the lonely, plain looking girl was bringing home. The act of killing her was intensified as he listened for the phone to ring or the sound of the doorbell. Even as he left and walked past the darkened houses of the quiet little neighborhood he half expected to hear the sound of sirens and had to force himself to walk casually. It was his favorite killing yet, but as with all of his killings, the feelings quickly faded, leaving him longing for the next thrill.

****

Thomas Reardon watched anxiously as the second hand slowly dragged its way around the clock on the wall. He couldn't wait for the bell to ring, bringing an end to yet another school day filled with isolation. Thomas didn't have any friends; in fact no one spoke to him at all. He was considered one of the "Weird" kids. People talked about him, often laughing behind his back, but never talked directly to him. It was so bad that he envied the kids that were picked on by bullies. At least they were getting attention, even if came in the form of abuse. A punch in the arm or a 'nuggie' was still human contact, something he had no recollection of experiencing. The clock's hands aligned to form the magical combination that would cause the bell to ring, often catching a teacher in mid- sentence, making the students laugh. Thomas gathered his books and papers from his desk and quickly made his way past the other kids who had gathered with their friends to talk and laugh together. Some days this bothered him, but today he had something else on his mind.

A quick stop at his locker to get his jacket and make sure he had his homework and then he was rushing through the hallway, weaving in and around those that were not in such a hurry. He pushed open the door and was greeted by the afternoon sun, causing him to squint. It was five blocks to his house and he was determined to run the whole way. Before he left for school that morning, he had set up an experiment and he was dying to know if it had worked. Block after block he ran, the houses that flew by in his periph-eral vision getting progressively more run down. In one yard was a dog that ran alongside of him, barking furiously the whole way. Every day that dog barked at him and he grew to hate it.

The block that Thomas lived on was right at the edge of the school zone and what lay beyond it were no more than shacks. His lungs started to burn, his legs feeling weak, until he could see his house before him. With renewed strength and energy he sped up once again from a fast walk to a full on jog, gasping for each breath. As he reached the front door, he had to stop momentarily to catch his breath, sweat dripping from his forehead. His hand fumbled around in his pocket in search of the key and closed in on its target. Frantically unlocking the door as if being chased, he pushed his way in to the silent home. As usual, there was no one to greet him.

Thomas's parents were very much in love when his mother became pregnant. Newlyweds that had not planned to have a child so soon; they were not financially prepared for a baby. His father had been going to school and working part time while his mother worked as a waitress to help with the bills. With a baby on the way, that all changed. His father would not let his beloved wife work on her feet all day while carrying a child, so he quit school and got a job at the factory. Putting his dreams aside was worth it when he saw how happy his wife was. Her life became consumed by the pregnancy. She loved feeling the life grow inside her. Her own parents had adopted her and she spent her whole life not feeling connected to anyone the way she thought others were. With no biological family, the life that grew inside her was the strongest bond she had ever felt.

As the months passed this put a strain on the marriage. A streak of jealousy developed as Thomas's father realized he was no longer the most important person in his wife's life. The disconnected feeling she carried all her life had made them closer as a couple, but now she didn't seem to need him anymore. Day after day he worked in that factory to provide her with the best life he could, longing for a future that would no longer be, as his dreams of college and a real career faded away. Once the baby is born she'll feel different, he would tell himself. She'll come back to me.

Things were different alright, but not at all how he imagined they would be. At first, she seemed anxious to finally see her baby face to face. They sat in the hospital room together, tears running down her face, and together they gave him his name. But before long, her attitude began to change, subtly at first and then drastically. By the time they brought baby Thomas home, she was no longer happy. She slept often and didn't eat properly. The doctor told them it was called post partum depression. It was common for new mother's to feel a loss or disconnection after carrying a life inside them for nine months and then being separated. At the time there was little help for this disorder and so they simply waited for it to go away.

One day, when he arrived home from work, he could hear Thomas crying in his crib. He called out for his wife but got no response. He checked the baby's room and only found the infant screaming. He continued on to the bedroom where he found his wife lying still. At first he thought she was only asleep. On the bedside sat a prescription bottle of sleeping pills his wife's friend had given her to help her rest. When he checked the bottle he found that it was empty. He tried to wake her, shaking her and screaming, but she was gone.

Out of a sense of duty, his father raised Thomas, but he would never forgive him. If Thomas would never have been born, or better yet, not even been conceived, he would still have his wife and his dreams. Now that was all gone, and it was Thomas that had taken it all away.

Beyond providing for his most basic needs, Thomas had no relationship with his father. He was always working and when he was home, very few words were ever exchanged. For the first few years, Thomas craved attention. He would cry out for the love that his father could not provide, because he was filled with only anger and hate. It was a lonely existence, devoid of emotion and love. He was forced to be independent and his own feelings began to fade to the point where he had trouble feeling anything at all.

His footsteps echoed through the empty house as he ran to the kitchen and set his books down on the table. The run had made him thirsty and anxious as he was, he needed to get a drink. He opened the fridge, the cool air feeling cold against his sweaty skin, he took out a pitcher of juice and poured himself a glass. He drank it so fast he was again out of breath, but this time would not be denied. Not even taking time to put the juice away he bolted out the back door, the screen door slamming behind him as he ran across the yard. At the far end of the yard was a tool shed, weather worn, paint pealing on all sides. Behind the shed stood a tall tree that provided shade to more than half of the yard. This was one of his favorite spots to spend time. It was mostly secluded from sight and he would often spend hours sitting at the base of the tree doing homework, reading or just thinking.

Recently, on one such occasion, he had been sitting there, knees up to his chest, contemplating the universe, when he saw a rabbit. It didn't seem to notice him at first and went about looking for food. He watched as its little nose flickered back and forth. His leg felt the need to stretch out and as his foot scraped the ground, it made enough noise for the rabbit to look over at him. It stood motionless for several seconds, then darted off and out of his yard. This gave him an idea.

He spent the next few days after school in the shed constructing a wooden box. He had seen on TV once that if you held up one end of a box with a stick and tied the stick to a carrot with a string, it could be used to trap an animal, like a rabbit. He hammered away making the box as close to the one he had seen as possible. Then he searched all over the yard to find just the right stick. Then all that was left was to tie it to a carrot, set it up and wait. That's what he did before leaving for school and now he had to know if he caught anything.

When he came within ten feet of the tree he slowed down and walked quietly. The trap lay on the other side of the tree and he let the tension build until in the final moment he swung his head around the tree's trunk. The trap had closed, but it could have just fallen. He crouched down and listened carefully at the side of the box. He heard nothing at first, but then he thought he could hear a light panting noise. Something might really be inside, he thought with excitement. Tapping on the side of the box, he put his ear right up to it and listened. Something stirred in the grass and he knew that the trap was a success. Carefully he lifted one side of the box just high enough to slide his hand inside. Feeling around, he came across something soft and furry and took a hold of it before lifting the box off completely.

His heart racing, he looked down to see what his hand held. Struggling to free itself was a rabbit. It was not the one he had seen before, though it had the same grey color, but this one was much smaller, a mere baby. The ears were smaller than the adult's and its eyes looked huge on the tiny, nervous head. He pulled the rabbit up to his chest and held it firmly, stroking its fur, and carried it into the shed.

A hot, musty smell made of oil and grass hit him as he entered. The ceiling was made of a thick green plastic that allowed some sunlight to penetrate, but there was little if any air circulation. The humid air hung heavy and took effort to breath. A lawn mower sat in the corner, still covered with grass from its last use. The walls were covered with tools, shovels and garden equipment, casting eerie shadows on the floor.

Using his hand, he swept the sawdust off of the gasoline stained counter and set the tiny, helpless rabbit down, keeping his hand on it to prevent it from escaping. He reached up and turned on the fluorescent light that hung loosely from the ceiling. It rocked back and forth making the shadows even stranger, but Thomas didn't notice as he stared intently at the life he held in his hands. Bending down, he looked right into the rabbit's large brown eyes, the little nose and whiskers twitching nervously. For no explainable reason he began to tighten his grip, ever so slowly. The rabbit's eyes seem to grow as he squeezed. He placed his other hand on the creature and as his grip increased it let out a strange howling sound. Then he felt the bones break under the fur, the tiny heartbeat racing under his fingertips until suddenly it stopped and the body went limp. He released his grip with both hands, allowing the ball of fur with exaggerated eyes to drop to the counter with a slight thud.

After a minute or so he sensed that his own heart had been racing as well. His breathing was heavy and he felt dizzy, but in a good way. He was feeling something new, a strange sensation like he had never felt before. There was a sense of excitement that he could not explain, but knew he wanted to recapture, somehow.

He stepped out of the shed to the fresh air and sat down in his spot beneath the tree. What had caused him to kill the rabbit? More importantly, why did he enjoy it so much? Knowing that he should feel some sort of remorse, he was surprised to find he felt only joy. Perhaps it was a sense of power, of control that was not present in his own life. Whatever it was, he knew he had to get that feeling again no matter what the cost.

The success he had with the trap was short lived, in fact so much so that it never worked again. He threw a rock at a squirrel, hitting it in the head and killing it as it fell from the tree to the ground, but it was not the same. He needed to feel the life in his hands and then feel it slip away. One day as he was at recess and leaning against the wall of the school alone, watching the other kids playing and laughing together, a bird flew into the window a few feet from him. He walked over and stood looking down at the bird lying on the ground by his feet. It looked dead and he was about to walk away when he saw a twitch. He bent down, picked it up and held it in his hands. Suddenly the bird sat up and he had to react quickly to keep it from flying away. The bird appeared to be dazed, but the clouds soon lifted and it fought to free itself. Thomas turned and looked at the sea of children running and playing without him, then turned his attention to the bird. He began to squeeze and saw a terrified look come to the bird's eyes. The bones crushed much like the rabbit and he felt life cease. Looking again at the playground where he was not welcome, he allowed the dead bird to fall to the ground. Several of the kids stopped playing and looked in his direction. The rest of the day he heard whispering around him, but no more laughter. It was then that he first realized that killing not only affected the life he took, but it allowed him to manipulate others as well.

Though he continued to come up with ways to catch small animals alive, even if he had to nurse them to health before killing them, it wasn't long before it lost its thrill. To feel that excitement again was going to take something special. It was then that he had an idea. Walking home from school he came to the yard with that dog. As he walked along the fence he waited for it to come out and bark at him. When he made it halfway past the yard with no sign of the beast, he relaxed and thought maybe it was inside the house for once. Just then he heard a rustle in the bushes where the dog was doing his business and then that sharp bark that shocked him every time. This time he stopped and looked the dog in the eye as it jumped up and down, barking and slobbering all over itself. After a short pause he said in a cold voice, "I'll see you tonight you stupid dog."

That night when he got home from school, he did his homework, fixed himself something to eat and went to bed early. He slept lightly, listening for his father to come home. When he did, it was late as always and he went to bed soon after. Giving him time to fall asleep, he quietly got out of bed and put on his shoes. He tiptoed out into the hallway, pausing every few steps to listen for signs that his father was awake. When he was met with only silence, he felt safe going out the front door and into the night. It was cooler out than he expected and he wished he had taken a jacket, but he dared not risk going back now.

Staying in the shadows, he made his way to the yard where the dog lived and sat still for several minutes. Once he was convinced that the dog was not out, he hopped over the fence and found a spot in the bushes to wait. There was no guarantee that the dog's owner would let him out again that night, but it was a chance he was willing to take. He sat and waited for what felt like hours. Discouraged, he looked around and thought about going home, but then the porch light came on, followed by the door swinging open. The owner was a mere silhouette behind the screen door, but out came the dog, tail wagging as it trotted down the steps.

Thomas looked at the dog and thought it seemed bigger from this side of the fence. He then realized he had not yet come up with a plan for how he was going to get control of the dog. Images of the teeth he had seen as the dog barked and growled at him in the past came flooding to his mind. Suddenly he felt fear and hoped the dog would not notice him.

The dog went to the nearest tree and raised its leg to urinate. When it finished it started to run back up the steps and Thomas felt a wave of relief. But at the top of the steps it stood and sniffed the air. With a low growl it ran back down the steps and straight towards the bush where Thomas sat. Running blindly at first, based just on the foreign smell his nose had detected, suddenly it caught site of Thomas and began to bark as it came right for him.

Thomas almost froze with panic, but managed to stand and just as the dog leapt for him, he kicked out and caught the dog right under the chin. Flipping over on its side, the dog let out a yelp before landing hard on the ground. It lay stunned and motionless. The fence was only a few feet away and he would have no trouble leaping to safety before the dog recovered, but as if by instinct he jumped on top of the dog instead. With both hands around the dog's throat he squeezed and proceeded to choke the life from it. As if it were the first time all over again, he felt a thrill sweep over him as the body went limp. However, it was what followed that changed him to his very core.

As he stood up and walked to the fence he heard the sound of the screen door opening. He quickly leapt over the fence and hid behind the hedge, afraid that if he tried to run at that moment he would be seen. A man appeared on the porch and began calling for the dog. When he received no response, he looked around, his eyes squinting to see in the dim light, until he saw a lump at the far end of the yard. Thomas watched intently as the man came down the steps and across the lawn. He tried calling out the dogs name one last time, but when the lump didn't move, he quickened his pace towards it. Unable to believe what he was seeing, he dropped to his knees as tears poured down his face. Reaching down with both arms he scooped up the dead dog's body and held it tight to his chest.

Through the hedge Thomas watched as the man cried in anguish, cradling the dog in his arms. The pain on the man's face fascinated him. It occurred to him that he was responsible for making the man suffer and it awakened something deep inside of him. He had a new sense of control that he had never felt before. With confidence, he stood up and casually walked away, smiling all the way home. As he lay in bed that night, trying in vain to fall asleep, he relived that moment over and over in his mind.

Something had awakened inside of him that let him feel for the first time he could remember, other people's pain. The anguish on the dog owner's face as he held the limp, dead body of his beloved pet, the torment he must have felt, was intoxicating to Thomas. There was no wrong or right, not really, though he knew in the minds of others it would be wrong, but to him it was an intellectual debate without emotion. Even if he could reason it to be wrong, it felt so right. Feelings, especially for someone thought to be devoid of them, nearly always won out against reason, and so he went about searching for ways to recapture the feeling.

It was easy to find opportunities in everyday life to inflict pain on others. In the hallways of school, Thomas would gently nudge another student at the top of the staircase and cause them to tumble into a broken, crying mass at the bottom. Between classes it was always crowded and hectic and no one would be able to tell what happened for sure. It would be seen as an accident.

Finding places to leave needles, razor blades and broken glass were among his favorite ways to catch someone off guard and watch them scream out in agony. The only problems Thomas ran across were being careful enough that nothing could be traced back to him, and making sure he was present when the 'accidents' happened. It wasn't enough to know someone would be hurt by his actions; he needed to see the expression on their faces, the look in their eyes at the moment of pain. The wave of realization that swept over a persons eyes the moment they knew someone was horribly wrong was what he craved, what fed his desires, what made him feel.

Eventually, as with everything else, the thrill died away and needed to be replaced by something bigger and better. Thomas had grown and was becoming a man. He was fairly thin as a teenager, but was tall and in good shape. As he lay awake one night, deeply unsatisfied and needing a fix, he decided to go for a walk. He was old enough now that he could take care of himself and as a result, his father treated him as if he didn't exist at all. No words were ever exchanged. Thomas was free to come and go as he pleased and if one day he never came back, it would make no difference.

It was around midnight when he had given up on sleep, pulled on a pair of jeans and a jacket and headed out into the night. He just started walking, not sure of what he was looking for, but knowing he needed to find it. Walking past the yard that years before had a dog in it, gave him a twinge of pleasure. The yard, which used to be kept so clean and well tended, was now overrun with weeds and tall grass. He heard that the man had fallen into a depression after the sudden and unexplained death of his dog.

His sense of purpose kept him walking from his neighborhood all the way into town. Grassy lawns gave way to concrete, homes to businesses. The neon lights glowed and buzzed as the sound of people getting drunk in the bars carried through the night air. Passing the hub of activity, the sounds faded. The wind blew garbage along the street's gutters and harsh white streetlights replaced the colorful neon.

Thomas came to an alleyway, barely lit by a lone, bare bulb that stood its ground against the surrounding darkness. Here the wind swirled like a mini-tornado, carrying dirt and garbage in its wake. There was an eerie calm that caused him to stop momentarily. Just before he continued on, he heard a sound coming from behind a dumpster that was overflowing and the main source of much of the garbage now dancing in the air. He paused to listen for it again, but heard nothing. Looking around and finding himself to be alone, he approached the dumpster. As he stepped cautiously along side it, he again heard a scraping sound. On the ground he saw a leg extend a worn out boot, almost tripping him. He peered around the end of the dumpster and found a man, heavily intoxicated, wearing several layers of dirty, torn clothing. At first he just stood there, staring at the man, watching his restless slumber.

The man opened his eyes, startled to see someone standing over him. "Who are you, what do you want?"

Not sure what to say, and entranced by the sight of this helpless person, sitting all alone in the dark, Thomas stood silent for several seconds. Not wanting to frighten the man into drawing anyone else's attention, he said "Sorry, I didn't mean to startle you. I heard you back here and just wanted to make sure you were okay."

"Oh, thank you young man. Say, what are you doing around here so late at night anyway? Shouldn't you be home in bed?" the man asked with slurred speech.

"I couldn't sleep." Thomas reached down to help the man to his feet and leaned him against the wall to regain his balance.

"It's not safe around here at night" the drunk said to him.

"I think you're right about that" Thomas said, and without warning began hitting the man. Again and again he struck. His reflexes deadened with alcohol, the man was helpless to defend himself as Thomas beat him to the ground. He tried to curl up and protect himself, but Thomas grabbed him by the hair and looked straight into his eyes as he continued to hurt him. The fear, his mind frantically trying to reason out what was happening to him and why, showed in his eyes and fed Thomas like blood to a vampire. Finally he let the man's head drop to the ground and stood up, breathing heavily. There was a glow on his face and he knew that he had found the next stage of his journey of pain and self fulfillment.

The late night journeys became a regular routine for him. He would steal bottles of alcohol from the liquor store and use them to entice homeless people into darkened places, where he would beat them unconscious and leave them for dead. But again, the feeling faded. It occurred to him that these people were so drunk that their feelings were numbed and inflicting pain didn't have the same effect. Sure they would plead with him, some even cried, but there was deadness in their eyes that lacked that true sense of terror.

As he walked around one night, contemplating this and desperately trying to come up with a solution, he found himself on a street he had not been on before. Instead of homeless drunks, he came across a woman. She stood under the streetlight, smoking a cigarette. Dressed in a leopard print skirt, fishnet stockings that had several holes in them, and a half shirt that revealed a hot pink bra, she clicked her stiletto heels together and approached him.

"Hey there cutey, you want a date?" she asked.

"Excuse me?" he said, confused at first.

"You know, a date." Seeing he still did not understand, she went on. "The kind of date where you pay me some money and you and I find a nice private place….and we make you feel good. You understand?"

"Oh, sure, I get it. Where would we go?"

"Oh we could step down to that alley back there. No one will see us, I promise."

"Okay, that sounds good." His heart was racing as he took her hand and let her guide him down the street to the darkened alley. There was just a shaft of light coming down across his face as she pressed him up against the brick wall. She placed her hand on his chest and could feel his heart racing. Mistaking that for nervousness, she smiled at his youthful innocence.

"What did you have in mind honey?" she asked.

"For starters, can we switch places? I want to see your face."

"Sure baby, whatever you want." He spun her around aggressively, taking her by surprise and bumping her head against the wall. "Calm down kid. I know you're nervous but that hur…"

Seeing the flicker of shock and pain as he took control and threw her against the wall, causing her to briefly step out of character, let him know that her senses were fully intact. That was all he needed. Without thinking, his hands went to her throat and began to squeeze. His face in the shadows, hers in the light, he stared into her eyes as they filled with terror. Unable to make a sound as her airway was forced closed, she did what she could, scratching at his face and kicking out with her heels. Her face turned red, tears welled uncontrollably in her eyes, she fought for her life, but he was too strong, too determined. The kicks ceased and her arms lost their strength, falling on his, then limply to her sides. Though she continued to stare, only eternal night filled her vision as life slipped away. He released his grip, allowing the now lifeless body to crumple to the ground. As he stood over her, he touched his face and noticed he was bleeding. A stinging sensation came over him and he knew his face was probably scratched deeply. He couldn't allow anyone to see him for there would be no reasonable explanation and instead did his best to keep to the shadows on his way home, careful to avoid the few pedestrians he came across at that late hour. As he walked he became aware of the pain in his shins where the woman must have kicked him repeatedly. Still, above the pain and fear of being caught was the utter excitement he felt from the experience.

Arriving home safely unseen, he went to the upstairs bathroom and looked in the mirror. His face was badly marked by the struggle and even after the blood was washed away, it was apparent that something had happened to him that he would not have an answer for. He lowered his jeans and found deep bruises along both legs. Fortunately, no one would care if he didn't show up at school for a few days. He decided to lay low until his face was presentable, satisfied with reliving his actions in his head.

The prostitute's body was found the next day. Though the technology existed at the time to examine the skin tissue under her fingernails, it was expensive and only used on more important cases. The reality was that no one really cared what happened to a prostitute and most people were happy to have her off the streets, figuring she got what she deserved for living that lifestyle. DNA evidence was still controversial and not widely accepted. Its many uses were yet to be discovered.

With plenty of time on his hands, Thomas thought much about his experience, but not just for pleasure. He realized he needed to find ways to protect himself during the act. Though he may be fortunate enough to get away with murdering the prostitute, his good fortune would not last if he continued to allow his victims to fight back and injure him.

The other conclusion he came to was that, like the animals he began his journey with, he liked the idea of strangulation, killing with his bare hands. He also knew that it would only please him completely if he could watch their eyes as the flame of life was extinguished. Though his upbringing was devoid of religious teachings, he had heard somewhere that most people believed that when the body dies, the soul escapes. Perhaps it escaped through the eyes and if he were there, watching as it happened, he could absorb it and that was why he felt so alive at that moment. Maybe it wasn't his own feelings coming to life, but the life of his victims passing through him that he could feel.

Though he stayed home for a week without giving the school any reason or notice at all, he did not receive one call to inquire about him. His father didn't even know whether he was there or not. The killing of the prostitute gave him two reasons to leave home. He was not aware of the state of the police investigation, and therefore unaware of whether they may be coming for him. But more importantly, he saw that by simply walking down a new street, he found a new way to feel alive. How many more opportunities lay out there in the world just waiting to be discovered?

He packed a small bag of clothes, took whatever money he could find in the house and in his father's room, and walked out the door. Without leaving a note or looking back he just kept walking, putting his past behind him. For a brief moment, he wondered how long it would take his father to realize he was gone, though he knew it wouldn't make any difference to him. It was the last time he ever thought about his father. His life was in what lay ahead, the world beyond his youthful borders. He was sixteen years old.

****

What seemed like a lifetime later, Thomas Reardon found himself still walking, still desperately searching for another way to recapture the thrill he once felt. There were plenty of prostitutes out in the world and many of them worked out of cheap hotels. He was able to refine his craft and find ways to protect his face from harm. Eventually they too became boring. It occurred to him that they were only half alive to begin with and that it seemed like most of them almost welcomed death. It also bothered him that no one really cared if a prostitute died, not the way that man so long ago had cared about his dog. He still thought often about the image of the man holding the lifeless form in his arms and crying out. The love the man had for the dog was what caused the pain. It was that, combined with the physical pain that truly made it exciting.

Working his way around the country, Thomas had begun to kill people who would be missed, who were truly loved. It was a dangerous game, one that kept him on his toes and forced him to develop the set of rules he now lived by. But as the years passed, the feelings faded and he began to think the only real thrill he had left would be the moment of his own death. One final thrill, and then it would all be over. He wasn't ready for that just yet. Instead he had begun this latest game with the police. He would string them along for a while, staying as close to the edge as he dared. Then when he decided it was time, he would disappear.

He walked along the roadside, dust swirling around his feet. His stomach reminded him that he had not eaten yet. It was time to find another McDonald's.

Chapter Thirteen

Jackson was weaving his way through the traffic, driving across town from Sally's Pancake House to the address he had been given for the latest homicide which, if connected, was becoming exactly what everyone feared, a series. Though the location of the killing was an odd choice for someone he figured to be very calculating, the description of the scene he was given, brief as it was, gave him that undeniable feeling in his gut that it was the work of their killer.

Driving faster than usual, but not at emergency pace, he found his way through the business areas, past restaurants and bars with names that gave away the crowd they were trying to appeal to. Some had definite sports themes; others portrayed certain ethnic qualities that identified them as Irish or German. There was one that stood out to him as he passed by, but he couldn't say why. Maybe it was because it was in contrast to all the other places he passed because it had little or no identity. In fact it looked as if someone had made it their purpose to have a place devoid of character, no fancy theme, plain looking exterior and a simple name. The bar was called Mickey's and was barely noticeable, yet it stuck in Jackson's mind like a small irritant that wouldn't go away.

The business district gave way to rows of houses, packed tightly together, creating a neighborhood. Though it was approaching mid morning and the sun hung brightly in the air making the neighborhood seem warm and friendly, Jackson knew that at night this was still not a safe place to walk the streets. Even so, he was certain that the homicide inside one of these homes would come as a shock to the residents who felt safe behind their locked doors. The worse a crime is, the more infectious the fear, the farther it spreads, like a virus. People who suffer a home invasion report feeling violated. Their very homes appear tainted by the presence of an unwelcome stranger. Some victims even have to move because they no longer feel safe or have tried in vain to clean their homes and just can't get past knowing or not knowing what someone touched without permission. Though this type of crime alerts those in the immediate area, the infection does not spread through other homes and is soon forgotten. When a homicide occurs in a home, the viral fear flows like a cloud of smoke and affects all those around it. No one feels safe, discussions of moving to a better neighborhood are inevitable, and as for the house of the victim, well that should just be torn down they say. If someone has been murdered in a house, it marks that house forever. If the house survives, even years later real estate agents will have to disclose the tragic circumstances of the fateful night long ago when someone's life had been taken. Children will be afraid to walk by on their way to school, daring each other to run up on the porch or ring the doorbell and see what happens. Stories, legends will be created and it will become the most infamous house around. Teenagers with morbid curiosity will drive by on Halloween and say simply "That's *The House*".

Jackson pulled down the street, not having to check the address he had written down because he wasn't the first on the scene. He came to a stop in front of what looked like an ordinary home that held many memories, both good and bad, for someone. He thought to himself, this is *The House*. He stepped out of the car and crossed the street before looking around and taking in the entire scene. This would include seeing how far away the nearest streetlights were to determine how well lit the area would have been at the time of the murder, how far off the neighboring homes were and what windows would look out on the scene and any possible escape routes and other general information that might help determine how likely it would be for there to be reliable witnesses.

There were two ways that a reliable witness could be helpful. The first one had a time limit. If a witness was able to give a general description of a fleeing suspect that included clothing and direction of travel, it would be helpful as long as it was within a certain amount of time. However, the more time passed, the less relevant the information became. A suspect could easily change clothes or turn in another direction within minutes of the crime. Of course if a discarded item of clothing were to be found in the general area that matched the witness's description, it could be analyzed and used as evidence, though circumstantial at best.

The other way a witness could prove helpful was in court. This type of witness required that someone could provide detailed information or could identify a suspect with a great deal of certainty. It meant that they had to be observant at the time of the criminal act and have a good enough memory to recall such details well into the future. Such witnesses needed to be trustworthy in the eyes of a jury. If the witness had a drug habit, a criminal record, dressed the wrong way or even spoke incorrectly, a jury might be quick to dismiss them as unreliable.

Witnesses made for great movie and television drama, but in reality, they were not the foundation of any good case. If there was just one witness it would be their word against that of the defendants. If there were more than one witness, any difference in their stories would be exploited by the defense attorney. People rarely had the same memories even if they were watching the same incident. People tended to remember things the way they wanted to and not how they really happened. Once you have several different versions of the same thing, the defendant's word becomes at least as reliable and the testimonies are negated.

All of this goes back to the most important part of any case, what Jackson was so adamant about preserving, evidence. Good hard evidence was hard to find and equally hard to dispel. If there was enough hard evidence, the case would stick. It was too late for a hot pursuit as the scene was several hours old. The lighting near the victim' home would likely prove insufficient for anyone nosey enough to get a good look at the killer. Therefore without seeing or speaking to anyone, Jackson had all but ruled out any reliable witnesses.

It was at this point that Bill Edwards, who was on the front steps of the house, caught sight of him and came towards him with a childish grin on his face. "Yes Bill, you drive fast, I get it. What have you found out?"

"The victim was discovered this morning by her friend Kate, who is inside right now waiting to talk to us. She's pretty shook up, but very cooperative."

"And the victim?"

"Female, name is Jill Hanson. Owns the home and resides here. Parents left her the house when they were killed in an accident a few years back. Lives alone, not many friends. Mid twenties. The body is in the bedroom."

"Have you seen her yet?"

"No, forensics is just finishing up now. I figured we could work the room together after everyone else clears out."

"That's fine." They reached the doorway and Jackson could see a young woman sitting on the couch in the living room. It was obvious that she had been crying and was still visibly upset. Before approaching her, he again turned to Edwards saying "So tell me about Kate."

"Closest and possibly only friend of the deceased. She told the uniform cop that she was supposed to meet the victim last night but didn't for some reason. She stopped by this morning to apologize and surprise her with doughnuts and found the victim dead. She called the police right away and was told to stay put and did."

"I noticed two cars in the driveway."

"One belongs to the victim, the other Kate."

"Alright, let's see what she has to say."

Jackson walked over and sat down in the chair across from the couch where Kate sat and leaned forward. He waited for her to look up at him and, speaking in a calm, quiet voice, he began "Hello Kate, my name is Detective Jackson. This is Detective Edwards. We are both very sorry about your friend and the loss you are feeling right now."

"Thank you" she said through blurry, tear filled eyes, followed by a sniffle.

"I know this is a difficult time for you and I don't want to keep you here any longer than necessary, but I'm afraid we do need to ask you a few questions."

"Okay" Kate nodded "I understand."

"Before we begin, is there someone you want to call to pick you up? You may not want to drive yourself right now."

"My boyfriend is on his way."

"Alright. When we finish I'll let the other officers know to let him in when he arrives because they are taping off the area. Then you'll be able to go home and get some rest."

"Okay" she nodded again and she seemed to be calming down.

"I guess the first thing I need you to do is just tell me what happened last night."

"I was supposed to meet Jill, you know" she gestured towards the bedroom where her friend's dead body sat. "Her boss was out of town and we were going to have a few drinks at this bar Mickey's."

"The one about ten minutes from here, real nondescript place?" Jackson asked and felt a twinge when she said it was, wondering why he had such a strange reaction upon seeing the place minutes before.

"Right, we go there sometimes. It's real low key and usually nobody messes with you, plus I think Jill had a crush on one of the bartenders. Anyway, I was on my way to meet her when I get a flat tire."

"What time were you supposed to meet her?"

"At eight. I talked to her in the afternoon and she said to meet her at eight. So I have this flat tire and when I check my spare I see it's flat too. I tried calling her cell several times, but she never answered. Maybe she couldn't hear it or something, I don't know. So I was stuck and frankly a little frightened because it was dark and no one was around, so I called my boyfriend."

"Sounds like you didn't want to call him."

"I didn't. I knew if I called him he would force me to stay with him instead of meeting up with Jill."

"Force you?"

"Maybe force is the wrong word, but I knew I would have a tough time getting him to just drop me off at Mickey's and I was right. We ended up going back to my place and, well, you know."

"Right, you can skip those details."

"Later on though, he makes it up to me by driving over and getting my tire fixed and even gets a buddy to drive my car to my place so I'd have it in the morning. Some times he can be pretty nice. So this morning when I woke up I was feeling guilty about standing Jill up last night and I got this idea to stop by. She told me she was going in late so I figured I'd catch her here and surprise her with breakfast."

"What time did you get here this morning?"

"I think between seven thirty and eight."

"When you first arrived, did you notice anything unusual or out of place?"

"No, not really. I pulled into the driveway and was happy to see her car was still there."

"Then what happened?"

"I know she keeps a key around the back, so I went to the back door and let myself in. I called out to her, but she didn't answer. I figured she was mad and just ignoring me so I started setting up breakfast. When I called out again and heard nothing, not even movement, I got concerned. I poured myself some juice and went to look for her. I tried calling her name one last time, but got no response, so I went towards her bedroom. It was dark, but I thought I could see her sitting there, so I turned on the light and..." she was overcome with emotion.

Jackson placed a hand on her and waited for her to settle down before he went on. "Let's not think about that right now. My partner and I are going to have a look for ourselves in just a minute. Instead, why don't we talk about what Jill was like before this? Did she have many friends?"

"No, not really. I guess she used to, but her parents were killed in a car accident and she went into a shell. She was just learning to open up a little."

"How long have you been friends?"

"Almost two years."

"Did she have a boyfriend or go out on any dates recently?"

"No, no boyfriend and if she had a date, she would have told me. I'm afraid I was pretty much all she had."

"Could she have met someone at the bar you think?"

"I guess it's possible, but I have a hard time picturing it. I really have a hard time thinking she would bring someone home with her, she just isn't the type."

"You say she was beginning to open up though, might she have done something outside of her comfort zone, especially when you didn't show up?" Edwards asked, chiming in for the first time.

"Oh gosh, this is my fault isn't it? You're saying that she did something different because I wasn't there like I was supposed to be right?"

"Not at all. This is not your fault." Jackson gave Edwards a subtle glare that burned through him and kept his mouth shut for the rest of the interview, wishing he could take back his question or vanish. As it was he felt about two inches tall.

"No, it's true. If I had been there instead of at home with my boyfriend, this never would have happened. She's dead because I'm a lousy friend, a lousy human being..." she continued to get more hysterical and was no longer of any use.

"Thank you Kate for your time. You can go when your ride arrives" Jackson said as he stood and patted her on the back, but he was sure she didn't hear him. She continued to mumble to herself through sobs and was lost in her own thoughts.

Jackson turned and walked towards the bedroom with Edwards following close behind. "Sorry" was all Edwards managed to say.

"We need to work on your interview skills."

There was a time when Edwards would have thought, or even said something to the effect of, 'Well if you would let me do some interviews, maybe I would be better at it.' But now he felt so awful that that line of thinking never came to the surface. Instead he was again reminded of just how much he still had to learn and how hard this job really was. There were so many aspects, so many little things to remember.

"We'll discuss it more at another time, but you need to remember one thing about interviewing a witness. Every word you say is chosen carefully to lead the interviewee in a specific direction. You control their thoughts and responses by what you say and do. It is all a game of manipulation. If you do it correctly, you get the information you seek. If you blow it, they either clam up or you get something like what you just did. Either way, they cease to be useful."

"Got it."

Jackson paused outside the bedroom door and waited as the photographer left the room followed by Dan Besson. Dan looked over at Jackson and shook his head. "I don't like where this is headed Simeon. This is getting ugly."

"Anything promising?"

"Nothing obvious. This guy is just toying with us. He's too good to leave me anything useful."

"I was hoping for better news so we could put an end to this before it goes any further."

"Me too, but I'm afraid it won't be that easy. Still, we're counting on you to pull something off here, you've done it before."

"Thanks Dan. Let me know if you come up with something." As Dan walked away, Jackson turned back to Edwards. "You're taking the lead in this one, are you ready for it?"

"Yes, sure." Edwards was anything but ready, but knew better than to blow such an opportunity. With a deep breath, he walked around Jackson and entered the room first and immediately regretted it.

Jackson followed wordlessly behind him and stood near the wall, just observing as Edwards scanned the room. He could tell how uncomfortable Edwards became the moment he saw the lifeless corpse of Jill Hanson, sitting in front of her mirror as if preparing for her date.

Edwards stiffened ever so slightly, but bravely pushed past it and made his way around the room, careful not to disturb anything. At first he was making a show of looking around because he knew that Jackson was watching him, but before long he found himself actually searching and analyzing things and trying to get an idea of just what happened to this poor girl.

As Jackson stood back and observed his younger counter part, he found it harder and harder to fight off his own instincts and soon, as if falling into a trance, he saw the events of the night before begin to unfold. Edwards and the room itself faded from his thoughts and vision and the corpse seemed to come back to life as the clock rewound in his mind.

The free flowing conversation between Jill and Mike that had begun at the bar continued in the car on the way to her place. He kept insisting that he would sleep somewhere other than her bed and she playfully suggested that he may not have to. The butterflies were a bevy of activity in her stomach and her heart raced with anticipation as she pulled into her driveway. It had been so long since she had been on a date, before her parents died, and if not for the incredible connection she felt to this man that she couldn't believe she had only met that evening, she would likely have made a fool of herself. She had no idea how to behave on a date, but it seemed to come so naturally with Mike.

They got out of the car and walked around to the front door and he held open the screen as she fumbled with the lock. He noticed her hands were a little unsteady and gave her a reassuring smile and placed a calming hand on her shoulder. She smiled back and tried to control herself and was finally able to fit the right key into the lock. She turned the key, pushed open the door and found it charming the way he hesitated as if waiting to be invited in. Before she could stop herself, she made a joke, asking "Wait a second; I saw this in a movie once. You aren't some kind of vampire are you?" She braced for his response and hoped he wouldn't find her silly or childish just when things were getting interesting.

"No, I'm not a vampire. If you have a mirror, I can prove it."

"That won't be necessary. You are officially invited in." A feeling of relief swept over her and she was amazed at how well they got along. It seemed too good to be true. She guided him into the living room and led him to the couch so he would not sit in her father's chair by mistake. "Would you like a bottle of water or something?" she asked as he sat down.

"No, I'm fine thank you."

"Let me just go freshen up a little then. Just relax and make yourself at home." He looked up and smiled that charming smile that made her heart race. She did her best to return it and went to her bedroom. She wanted to look and smell her best before she invited him to join her. Sitting down in front of her vanity mirror, she quickly brushed through her hair. Leaning forward, she checked her make up and found that most of it was still relatively intact. Her lipstick had worn off from drinking, so she put on a fresh coat. Finally she took her bottle of perfume and sprayed in a few key places, hoping it would cover the smoky bar smell that had soaked into her clothes and hair.

As she paused to double check her overall appearance, she noticed that Mike was standing in the doorway. He saw that she was aware of him and again flashed that smile as he walked towards her. A peculiar expression came over his face as he made a show of discovering her robe hanging on the corner of the closet door just behind her. As if he were on stage performing some sort of magic trick, he silently pulled the belt from the robe, like pulling a never ending string of handkerchiefs from his pocket. Continuing in this playful, silent attitude, he gently wrapped the robe's belt around her torso, trapping her arms against her body.

Though he was very gentle, Jill was a little concerned and became fully aware of just how little she knew about this man. She fought off any signs of panic and tried to convince herself that it would be fine. After all, if she over reacted, he might want to leave, and she wasn't ready for that. She decided to trust him and hope for the best.

He slowly began to tighten the belt and before she knew it, she really was trapped. The panic started to rise once more as she realized she could not lift her arms and was truly vulnerable. The belt began to burn as it dug into her arms and chest, and she was about to vocalize her objections, when a dark flash went past her eyes and startled her into temporary silence. That silence would become permanent as the next thing she felt was something tightening around her throat. Unable to turn around, her eyes, now filled with tears, looked in the mirror to see what was happening to her. They locked with the reflection of Mike's eyes and she could see great pleasure on his face. From what she could tell, he had wrapped a leather belt around her neck and was now strangling her.

For a brief instant, though she knew she was dying, her sense of humor kicked in. Seeing his reflection staring at her so intently, she thought to herself that it was at least true that he wasn't a vampire. Images of her parents soon followed as she came to realize she would soon be joining them. Her face was red and her eyes strained to break out of their sockets as the pressure increased on her throat, then suddenly the pressure and the pain faded away and there was only darkness. Jill Hanson was gone.

In much the same way, but in reverse, Jackson came out of his trance and again saw the present day crime scene before him. The body still sat in the chair, held upright by the belt. The head, like the head of a cloth doll, hung forward. Jackson could smell the mixture of stale smoke and moderately priced perfume.

"You okay?" Edwards asked, looking over at him, unaware that he had zoned out for several minutes.

"Sure, I'm just waiting for your observations." The fog had lifted and Jackson was back in the moment. He was never arrogant enough to assume that his version of events was correct, but he always had a feeling it was. In a way it felt like cheating to him as he watched other detectives' struggle their way through crime scenes, trying to piece them together. Of course it wasn't cheating, but merely the product of his own hard work that got him to this point.

Edwards was crouched down near the victim, looking intently at the wounds and position of the body. At last, he stood and joined Jackson at the edge of the room. "Okay, here goes. The victim was out at the bar, waiting for her friend that never shows. For one reason or another, she breaks out of character and strikes up a conversation with some guy. She gets a little too drunk and a little too bold and ends up inviting him back to her place. This fits with our guy because we think he doesn't have any place to stay anyway and may have even made that known."

"I like it. Go on."

"They get here; she excuses herself to freshen up or something. He finds her sitting in front of the mirror, which again is perfect for our guy, grabs the belt from her robe that is conveniently hanging just a few feet away. He gets it around her, either because she is too drunk or too lonely to stop him, and then ties her down. Once more, this fits our guy because he has learned the art of preventing defensive wounds."

"You are doing very well. Keep going."

"Alright, the final similarity is, like our rest stop salesman, it appears by the abrasions on her neck that the killer used some sort of belt to strangle his victim from behind."

"Wonderful. I would say you have come a very long way. You might even be ready to do this on your own."

"Really? That's awesome. I mean, that would be great. Still, there is one thing that bugs.

"What's that?"

"Well, as I said, there are plenty of similarities in the M.O. to indicate that this is our guy, and I'm almost convinced that it is, but why go from travelers in out of the way places to a local girl in her own home. We already decided that these were likely not personal crimes against the victims, so why the change?"

"Good question. I have only one explanation. This has to do with us."

"Say what now?"

"Maybe we aren't putting enough pressure on him. I suspect that the fear of getting caught has added to his thrill, which is why he has gotten progressively more risky. This was a bigger leap, maybe because he is frustrated by our lack of progress."

"So this really is some sort of stupid, twisted game. This really makes me sick, you know?"

"I do. I'd be concerned if it didn't. Just keep your feelings under control."

Together they left the bedroom, lost in their own thoughts. Jackson was proud of the progress Edwards had made and could see him becoming a very good detective. Edwards' assessment of the room brought him to almost the very same conclusions he himself had. Unfortunately, once again they knew what happened, without it helping them find and stop the killer. There was the small hope that the evidence team would come up with something useful, but it was unlikely. He felt like he was being played and wasn't sure what to do about it.

On the car ride over, Jackson had called another detective and sent him over to Mickey's, where the killer and victim likely met. Hopefully they could get a decent description of the killer and have something to go on. At least that would be something. Even so, Jackson was not too proud to admit they needed help.

"So what's next?" Edwards said, interrupting his thoughts.

"Meet me back at the squad. I think it's time we get some different perspectives on this thing. I'm going to ask some of the other detectives to meet with us so we can tell them what we've got so far. I have a feeling there is something we are missing and maybe together we can figure it out."

Kate's boyfriend had shown up and was walking her out. They had to pause at the front door to allow two men from the coroner's office to pass through, carrying a stretcher. On top of the stretcher was a body bag. When Kate saw this, it all became too real for her and she practically collapsed against her boyfriend, causing him to stagger. After righting himself, he led her through the doorway. He lifted the yellow police tape that surrounded the house and guided her under it before taking her to his car. As she fell to the front seat, she lost all control and began sobbing so hard she shook the car. Without a word, he got in and drove away.

"Once the body has been removed, go ahead and lock up the house. I think we're all done here, for now anyway" Jackson said to the uniformed officer at the door. Edwards had slid past him. As Jackson approached his car he noticed Edwards standing there, looking in his passenger window.

"Can I help you?" Jackson asked, startling him.

"No, no thanks."

"What were you doing?"

"Oh, nothing, just looking for something."

"Looking for what?"

"Nothing, never mind. I'll see you back at the station." Edwards hurried off to his own car, embarrassed at getting caught and still not finding anything of use. Maybe Palmer was just messing with him, having fun with the new guy. There probably was never anything on the front seat to begin with and he just wanted to make Edwards look stupid in front of Jackson. That had to be it, he thought to himself, but there was a gnawing suspicion that left him unconvinced.

Jackson watched Edwards walking off, looking like he was mumbling to himself. A smile came over his face as he sat down in his car and looked over at his passenger seat, which was empty. He opened up the glove box and removed something. With a chuckle he glanced in his mirror to see Edwards get in his own car and slam the door in frustration. Jackson dropped the object on his front seat, shaking his head as he started up the car. It was happening, again.

****

"Thank you gentlemen. The books look good. I guess I'll see you next quarter."

"Thank you Trevor. Have a safe trip home."

There were handshakes and smiles as he left the board room he had spent many hours in, going over financial records. Trevor had already forgotten the names of the men that were walking him out of the building and patting him on the back in a friendly attempt to push him out the door and be rid of him. There was nothing personal, but they had their own lives to get back to and he was just a stranger, standing in their way. It didn't really bother him anymore. To him they were like the motels he could no longer distinguish from each other. The names, the faces all seemed to blend into one interchangeable person. The sad part had always been that though he didn't want to stay, he had no great desire to leave either. Going back home to his 'cookie-cutter' home and mundane life was no real incentive to hit the road.

This time however was different. He had a new found sense of optimism. He was holding to his promise to make some changes and he actually looked forward to it. Glancing at his watch as he walked across the parking lot to his car, he decided there was time to grab a quick bite and still get some miles behind him before stopping for the night. When he had nothing to go home to, he usually took his time getting there. After all, the food and motels were paid for. But this time he was anxious to get going.

Pulling out of the parking lot he wondered briefly if the people he had just left were talking about him or if they had already forgotten he was ever there, but it didn't matter. It didn't take long to spot a place to get some fast food that he could eat while driving. He noticed that he was smiling and wasn't sure why. His thoughts went to the future and what life might be like in a year or so. Would he have a girlfriend or a wife? If so, he would probably dread these trips, having to leave her behind and be apart for so long. What about kids, was he too old to think about that? The smile remained. He had to laugh at the absurdity of it all. He didn't even know of anyone he could ask on a date and yet he was picturing himself as someone's husband, someone's father even. It felt good to think positive for a change.

As he pulled up to the drive thru, he thought about how easy it was to forget what town you were in at a fast food restaurant, or even what part of the country. They all looked the same. He did his best to order through the static filled box with pictures of all the food choices displayed in bright colors and wondered why it was so hard to find an intercom that actually worked. He pulled up to the first window and paid the high school student who did her best to look happy but really wanted to be any place else. She handed him a receipt and he looked it over to see if it was even close to what he ordered. They would get a kick out of this when he turned it in with his expense report. Usually he ate at fine dining establishments as a reward for the life he had been given. This would be something completely new and that in and of itself made it worth doing. The order was close enough so he proceeded to the second window.

There he was greeted, sort of, by a slightly older girl of maybe nineteen, wearing the uniform of a manager. She handed him the food they think he ordered while talking into a headset and never actually looking at him. He wanted to ask for napkins, which they neglected to give him and would likely come in handy, but she had already closed the window and walked away. He took a few fries and set the bag on the seat next to him before checking to his left and pulling out into traffic and heading out of town.

****

The sound of multiple conversations filled the briefing room next to the detective's squad. The men Jackson trusted and had asked to join them were gathered around in groups of three or four, waiting for the impromptu meeting to begin. When Jackson and Edwards walked in the noise fizzled out and the men began to take their seats. Jackson made his way to the podium at the front of the room and began. With a nod, Edwards placed a large board with a map of the city and surrounding area behind Jackson, then set several file folders on the table in case anyone wanted to flip through them.

"First of all, thank you for coming. I know you all have your own cases to work on and Edwards and I are grateful to each of you for giving us a few minutes of your time. I will try to keep this as brief as I can. As some of you know, we seem to have a series of killings on our hands, three that we know of. We believe the same man killed all three. The psychological profile we have come up with is available, Bill can you give everyone a copy of that please? Our guy prefers strangulation. He is likely a drifter with no fixed address. We have what we believe to be a DNA sample from the first crime scene and hope to have a good description later today." Jackson went on to fill them in on the rest of what they knew, which wasn't much. "Basically we have reached a point where we need some fresh eyes on this. Even the killer appears frustrated by our progress and frankly I don't know what to do next. Does anyone have any suggestions?"

The question hung in the air and was met with blank faces and silence, only to be broken when someone took a sip of their coffee. The detectives began to look around at each other as if they expected someone else to speak and take the responsibility off their shoulders. When no one seemed willing to break the stand off, Jackson made another appeal. "Come on guys, I know there isn't much there, but please, someone say something. Together, those of us in this room have worked every kind of case imaginable. I just know there is something we haven't explored yet."

"Where are you expecting to get a description from?" Someone asked.

"We believe the third and latest victim met the killer at a bar not far from her home. I have Detective Coffield over there talking to the bar staff now. Hopefully they will remember the guy. The girl did go to the bar semi-regularly."

"So we could have a description, a DNA sample and an M.O. by tonight, right? What don't we have?" The same detective spoke up and hoped that others would begin to join in.

"Just to put it out there, we sort of know the killer, we know what he likes to do. What we need is the when and where, right?" someone else chimed in and the ball had finally started to roll.

"Right. Let's focus on that. How can we get some idea of where, assuming the when will be anytime in the next day or two?" Jackson asked the now responsive group.

"You said you believe he is a drifter. Any idea which direction he is drifting?" A third detective had joined the discussion.

"That might be it. Let's mark the scenes on the map and see what we get." Jackson used stick pins with red flags on the end to mark each crime scene on the map behind him, then stood back for a second. "Wait a second; I think this could be something. I think I broke one of my rules and assumed the drifting was aimless or possibly moving away from the city, but that isn't it at all."

"What do you see?" Edwards asked on behalf of the puzzled group that had collectively wondered the same thing.

"He isn't doing either one. In fact, he is surrounding the city."

"Huh?"

"Each killing took place almost exactly the same distance from the center of the city. They also are equidistant from each other. Therefore, if we take the same distance from between the other victims and cross that with the same distance from the city center, we get a location right about here." Jackson measured it all out with a ruler and placed a pin with a blue flag at the spot. "I think there is a good chance this is where he will strike next." He stood back to get a better look and allow the rest of them to see what he was seeing.

"My goodness I think you're right. We have a pattern" one of them said.

"But why this pattern?" Edwards said, still puzzled.

"I have no idea. Maybe there's a reason, maybe not. It could be that he is using it to give us something to go on. He would know that we would figure it out sooner or later."

"So he could be just setting us up. We need to beef up the patrols in the area and show him some police presence."

"Wrong. Right now he doesn't know if we figured out the pattern yet and until we have a good description of him, we need to keep it that way. For now I want unmarked cars and non uniforms only. The last thing we need to do is scare him into hiding. We could lose the trail permanently if we over play our hand."

"You're right, sorry" Edwards admitted. It was a rookie suggestion, but Jackson was pleased with how he handled the criticism.

"Alright, thanks guys. I knew you could help us crack this thing. Anyone able to help us tonight, please let us know. Otherwise you can go with our gratitude."

The chatter began to build as the detectives stood and filed out of the room. A few of them came up and offered to help patrol the target area, even though they would be officially off duty. This was turning into the kind of case that everyone was eager to have resolved. It was a miracle that the media had not yet picked up on it and started to cause problems for them. The detective squad was a very diverse unit made up of multiple races, ages and beliefs, but they knew when to come together and work as a team and Jackson was grateful for that. For the first time he felt like they might actually catch the killer and end his reign of violence.

As the last men left the room and near silence returned, Edwards gathered up the files he had spread out. Jackson stood before the map and studied it hard as if to work through the mathematics of his hypothesis and discover any flaws.

"So it worked, we found something helpful we hadn't seen before" Edwards said, snapping Jackson's concentration.

"It sure seems that way. I've got a good feeling. You understand what we need to do tonight?"

"Yes, I do now. Sorry about before, I just got a little too excited thinking we might know where this guy is going to be."

"Don't worry about it. Listen, I'd like you to be in charge of setting up the canvas. Organize the volunteers we have and check with the watch commander to see who we can pull off patrol and out of uniform. I'm sure they will cooperate. It is of the utmost importance that we keep this low key until we get that description and know who we are looking for."

"Right, I got it."

"I know, sorry. I just want to make sure we do this right. I'm going to go fill the Lt. in on what's going on and then hopefully I'll hear from Coffield. Go ahead and start getting organized."

Edwards had a definite bounce to his step and looked an inch taller as he left the room. His lifelong pursuit had finally started to come to fruition. Before the night was over, he may even be chasing down the bad guy. Then in the morning he would stand before the media the hero of the city, having saved the lives of countless of its citizens. That would follow with a promotion and of course the end of his training. He had to stop walking to get his thoughts under control and focus on the task at hand. If he blew this, everything he dreamed of happening would be destroyed with a vengeance.

Jackson took a few more moments to analyze the map and strategically placed flag pins, concentrating on the blue one so hard he could almost see the neighborhood come to life before his eyes. "I think we just may have you" he said softly to himself before turning to leave the room.

Seconds later he stood knocking on the door to the Lieutenant's office. "You have a minute?" he asked.

"Sure Simeon, come on in. How did the meeting go?"

"Very well actually. It took a little prodding to get them going, but after that we did some brainstorming and I think we came up with something useful."

"Great, what is it?"

"We may have uncovered a pattern to the locations of the killings and have a projected site for the next one."

"Very good. I assume you are setting up a canvas right away?"

"I have Edwards pulling it together right now."

"Are you sure he's ready? We can't blow this."

"He's actually come a long way recently. He's ready."

"Alright, if you say so. Now if we can get this wrapped up before the media gets wind of it, it will be a miracle."

"I was just thinking the same thing."

Chapter Fourteen

Making his way through the maze of desks, Jackson felt pretty good returning to his work space. Since the beginning of this case, there had been the overall grim feeling of a dark cloud hanging above him, constantly threatening to open up and unleash a downpour. The feeling of never quite getting a grip on just who he was chasing was unsettling to say the least. Now, for the first time, he had a sense that the net was closing and if played correctly, their next move could prove victorious.

Though he hadn't noticed at first, it suddenly occurred to him that the squad was unusually quiet. There were plenty of people around, busy with activity, yet there was an unmistakable hush to their tone. Once he reached his desk he knew why. Sitting in the middle of his well organized desktop was a newspaper; the headline read *Killer on the Loose? Third Victim Found and may be Linked.* His heart sank as he read through the article. How do they do it, he wondered to himself. This was the late day edition, which meant the reporter had to have found out about the victim early that morning and had the story ready to go to print before he had even finished searching the room. There were some reporters that had a real future as detectives if they ever chose to go that route, he thought.

The details were sketchy and gave nothing away that would seemingly hurt the investigation; however the panic factor would rise immediately. As detectives, they had to prove beyond a reasonable doubt that the murders were connected. Reporters could draw any conclusion they wanted that would help sell papers. They would stand behind the noble cause of the "People's right to know," but it was always about the money and beating out the competition. Of course if the paper did step out of line and print something they shouldn't and got called on it, it would simply be a matter of printing a retraction buried deep within its pages. If the detectives made a mistake, the ripple effect of pain and injustice would carry farther than anything a pebble was capable of producing in the smoothest of ponds.

As he came to the end of the article he was resigned to the fact that it was likely to happen sooner or later, even the Lieutenant said it would be a miracle to avoid it much longer, and he was happy at the superficial nature of it, making it relatively harmless. That is until he got to the end. There in the final paragraph was his own name in black and white. Not only was he mentioned as the lead investigator responsible for capturing the killer and making the streets safe again for all the readers, but it went on to give a mini-bio that mentioned that he had an ex-wife and daughter living in the area. This infuriated him. Not only was it unnecessary, but it directly threatened the safety of his family. Why this was included was unclear and beyond irresponsible.

The room had gone completely silent around him and it was as though those present were waiting to see the old Simeon Jackson burst free in all his angry glory. What they saw was Simeon Jackson set down the paper, take a deep breath and close his eyes for several seconds. When he opened them, it was obvious that he had calmed himself and was in clear control. The normal sounds of the room slowly built back to a crescendo and everyone went about business as usual.

Jackson's state of mind returned to normal and he was going to show the article to the Lieutenant merely for information, not out of anger when his phone rang. "Jackson" he answered.

"Yeah Jackson, this is Coffield. I'm leaving that bar Mickey's now."

"Tell me you got something."

"Actually yes. Seems the girl was a regular that the bartender knew and the guy was someone he'd never seen before. He found it odd that the girl was talking with him so he was able to give me a good description of him."

"Excellent. I need you to call Edwards on his cell and get him that description. We think we have an idea of where the killer might strike next and Edwards is setting up a black canvas right now. The description could open up some better avenues for us since we will know what to look for and won't have to stay so hidden."

"Will do. Before I take off here is there anything else you need me to do?"

"Yes, tell them not to touch anything. I just had a thought that may be helpful if it pans out."

"Well they won't like that too much. They aren't open yet, but the place is still a mess from last night and I think they want to get it cleaned up before long."

"Tell them I am on my way and if they cooperate they can clean within the hour. Otherwise I will close the place down and bring in a full team to search the place, costing them several hours of operation. That should keep them quiet until I get there."

"Alright, you got it. I'll call Edwards and see if he needs me tonight as well."

"Thanks Coffield, you did well."

It was all coming together now, which was even more important when he considered that his family had been dragged into this. His anger had subsided, but he still planned to have a little chat with that reporter when this was all done. Moving swiftly he again dodged his way past the desks and out the door. Something had occurred to him that was only confirmed when he was told the bar had not been cleaned. If he was right, the killer just may have made a rare mistake. The thought kept up his feeling of urgency and he drove closer to the speed Edwards had quickly become known for than his own. He wanted to finish this and be ready for the night's events of which he wanted to be a part.

****

Gas station bathrooms are like the carpets of a pet owner, no matter how often you clean them, there is still a peculiar and unwelcome smell. Thomas Reardon stood in such a bathroom, looking at his own reflection and trying to see life behind his eyes, but that life, if it ever existed, had long since died away. The only thing he saw in his eyes was the need to kill. They made him think of the eyes of his victim as they died and how ironically, it was at the moment of death that the eyes seemed to contain the most life. It was as if he squeezed the life of a person like a tube of toothpaste and it rose to the top and filled in behind the eyes before disappearing forever. Something about that moment made him feel alive, made him feel, period. To him it felt like the life that passed from his victim somehow passed through him momentarily and allowed him to taste life, however briefly.

Standing shirtless he proceeded to splash water on his face and armpits, rubbing at the dirt that had built up and trying to remove the smell that came from not showering for days. He knew it was risky to take showers anywhere the police would be investigating because there were just too many DNA samples that could be left behind. Unfortunately as he often found, the soap dispenser was empty, leaving him only water to rinse away the grime.

He began to think about the game he was playing. It was time to step things up because he was getting bored by it. The killing itself wasn't enough anymore. He needed to add to the thrill, throw in a new twist. Toying with the police and the fear of getting caught had helped some, but it wasn't enough. Perhaps by now they would have picked up on the pattern he had laid out for them, making the threat even greater. It would get them excited and renew their energy, but in reality there were just too many places to hide, too many places to kill and not be seen. He could kill right under their noses and just walk away and they would never know it.

He took several paper towels and tried to dry himself off, but the towels were so stiff they had almost no absorbency. He pulled on his dirty shirt only to have it stick to his skin in the spots that just would not dry. After sniffing under his arms he realized the smell was still there, but at least not as strong. If he didn't take a shower soon he wouldn't get close enough to anyone to kill them. What a headline that would make, *Killer Stopped, not by Police, but by the Killer's Own B.O.* He smiled to himself as he looked down at the newspaper someone had left in the bathroom and read the headline again that referred to his game. His eyes focused on the last paragraph and he thought he may know how to make things more interesting.

It had become part of his routine to take a few dollars from his victims. Never enough that anyone would notice it missing; after all, he didn't want anyone confusing his work with that of a lowly robber. The few dollars came in handy to buy food and supplies that he needed to keep going. As he walked through the little mini-market that every gas station seemed to have these days, he reached in his pocket and pulled out a wad of wrinkled bills he had taken from the purse of his last victim. He could no longer remember her name and her face was fading fast, but the eight dollars he held was nice to have.

Down the snack aisle he took some granola bars and a bag of chips before rounding the corner and getting a bottle of water from the refrigerated section. He paused in front of the first aid and personal hygiene area and gave a long hard look at the deodorant. They were all priced at around four dollars, which could pay for a lot of food. He considered his options and just how long it could be before he showered again, then he noticed a display rack on the top shelf that contained car air fresheners, the kind that hang from the rearview mirror and make the car smell like flowers or pina coladas. They were on sale for a mere ninety nine cents. He decided that he could rub one on his clothes or even keep it in his pocket and save the extra money instead of using it to buy real deodorant. He chose one that seemed fitting when he looked back on how this game began. It was *pine* scented.

As he made his way up to the counter to pay he thought how funny it was that he could kill someone with his bare hands and yet wouldn't steal a stick of deodorant. Of course, to get caught shoplifting deodorant when he had been getting away with murder would be more than he could handle. He resolved himself to smelling like pine and placed his items on the counter to be rung up. After straightening out enough dollar bills to pay the total, he was happy to have a couple left over to shove back down in his pocket. Small plastic bag in hand, it was time to get walking. He still had some distance to cover if he wanted to get to where the police would undoubtedly be looking for him before nightfall.

****

At the pace he was driving it was only a few minutes before Jackson found himself once again driving down the busy street lined with bars and restaurants he had taken on his way to Jill Hanson's home. He slowed down to make sure he didn't pass his destination, but knew that he would be able to sense it when he was close. As expected, the bar that should have blended inconspicuously into the background all but called out to him. As he pulled into the parking lot he could not identify or shake the strange feeling that came over him. He wasn't sure why he had felt that connection to this place from the first time he passed it, but there was definitely something to it and it made him uneasy.

The lot was empty and next to the front door was a sign that told him it was less than an hour before the bar was scheduled to open. Hopefully it would not take long to get what he needed and be out of their way. After all, it wasn't their fault that a killer met his victim in their place of business and there was no reason they needed to suffer for it. The door was locked and he knocked loudly to get someone's attention quickly. As he listened for a response, the sound of heavy footsteps could be heard approaching from the inside. "Yeah, who is it?" a rough voice asked from behind the door.

"The police, open up" Jackson responded.

"You Jackson?"

"Yes." He could hear the sound of multiple locks being turned before the door swung open. Greeting him was a mountain of a man with a mean disposition, blocking the entrance almost as thoroughly as the door had a moment before.

"Let me see your I.D., I was told not to let anyone in but Detective Jackson or the bar wouldn't open on time."

Jackson sized him up and figured him for the bouncer. He obligingly took out his badge and I.D. and showed the man. After looking from the photo to Jackson and back a few times, he handed it back to Jackson and stepped aside, allowing him entrance before closing the door behind him. The sound of the locks being turned back to the locked position soon followed as Jackson stepped into the darkened bar and waited for his eyes to adjust to the low light. Looking around it was just as Coffield had described. Perhaps the staff was too tired to clean up at closing time because it looked like the last customer had just left based on the state of things. Bottles and dishes were everywhere and the floor was in serious need of a good sweeping. Of course this is exactly what he had hoped for.

His eyes were just getting used to the light when a shape approached from somewhere behind the bar that turned out to be an older gentleman in his late fifties to early sixties. He didn't look too happy as he came over to

Jackson and said "As you can see, we have a lot of work to do before we can open up and that's less than an hour away, so can we move this along?"

"Are you the manager?"

"Yeah, I am."

"Are you Mickey?"

"Sam actually. What do you need from us?"

"I need to talk to the bartender that was working last night, the one that remembers the girl and the man she met here, and I need you to leave things as they are until I finish."

"That would be Joey. The other cop already got the full story from him."

"I need to ask him something else."

"And just why does this require me to not get my bar cleaned up?"

"I'll let you know when I have my answer. If you were a little more cooperative, this would go more quickly and I can be out of your way."

"Alright, I'm sorry. This girl that was killed, she was a sweet kid. She never hurt anybody, you know? We all liked her a lot. She was lonely, we all knew, quiet type, but a good kid. Nobody here is happy about all this, believe me. We want to help, but we also have a business to run. I'll get Joey. Let me know when you're finished so we can get this place put back together and try and put all this behind us, alright?"

"Thank you, I'll make it as quick as possible."

Sam went back the way he came, and now Jackson could see that there was a door behind the bar that led to what was likely an office. He walked over to the bar and looked around behind it, hoping something would occur to him. As he looked at the wooden stools that lined the bar he wondered where Jill sat the night before, unwittingly meeting the man that would kill her in her own home just minutes later.

A younger man, tall and handsome, came through the door and over to Jackson, the bar separating them. He stood like he was ready to take Jackson's drink order, a force of habit, before he spoke. "Detective, I'm Joey. Listen, I feel awful about this. Jill was a really nice girl and didn't deserve this. How can I help?"

"I understand you remember seeing her last night."

"Yes, that's true. She came in around eight, alone. She sat here at the bar and had a couple of beers. I think she was waiting for her friend that rarely shows up. Then this guy comes in. I've never seen him before and he looked kind of rough around the edges, worse for wear. There was something about him I didn't trust. Before I knew it, they were talking to each other."

"Do you remember who started the conversation?"

"Well that's the thing. If he had started hitting on her I might have said something, but as I recall, it was actually her that started it. This was really unusual for her because she's so quiet, or was I guess. She talks to me quite a bit, but I've never heard her talk to any other customers except her friend."

"Can you remember what they were talking about?"

"Oh, nothing special that I noticed. Small talk at first, but after a while she seemed more relaxed and like she was enjoying his company. She wasn't watching the door for her friend anymore and she was smiling a lot. I decided to just let her enjoy herself and left them alone. At some point he changed seats to move closer to her and I thought that was odd, but she seemed happy about it. I didn't want to cramp her style if she was really interested in the guy, you know? I mean I wanted to watch out for her, but there was nothing going on between us so if she found someone she liked, great. I guess I didn't do such a good job of watching out for her though did I.?"

"You can't blame yourself for this. You had no control over what happened and no way of knowing what this guy was capable of. Don't beat yourself up over it. Do you remember anything else they said, anything about where they were going perhaps?"

"As I said, I was trying to give them their space, but it wasn't very crowded here last night, especially that early. I heard him asking about where he could find a motel. I get people asking me that sometimes, so my ears perked up a little. I was prepared to step in, when she answered it to his satisfaction. At around that time I went in the back for something and when I came out they were both gone. She left a nice tip as usual, he left a crinkled up dollar bill. I assumed they left together."

Jackson sat down at the place Joey had indicated the man had sat and just appeared to be soaking in the surroundings. He allowed Joey's story, which was not unlike the one he had imagined himself, to flow through his mind from the perspective of the killer's seat. After several trance like moments with Joey standing silently staring at him, unsure of what was happening or what to do, Jackson finally broke the silence saying "What was this man drinking?"

"He had a beer."

"Did he use a glass or drink straight from the bottle?"

"He drank from the bottle, why?"

"Are you sure?"

"Yes. Guys usually drink from the bottle. I don't give them a glass unless they ask for one unless it is a specialty beer, one that requires a lemon or orange slice or something like that. He didn't ask. It would have stuck out in my mind if he did because it is rare. There is some macho code that says a man drinks from the bottle."

"What do you do with the bottles?"

"They get thrown in this garbage can under the bar. The next morning we take them out to the recycling bin."

"I see that there are still bottles in it. Would that particular bottle still be in there?"

"It should be. We didn't feel like cleaning up last night so I'm sure it's in there."

"Do you remember what he was drinking?"

"MGD" Joey said after thinking for a moment. "Like I said, it wasn't very crowded last night."

Jackson pulled on a pair of rubber gloves and walked around behind the bar. The garbage can contained about twenty beer bottles of various brands. One by one he set them on the bar; separating the MGD bottles from the rest. When he had finished, there were three bottles in front of him that he was interested in. "You are sure that one of these three bottles is the one this guy drank from?"

"Yes. I was here until closing. Like I said, we didn't feel like cleaning, so all the bottles would still be in there."

"And he couldn't have taken the bottle with him?"

"No way. You can't take the bottles out of the bar, besides, I remember that the dollar he left was under the bottle. It was so wrinkled I kind of felt sorry for him. I figured he could probably use the dollar more than I could."

"What about the dollar, is that still here somewhere?"

"No, that's gone. We take care of the cash every night so there isn't too much here at once. That bill would be at the bank already."

"You've been a great help Joey, thank you. I'm going to keep these three bottles, but you can tell Sam I'm all finished and you guys can clean the place now."

Jackson removed an evidence bag from his pocket and carefully placed the three bottles inside. As he walked towards the door and waited to be let out, he took out his cell phone and called Dan Besson. "Dan, this is Jackson."

"Hey, what's up?"

"I need you to clear some time for me. I'm bringing in three beer bottles. One of which should have our killers fingerprints. We're setting up a canvas for him as we speak and being able to positively identify him could be invaluable."

"No problem, bring them in and I'll work on them right away."

"Thanks Dan." Jackson hung up and had just reached his car door. The sun was going down and there was electricity in the air. One way or another, this case could take a dramatic turn in the coming hours. Sometimes all it takes is one mistake and it looked like their guy may have finally made one.

Chapter Fifteen

Bill Edwards sat at his desk in the squad, a place he secretly had begun to call 'Command Central', but of course only to himself. He had received a call from Coffield with the description the bar tender had given of the man believed to have left with the latest victim and the last one known to have seen her alive. Though Bill had begun to understand that nothing could be taken for granted and that things were certainly not always as they appeared, he couldn't help but feel like real progress was finally being made.

As he hung up the phone after getting the latest information out to all patrol cars, especially those involved in the canvas, he began to have those delusions of grandeur once more. He pictured himself standing on the front steps of some Hollywood style city hall, a crowd of reporters filling the steps and sidewalk below. The flash bulbs and spotlights attached to television cameras were everywhere and the sounds of a flurry of questions being asked would go silent as he began to speak, everyone hanging on his every word as he began to describe the harrowing way in which he chased down and apprehended the serial killer that had been plaguing the city for these many days. He would describe in detail how it was he who had put it all together, it was he who had organized the final search and he who had placed the cuffs on this horrible man, thus ending the nightmare of fear.

Though even he had to laugh at himself, he was experiencing a child-like resurgence and finally knew what it was like to be a real detective. He was handed the responsibilities of a veteran and it felt good. As he sat back in his chair, arms folded behind his neck and the breath of satisfaction slowly escaping his lips, he saw Jackson enter the squad and make his way over. There was a definite pep in his step as he weaved his way between the desks to his own and if Bill was not mistaken, there might have even been the almost undetectable beginnings of a smile. This could only mean that he had news and Bill waited anxiously as he pulled out his chair and tossed his coat over the back before sitting down.

"You seem unusually cheerful. Did things go well at the bar?" Edwards prodded.

"Actually they just might have. I followed a hunch and came up with three beer bottles, one of which should contain our guy's fingerprints. I have Dan working on them as we speak and with any luck, we could be putting out a full APB within an hour or so."

"That's fantastic! Good work."

"How's the canvas coming along?"

"It's all set. They will begin in earnest at sundown, though I have the usual patrols on high alert already."

"And did Coffield get ahold of you with that description?"

"I just finished getting it out to everyone. If we get a name and photo to go along with it, we can go all out, right?"

"Absolutely."

"So if this works, we could have fingerprints, DNA, a photo and description and a high probability target area. We've come a long way haven't we?"

"Yes, especially from where we were just a few hours ago. Are you beginning to feel like a real detective yet?"

"Actually yes, I am. And thanks. I realize now how invaluable you have been and what a punk I have been acting like. I'm sorry for …"

"Don't mention it. Everybody starts out that way."

"Even you?"

"I'm afraid so. If people knew what police work was really like, there would be a lot less interested in joining up. We all have to fight past the Hollywood version and get down to reality. Only then can you figure out if it's really for you. In your case, I truly believe it is."

"That means a lot to me, thanks."

"To be honest, you're actually ahead of the game in many respects."

"Well having a big case doesn't hurt."

"No, you're right there. But a big case can hurt you too. If things don't go well it can kill your career before it gets a chance to start. You've caught on well and you already show signs of thinking like a detective. I could tell by how you worked the crime scenes that this was the right job for you."

"I was scared to death! I've never even seen a dead body, much less spent an hour in a room with one and studied them up close."

"That's something else we all had to get used to, but you handled it, fought through and by the next one you were very professional."

"Yeah, that was a little unnerving in and of itself. I mean I really could feel myself getting into the mind state of a killer, thinking like one."

"Unfortunately that is a crucial part of this job. Not everyone can do it, only the good ones. It can definitely be disturbing sometimes. In a way it's like tapping into a side of yourself that you don't ever want to come out. The thing is, you can't ever let it get to you, you have to keep it under control."

"How? Doesn't it ever get to you?"

"Sometimes. You just have to be stronger that it. Keep in mind why you are doing it and don't give in to it. It's best to have your life centered around something, something that can always bring you back."

"Interesting. Well thanks again. I'm starting to see just how much there is to learn, but for once I'm looking forward to it."

"Good. Say, it might get a little hectic tonight. Since we are waiting on those fingerprint results anyway, why don't we grab something to eat? Dan has my cell number in case he has any news."

"Sounds good to me."

Pulling on their coats, they made their way through the squad and out the door. Edwards had yet another pleasant surprise when Jackson began walking towards his own car and motioning for Bill to follow. Bill's heart rate increased, as did his pace, wanting to reach the car before Jackson would have a chance to clear off the seat. This might finally be it, the moment of truth, the end of the mystery. He would finally find out what had made such a dramatic change in Jackson, turning his life around.

He stood at the door, waiting for Jackson to unlock it, and looking through the window his eyes darted in all directions. Nothing. There was nothing there. The lock clicked open and he quickly got in hoping the change of view might lead to something. No longer hiding his curiosity, nor his growing frustration, it became obvious that he was up to something. With his goal once again seemingly out of reach and believing even more that the whole thing was just made up to drive him crazy, he put on his seatbelt and looked over at Jackson. There was a peculiar smile on the other man's face that made him uneasy.

"Looking for something?" Jackson asked, almost laughing.

"Huh? No, what do you mean?"

"Well, I saw you looking in my car earlier and now you seem to be doing it again. Would you care to explain?"

"Not unless I have to."

"Please do" Jackson said as he started the car and pulled out of the parking lot.

"Alright, but it's awkward."

"For you or for me?"

"Maybe both. When we first started to work together you were somewhat... reserved to put it politely. I didn't know if it was me or if that's just how you were so I started asking around."

"And someone told you about the child molester case, right?"

"Yes. They said you were different before that, but you found something that literally changed your life and you were never the same."

"That's true. Go on."

"But they wouldn't tell me what it was."

Jackson chuckled. "I'm not surprised. But what did they tell you?"

"That I could figure it out on my own if I saw what was on your front seat. It sounds stupid, I know. It was probably just somebody messing with the new guy."

"Not necessarily." As Jackson stopped at a red light, he reached behind Edwards and retrieved something from the backseat and dropped it on Edwards lap. "I believe this is what you are looking for."

Edwards looked down at what now lay in front of him and took a second to figure out just what he was seeing and why. "A Bible? That's it? That's the big secret I've been trying to figure out that no one would tell me about, you found religion?"

"I guess so."

"I have to tell you, I'm a little disappointed."

"Why, what did you think it was?"

"I don't know, just something a little more interesting."

"Have you ever read it?"

"Yes, well a little. Not really, but still."

"It's pretty interesting stuff."

"Still, for such a drastic turn around, I was hoping there was some answer I had not heard of."

"Maybe you haven't really heard it yet. In order to really hear about God you have to be ready. I was at a real low point in my life. I had come dangerously close to losing my job, setting a child molester free and was still dealing with my divorce, which not only cost me a loving wife, but my daughter. The rage I had inside that had erupted that night when I went to make the arrest was still there, waiting to boil over again. My life was headed nowhere. I took a couple of days off to try to clear my head. One night an old friend stopped by and we sat and talked, at first about nothing in particular, but then he changed gears on me and started talking about God. I looked at him the same way you are looking at me right now. That was the last thing I wanted to talk about. Like most people, when things are at their worst, I said things like 'If there's a God, how could He allow such misery.' Yet my friend just kept talking. Nothing forceful, just calmly talked about Jesus and love and forgiveness. He said that he could tell that I was unhappy and it was because I was missing something in my life. As he went on he talked about the fact that only God could have kept me from losing my badge and kept that animal behind bars, nothing else made sense in this age of lawsuits. I spoke very little but found myself really listening to what he was saying. I don't know if I believed it at the time, but when he said God had plans for me it felt good. Then he simply made a promise to pray for me and left."

"So what did you do?"

"I sat there for the longest time. My cynical side arguing with everything he said, but a growing part of me wanted to believe him. I had no interest in becoming religious. I did my best to dismiss him and think about something else, but his words haunted me. There was a truth there that could not be denied. That's when the strangest thing happened."

"What?" Edwards asked, more interested than he intended to be.

"Almost as if by some exterior compulsion I found myself falling to my knees. Now I hadn't prayed since I was a kid in Sunday School, yet the words and emotions began to flow out of me effortlessly. I broke down and through my tears I accepted Christ and asked Him to be Lord of my life."

Edwards was caught up in the moment. This was the last thing he expected to hear from this hardened, serious detective with the violent past. He wasn't sure how to respond. God had never been a part of his life. It's not that he didn't believe, he didn't care enough to even consider the question. His pessimistic side started to fight its way through the emotional story Jackson had just told. "I know you were in a bad way at the time and I can see you being vulnerable or maybe open to your friend's suggestions, but with all that you have seen and still see on this job, the very worst of humanity, you can still believe in God?"

"Yes, and that belief is what gets me through. Without Him, I would have lost my mind years ago."

"Interesting. Well I guess if it helps you, I'm fine with it."

"Thanks."

"I don't mean it like you need my permission or anything. I just mean that I'm comfortable with it."

"I understand" Jackson said as they arrived at a nearby restaurant.

****

After several hours of nothing but farms and cornfields on both sides of the road, no longer able to discern one decrepit old barn from the next, Trevor Simmons was ready for a break. His stomach grumbled and he began to watch the billboards and advisory signs to find the best exit to take, one that offered a variety of food choices as well as gas stations from chains that he had actually heard of before. He was leery of the gas stations that looked like the people made the gas themselves, right next to the moonshine still out in the woods someplace. He also didn't like places where the names were just too cute. If it wasn't a nationally known name brand, he wouldn't risk putting it in his tank. Even though it was a company car, if something went wrong with it, he would be the one stranded on a dirt road, next to some farm that looked like it was right out of a horror movie. It was worth spending the company's money to get reliable gas.

There were several billboards advertising fine and not so fine dining at an exit a few miles away and he made the decision to follow their advice and stop. When it came to food, ironically he looked for the most local places with food he could not get other places. He found it strange that he was more willing to take a chance on what went into his body than what went into his car, but he figured if he had to travel for a living, he might as well get a taste of the places he went to, literally.

As he slowly came to a stop at the top of the ramp and looked for a clue as to which way he should turn, he spotted the perfect place off to the right. There was a recognizable gas station with decent small town prices and within walking distance was a real down home restaurant. He drove over to the station and stopped at an open pump. Stepping out into the evening air that had cooled considerably since he had last breathed it earlier in the day, he took a moment to stretch and with a yawn took out his business credit card and slid it into the slot. He selected the cheapest variety, after all, he was still an auditor, and began pumping the gas. Looking at his windshield, he briefly considered trying to wash the dead bugs off, but he knew it would be futile. They would just smear and make things worse. As long as he could still see, it was better to let sleeping bugs lie, or dead ones as the case may be.

A loud click told him his tank was full. Following the clearly printed instructions not to 'top off', he replaced the hose, took the receipt and got back in the car. The restaurant next door was a quaint little place that promised home cooking. That being something he never actually got at home, he drove the few feet to the adjoining parking lot and parked. There was a hand painted sign in the window that said 'Just like your Momma makes'. He'd have to see about that.

As he opened the door a bell rang over his head to announce his arrival. There were antiques everywhere. The floors were all hard wood and the air was filled with a mixture of pine trees and food cooking on a hot stove. In a way it had already reminded him of his mother's kitchen and it brought a smile to his face. He was grateful for the nostalgia. He hadn't thought about what it was like to have a real 'home' for a long time, and this had put him in a good mood.

An older, grey haired lady approached him and asked if he would be dining alone, he indicated that he would and she led him to a table near the back. He wondered if she was hiding him and if so, was it for his benefit or theirs. Either way, he was feeling good and he wasn't going to let it bother him. She handed him a menu and made her way back to the front.

He opened the menu and found he had a choice of several styles of chicken and ham, as well as roast beef and steak. A warm feeling came over him just being there and it prompted his mind to again drift towards his imaginary future. Would it be like this? Would he come home after a long day at the office or a trip like the one he was on now to a place filled with the smell of food cooking? Would there be a kind and beautiful woman awaiting his return? He began to picture what his house would look like with a woman's touch.

A woman that was a little younger than the hostess, wearing a big smile and a lot of make up came over to his table to take his order. She was chewing gum like it was a natural function, like breathing, and the smile seemed to be permanent. She called him Hon'. He did his best to order something that his mother would have made him and she said she would be back in a "Jiff" with his drink.

Looking around at the other patrons he saw older couples everywhere, a family sat in the corner booth and it was clear the children, not the parents, were in control. Then his eyes rested on a beautiful young lady sitting alone. She must have come in while he was ordering because he would certainly have noticed her. She was still looking at the menu and had not returned his gaze. He tried to stop looking to avoid staring, but found it difficult to keep his eyes off of her.

A thought came to his mind, a crazy thought, one that even if it had surfaced in the past it would not have survived for more than an instant, but on this evening he allowed it to flow freely through his brain like a kite in the sky swirling over a child in the park. Here they were, two grown people, sitting alone just feet apart. Sure they did not know each other, but no one knows anyone at first. People had to meet somehow, so why not here, in this restaurant, on this night. Though he was far from home and had no idea where she was from, the idea of just having dinner and pleasant conversation with an attractive woman was too compelling to pass up. With courage he wasn't aware he even possessed, he looked himself over and determined that he was presentable, still wearing his suit, and stood up. He closed his eyes and cleared his mind and found himself almost involuntarily walking over to the young woman's table.

From somewhere deep within him a voice that he almost didn't recognize came out full of hope brought on by the nostalgic atmosphere, his new found outlook on life or some undetermined source and said "Excuse me. I couldn't help but notice that you were dining alone. I'm alone myself and I wondered if you might like to join me for dinner and polite conversation?"

She looked up at him and her expression changed from friendly to annoyed. "I don't think so" she said as if she had a bad taste in her mouth.

"I'm sorry; I know this is a little strange since we don't know each other. I just thought that perhaps…"

"Listen. I don't care what you thought. Please just leave me alone." Her attention quickly returned to the menu as she pretended that he was not there. For a moment all he could do was stand there in stunned silence. As he slowly gathered himself he turned and walked back to his own table. Suddenly this place no longer had a warm feeling, but it was as if someone had opened the doors and windows in the middle of winter, sending a chilling wind through the entire building.

He was tempted to just walk out, but with his food already ordered, it would not be right to stiff the restaurant. His appetite lost and his mind on other things, he would never know if the food was truly like his mother used to make. When it arrived, he ate quickly, but to him it had no taste. There was just the bitter bile in his mouth from the memory of the young woman's face and harsh words. There she sat, just a few feet away, already forgetting about him.

When he finished eating, he walked past the woman without looking at her. He was tempted to give her a piece of his mind. He wanted to tell her that it was people like her that were what was wrong with the world these days. It was attitudes like hers that kept people isolated, afraid to speak to others, afraid to reach out and trust and feel. All he wanted was someone to talk to and share a few minutes dining with someone. But instead, she had to treat him like he was less than human, a disease of some kind, not worth wasting her time on. That is what he wanted to say, but instead he left in silence. The hostess tried to thank him for stopping in and invite him back, but the sound of the door closing behind him cut off her kind, well rehearsed words.

He got back into the car and pulled away. No matter how hard he tried to recapture the optimism he felt just a few minutes earlier, it just wouldn't return. Instead, his mind flooded with the woman's scornful face, his thoughts of a brighter future just seemed silly now. In just moments he had gone from such a profound and determined high, to the lowest of lows. That was the price he paid for feeling, for reaching out. Was it worth it to subject himself to such rejection? What if that was all that awaited him, over and over? What if happiness would always somehow elude him? His mindset had changed completely as he returned to the highway. There was no longer an urgency to get back to the empty house that lay at the end of his journey. It would be dark in an hour. Maybe it was time to find a motel to spend the night.

****

Stomachs full, Jackson and Edwards were walking back to the car when a cell phone began to ring. Reaching into his pocket and pulling out his phone he answered "Jackson".

"This is Besson. I have your finger prints lifted from the bottle you gave me."

"You think you found some from our guy that we can use?"

"All three bottles had one set in common, I assume those belong to the bartender. Two of them contained a second set, and the third had a set all its own. If you're sure your guy only drank one beer, it seems likely that those would be his."

"Great work Dan, we're about ten minutes out and on our way. Can you have someone there start running them through the system?"

"They're already on it. I gave it to them just before I called. With any luck, you may have a winner by the time you arrive."

"Thanks so much Dan, you really came through for me and I won't forget it."

"No problem. Good luck tonight."

Jackson hung up and was excited to fill Edwards in on the part of the conversation he hadn't heard. He drove a little faster than usual, anxious to find out if they could put a name and face to their killer.

"I'm curious about something" Edwards said, breaking the silence.

"What about?"

"Well, I don't pretend to be an expert on religion or anything, but I always thought Christians felt it was their duty to go around telling everyone about Jesus and trying to recruit everyone. Yet I've never heard you mention your beliefs in all the time we've worked together and I had to go out of my way to find out."

"Some people are very vocal about their beliefs. I'm a little more subtle. It takes all kinds."

"So you don't think it is your place to tell people about God?"

"I didn't say that. I am more than happy to share my beliefs. I just think God has different ways to use us to spread His word."

"But if you don't bring it up to people, how can you talk about Him?"

"I didn't seek you out and here we are having our second conversation about Him already. Both of which were initiated by you. God has His ways."

"Yeah, but I'm not interested in God."

"Neither was I."

Chapter Sixteen

It had been a long day and Kelly Sanders did not feel like cooking or worse yet, cleaning up afterwards. There was something about washing dishes on a full stomach, the smell of dish soap combined with the food, now wet, in addition to the effort itself that made it so much more appealing to eat out and let someone else deal with the work. She was not a wealthy woman who could afford fancy dining and so she found herself sitting at the counter of the Denny's near her apartment building.

She needed time to just clear her head from the hassles of the day so she sat and read a book while waiting for her food to arrive. Though she found it difficult to devote her full attention to the book, as she was taught by her father to always be aware of her surroundings, especially when out in public, she did manage to get a vague grasp on the general intentions of the author.

There was a certain comfort she felt just being in the presence of other people, even if she was not interacting with most of them. Too many nights alone in her small apartment left her wanting the sounds of people's voices that did not come from her television. There was a stigma to dining alone that she was wary of, but sitting at the counter afforded her the chance to not look as awkward as if she were in a booth. She had tried sitting in a booth before but had the strange sensation that the booth was swallowing her up, making her look small and insignificant and announcing to the world that yes, she was dining alone. "No, I don't have anyone special in my life!" she felt like screaming out. Since when did it become such a negative thing to dine alone anyway? What was wrong with a little solitude, even in public? The world revolved around couples, families and groups of friends. Those that tried to do anything alone were not heralded as independent, they were considered outcasts. She would have been fine being alone if not for the nagging suspicion she had that people were staring at her and whispering.

"Look at the woman eating all alone. There must be something wrong with her" she imagined them saying. Maybe there were times when a person just wants to be alone, hadn't they considered that? So what if she didn't really have a choice in the matter, it wasn't really any of their business anyway.

She did her best to concentrate on her book, but occasionally she gave in to the urge to glance over her shoulder and see who was looking at her. Everyone appeared to be just enjoying their food and conversations so she would go back to reading, though in her mind she wondered if maybe she just wasn't quick enough to catch them looking. No sooner had she thought this when the busboy started to laugh. Had he been looking at her? Did he somehow know what she was thinking? No, that was impossible. But why was he laughing? She was sure he saw plenty of people dining alone and surely it would no longer seem strange or out of place to him. Besides, he was just a bus boy. Who was he to laugh at her anyway?

Her food arrived and she found herself watching the server very carefully for any signs of laughing at her expense. I have to stop this, I'm just being paranoid. I'm not crazy and this is crazy, she thought to herself. Maybe she was just lonely. Maybe instead of the world telling her she was strange; something inside her was saying it was time to meet someone, someone to spend time with, talk to and do things with. Maybe she could find a friend or even a nice man to date. She set her book down and looked over her food. Taking in a big breath to both clear her mind and whet her appetite with the aroma, she began to eat.

As she let the taste of her first bite trigger the various taste buds along her tongue, savoring the flavor and enjoying the fact that there would be no dirty dishes to clean at the end of her meal, not for her anyway, she heard the door open behind her. Glancing over to see who had come in she saw an interesting looking man, a little ragged but not entirely unattractive.

She temporarily forgot about her food and gave him the once over. His clothes were certainly a little worse for wear and his hair was greasy. Still, there was something about him that intrigued her. He too was alone and her heart sped up with an undefined excitement when he chose to sit just one stool over from her.

Her face felt flush as she was reminded of her earlier thoughts. This could be just the opportunity she was looking for. It seemed natural that, sitting so close and sharing the same activity, the two of them might strike up a conversation. From there, who knows? She had to at least entertain the thought, right? Her stomach felt strange, her food forgotten as she tried to think of a way to break the ice. To her delight, he looked over and smiled at her. He had an infectious smile and she could not help but return it.

"Hi, my name is Justin" he said in a smooth voice.

"I'm Kelly. Nice to meet you" she somehow managed to say. He looked more handsome now, though she noticed he smelled like one of those car fresheners people buy at gas stations and hang from their rearview mirrors.

****

Jackson and Edwards arrived at the station just minutes after speaking to Dan Besson on the phone. They wasted no time making their way through the hallways to the part of the station referred to as the computer lab. Though everyone had a computer on their desk, this was the place for the special computers. The one they were interested in this evening could take a set of fingerprints and compare and cross reference them with prints on file in data bases all over the country.

Jack Palmer sat in front of the screen watching a flurry of fingerprint images flying by on the right side of the screen, occasionally pausing to compare points of similarity to the stationary print on the left. Noticing his observers, Palmer turned saying "As you know, this can take hours. You want me to stick with it or do you want to take over?" Instead of a verbal response, Palmer saw Jackson's face light up. He quickly turned back to the screen and saw that the flurry of prints had come to a complete halt, revealing a match. At once, all three leaned in towards the screen, narrowly missing each others heads.

No one seemed to be breathing until at last Jackson said aloud what the others were reading for themselves. "Thomas Reardon. Served time in juvenile hall for killing animals. Psychiatric evaluation revealed very little. He must have out smarted them. No recent photo, must not have a driver's license. At least we have a name to go with the description now. Thanks Palmer."

"Yeah, it's been a rough ten minutes" came the sarcastic response.

Jackson and Edwards turned quickly to head back down the hallway and towards the parking lot. Without being told, Edwards took out his cell phone and began reporting the latest information to those on his canvas operation. Word would spread quickly as those in the field would be happy for all the help they could get, wanting to wrap things up as quickly and easily as possible. Jackson was pleased to see him act on his own. He had taken responsibility for the canvas and was making it his own. With a sense of pride he slapped Edwards on the back, taking him by surprise, but a welcome one.

On the way back to the parking lot they stopped by the dispatcher. With the name of the suspect, they could now request an All Points Bulletin, alerting all officers in the surrounding area, including adjoining cities, county and state police. The time for subtlety had passed. They knew who they were looking for and did not want to afford him the luxury of hiding.

****

Though she immediately felt a certain comfort with Justin, Kelly waited until he spoke again. She didn't want to seem too forward and a part of her was still not convinced that this was all real. If he didn't speak to her again, it would be a devastating blow. After all, she had allowed herself to start down a path that she could not quickly turn from, though it was in her mind and no one else was aware of it. Fortunately, she did not have to wait long. He lowered his menu and turned to her, again smiling and said "I can't seem to decide what I want. Forgive me for asking but what's that you are having, it looks really good?"

"I decided to go with breakfast for dinner. This is one of those skillet things, the one with ham and peppers..." he leaned towards her and held out the menu. "There, that's the one." She liked having him close and felt a surge of electric excitement as she could feel his body heat.

Just then the waitress reappeared and he leaned back to his own seat.

The lack of warmth with his sudden absence was evident and she didn't like it. He held up the menu and pointed to the picture she had shown him, saying "I believe I will take the lovely lady's advice and have this as well."

She smiled shyly at the compliment and said "I think you'll enjoy it." This was easier than she had imagined. Why had she not tried this long ago?

"I'm sure I will, thank you. But to be perfectly honest, if not a little bold, what I'm really enjoying is your company."

"Thank you. I am too, yours I mean." Now she was blushing on the verge of giggling.

"Well there is no sense in us both dining alone is there? Would it be alright if I moved down and joined you, or am I being too forward?"

"No, not at all. I'd be very happy if you would join me." She gave a slight wave of her hand, indicating the stool next to hers and hoped her face was not as red as it felt. If it was, she must look like a tomato by now.

She found it difficult to eat, not just because she had lost her desire for the food with something so much more interesting to think about, but because since his food had not yet arrived, he would likely be watching her. She also did not want to get caught with a mouth full food or heaven forbid something stuck in her teeth, should she need to speak. Besides, there was a smile on her face that would not be denied and that alone made eating politely nearly impossible.

There was a way about him that made her feel calm and comfortable. The way he spoke was flattering and his personality gave life to his rugged features. She was enamored with him and didn't try to fight it. As she put her book away in her purse, certain she would no longer be needing it, his food arrived. He looked it over approvingly and as he took his first bite he made a big show of just how much he enjoyed it. Perhaps it was for her benefit, but it wasn't necessary.

After doing her best to eat enough, she indicated to the waitress that she was finished, but as the plate was carried away she realized that now she would be responsible for carrying the conversation. She did her best to keep him interested as he ate every last bite, talking about current events, the situation of the world, hoping that she was not boring him.

With her food cleared away she needed an excuse to stay and though she was not at all hungry, she ordered dessert. She kept on talking and he listened intently, seemingly hanging on her every word, occasionally making a comment between bites. She was determined to make this last. What had started out as a lonely dinner among strangers had turned into a glorious bonding with another human being, one that she now found very attractive. She was not about to just get up and walk away.

Eventually he pushed away his plate, now completely devoid of food, and sat back patting his full stomach. Her untouched ice cream that she hadn't even noticed in front of her was beginning to melt. Suddenly she was filled with dread as she realized he may be about to leave. What could she do to stop him? Coffee! He hadn't had coffee. Maybe she could invite him to her place for a cup of after dinner coffee. The very thought both scared and excited her. Her father, if he were still alive, would be furious with her for even thinking of inviting someone she had just met, a man on top of it, back to her apartment. Though she respected her father, she pushed away the thought and decided that if that's what it would take to continue this rare human interaction, then so be it. She almost gasped as he stood up, but he was merely excusing himself to use the bathroom. With a wave of relief, she began to come up with just the right way to invite him home.

With the added information at their disposal, uniformed patrol officers were now added to the unmarked cars searching the target area. Police presence was greatly increased and officers were instructed to check every bar, diner, coffee shop or anyplace that was open late. Thomas Reardon seemed to enjoy killing as a nightcap and would likely seek someone's company after nightfall.

Officer Beck drove car thirty four slowly through the alleyway as Officer Ramirez worked the spotlights to brighten the many dark areas along the way. Seeing nothing unusual they pulled out onto the main street and continued on. After passing several store fronts, most of them closed for the night, they came upon a Denny's restaurant.

"What do you think?" Beck asked.

"It fits the description" Ramirez replied with a shrug of his shoulders. "I could use a cup of coffee anyway. Let's go in."

Beck pulled over and stopped in front of the entrance. The officers got out and gave a quick check of the buildings exterior before making their way inside. Standing by the hostess stand and looking around, they were suddenly approached by the manager who hurriedly picked up two menus before asking "Table for two officers?"

"No, we just need to look around. We're looking for a white male, in his thirties, longish brown hair, kind of dirty, thin…have you seen anyone that matches that description here tonight?"

"I've been in the back off and on and haven't paid that much attention, but I don't recall anyone like that. You might want to ask my hostess when she returns from her break. Until then, feel free to look around all you like."

"We will. Get us a couple of coffees to go. Large coffees."

The manager rolled his eyes as he headed back to the kitchen, knowing he wouldn't see a dime for those "large" coffees. This was the modern version of protection money. The officers walked around looking over each customer one by one. Satisfied that no one fit the description they were content to take their coffees and leave when Beck noticed a woman sitting at the counter alone, looking very nervous. In front of the seat next to her was a dirty plate, but no one was sitting there.

Kelly was watching the police officers walking around and wondered what they were doing there. She knew there was no reason for them to be looking for her, she had done nothing wrong, but she couldn't help but feel nervous by their presence. If they weren't here to eat, there must be something wrong. She wanted them to leave before they ruined everything. The good feelings she was having were gone and she was beginning to lose the confidence she had felt. If they were still here when Justin returned, she would never have the courage to invite him over. Then it occurred to her that maybe he was the one they were looking for. No, that couldn't be. He was so nice, such a gentleman and he treated her well. There was no way he could be a wanted criminal. Still, she couldn't help but question her decision to invite a stranger into her home when the police were obviously looking for someone. She decided it was best to just leave, but before she could get more than a step she realized the officers were looking at her.

She froze in her tracks as they looked at each other and walked in her direction.

"Is everything okay Miss? You look a little frightened" Ramirez said.

Thomas Reardon dried his hands off on the paper towels and looked into the bathroom mirror. He was amazed at just how many desperate women were out there, so willing to trust him with their very lives. Though it hadn't happened yet, he was certain that when he returned Kelly would invite him back to her place. He could probably even convince her to pay for his meal, which was a good thing since he didn't think he had enough money to pay for it. She was cute, though she was nervous and completely boring. He would enjoy killing her. The thought got his blood pumping a little faster and there was a flicker of excitement in his eyes as he turned away from his reflection to go seal the deal. He opened the door and looked to make sure she was still waiting for him and was surprised to find her speaking to two police officers. He quietly let the door close again and stood against the bathroom wall feeling a surge of adrenaline through his entire body.

"Yes, everything is fine. If you'll excuse please…" Kelly said, trying to squeeze past the officers who refused to budge.

"We're looking for a man" Beck said.

"Aren't we all?" she replied, trying to lighten the mood and not seem so nervous.

Ignoring the levity, Beck gave her the description of Thomas Reardon. "Have you seen anyone that looks like that this evening?"

She considered lying to them. Even though Justin fit the description perfectly, whatever he had done could not have been too bad. Her conscience got the better of her as she looked over at the spot in which Justin had eaten his dinner. There eyes followed her gaze and it was clear that lying would be useless. She decided to just give in and tell them the truth. "Well there was a gentleman sitting next to me that may look like that, but I'm sure he's…"

"Where is he now?" Ramirez interrupted.

"He went to the men's room" she said, sounding defeated, and sat back down heavily on her stool.

No sooner had the words left her lips, the officers were moving past her and through the restaurant towards the men's room in the back. Standing silently outside the door, guns drawn, they nodded to each other and swung open the door. Waiting for a response that didn't come, they went inside and looked around, but there was no one there. Beck kicked open the stall door and cautiously checked inside, but it too was empty. "Check the window" he said urgently.

Ramirez looked it over and ran a finger along the bottom edge and it came up covered in dust. "Doesn't look like anyone has touched this for a while." They both stepped out of the room a bit baffled and were about to walk away when they noticed the entrance to the ladies room. They shrugged and again took up position on the sides of the door before swinging it open. When once again they heard nothing, they went inside, hesitantly just in case it was occupied for its original purpose. They found it empty and turned to walk out.

"Hang on, let me check the window." Beck stepped over to the window and saw something strange. There was something sticking out from the window. He raised it just enough to remove a piece of paper and let it close again. His heart sank as he understood what he was looking at. With a sense of panic, he ran from the room. "He went out the window, let's go!"

Kelly watched as the two officers ran past her and out of the restaurant. Moments later it began to sink in just how close she came to inviting a man to her apartment that was now being chased by the police. She wasn't sure what he had done, but suddenly eating alone didn't seem so bad anymore.

Out behind the building, hiding in the shadows, Thomas Reardon watched the window as the silhouette of the officer grew stronger just before he raised and lowered the window from inside the ladies room. "This is amazing" he whispered to himself as the adrenaline pumped through his veins. Just moments before he could hear them bursting into the men's room as he was climbing out the window. They had come so close to catching him he thought his heart would burst through his chest. Now as he watched them through the frosted window, he saw them run from the room and back through the restaurant. Thomas shook his head at this mistake. Had they simply opened the window all the way, they might have seen him and even had a chance to catch him. However, the little gift he left them worked just as he had hoped, distracting them just long enough to put him out of reach. Precious seconds were all the difference he would need to disappear.

Using this time to break from cover, he rounded the corner, crossed the alley and walked around the building behind Denny's. In moments he was on the sidewalk, blending in perfectly with the other pedestrians. After walking for a block and a half he cut across a yard and faded into the darkness of night.

Not sure if he was armed, but certain he was dangerous, Beck and Ramirez were following the book as they rounded the corner and searched behind the restaurant. The lighting was less than adequate making for many shadowy areas for their little flashlights to penetrate as they continued towards the alley. Feeling they were probably too late, they relaxed a little.

"Call it in, I'm going to look a little more."

Beck used the radio attached to his collar to report to headquarters. When Jackson came over the radio from his car, Beck asked him to call him on his cell phone. "Hello?"

"This is Jackson. We're on our way there. What's up?"

"Detective, there's a little more to the story that I thought best to tell you off radio first."

"What is it?"

"Well Reardon left a little something at the scene that I think was meant for you."

"What is it Beck? Spit it out."

"He left a newspaper clipping about his killings next to his escape route and that's not all. He circled the part of the article that mentions your name and your family."

"Okay, thanks" Jackson said after a short pause. "We'll be there shortly."

Chapter Seventeen

Once the dispatcher at police headquarters had received the call from Beck regarding the close call they had at Denny's, all patrol cars in the immediate area were redirected to search everything in a two mile radius of the restaurant. Jackson and Edwards monitored the radio traffic from their car while en route to the Denny's for further questioning of the witnesses, in the hopes it might provide some insight into the direction that Thomas Reardon may have headed, though Jackson knew deep down it would not help.

"So what was all that about?" Edwards asked, curious about the call Beck asked Jackson to place.

"There was something he didn't want going out over the open radio. It seems that the newspaper article effectively alerted Reardon of both my name and my family status."

"Why, what happened?"

"He circled that part of the article and left it behind on his escape route where we would be sure to find it."

"That's a direct threat! We have to catch this guy, now." Edwards had begun to panic and looked over at Jackson, expecting him to be on the verge of losing it. To his surprise, he didn't see the return of the violent, raging man that he had heard about, but a man that was the picture of calm, though he had taken a page out of the Edwards driving manual and was driving as if on an obstacle course, not a city street.

Jackson pulled the car up next to car thirty four, which still sat near the front entrance to Denny's. Edwards threw open his door and rushed out, anxious to do something, anything that would help move things along. Though he did not know Jackson's ex-wife and daughter personally, the idea of a killer so directly threatening the safety of an officer's family made him ill. He had nearly reached the front door when he noticed he was alone.

Turning back to see where his partner was, he saw him still sitting behind the wheel of his car. Like he had seen once before, his head was down and eyes were closed. Only now did Edwards realize that Jackson was not sleeping, but praying. Hurriedly he returned to the car and flung open the driver's door and felt justified in interrupting. "What are you doing? Some maniac just threatened your family and you take time to pray?"

Jackson seemed not to notice him at first, but after several seconds that felt like minutes, he opened his eyes and looked at his young associate. "There is always time to pray. I would rather proceed with God's help, then to just run into it in a blind rage. Believe me, I've tried it the other way and it doesn't work so well."

"Still, how can you stay so calm?"

"Because I prayed. If you place things in God's hands, you have merely to do your part and leave the outcome up to Him."

"Even if that means the death of your only child?"

"If that's what He decides is the best thing, then yes."

"Just like that?"

"I'm not saying it would be easy and I certainly don't want that, but if God says someone's time is up, do you really think I can stop it?"

"Then what is the point of what we do anyway?"

"Like I said, we still need to do our part. God uses us how He sees fit. We have to trust that whatever the outcome, it is somehow for the best."

"I don't know if I can buy that. That seems like a lot to ask."

"It's a matter of faith."

"But even faith in something you can't possibly understand?"

"The Bible says to trust in the Lord with all of your heart and not to lean on your own understanding. If we had to rely on our own understanding, we would be in a lot of trouble. Now, I have enjoyed this little talk, the third that you initiated by the way, but we do have a job to do. Shall we?"

Edwards head was spinning, but he was glad to get back to the matter at hand and so he turned and headed back towards the front door, this time with Jackson in tow. Just inside the door were Beck and Ramirez and a room full of people anxious to be on their way. Everyone had been asked to stay until they were questioned and cleared by the detectives and some were getting very impatient.

"So Officer Beck, what do you have for me?" Jackson asked.

"First of all, I am so sorry we blew this thing. I can't believe we let him escape."

"Don't worry about it, everyone makes mistakes and this guy knows what he's doing."

"Thanks detective." Beck was both relieved and surprised in how calm Jackson remained under the circumstances. "We kept everyone here. The woman at the counter tipped us off. Apparently they sat next to each other but had never met before."

"Let's see if we can move this along. There's no need to inconvenience these people more than we have to. You guys get out your notepads." Jackson stepped into the dining area. "May I please have everyone's attention? My name is Detective Jackson. I'm sorry we had to keep you here, but if everyone will cooperate, we can get you out of here very soon. Now, aside from the lady at the counter, does anyone remember or have knowledge of the man that was sitting next to her beyond a general description?" He waited a moment and looked for anyone to raise their hand. When no one did, he continued "Alright. Then please take out your photo I.D.'s and form a line, without pushing please. Give the officers at the door your name, address and phone number where you can be reached. After that you will be permitted to leave. Make sure you pay your checks first! Thank you for your patience and cooperation."

After giving everyone a chance to get in line, he asked the manager to come over by the place that Thomas Reardon had sat. "I'm going to need a few things."

"Of course you will. What I need is to get my restaurant open again. I'm losing money here."

"I apologize for that, and with your cooperation, you will be open within the hour. Now, is this the place setting the man in question was using?"

"I don't know, I guess so. Like I told the other guys, I don't even remember the man."

"Yes, that's his plate" Kelly said nodding towards the counter next to her.

"Thank you Miss." He returned his attention to the manager "I'll need to take all of these items with me for now to test for prints and DNA."

"Fine, take them. What else?"

"I'll need to speak with the young lady. Then we should be able to clear out."

"Is that all?"

"I would love a soft drink."

"I'll see that you get one." The manager walked off quickly, not at all happy.

Jackson waited for him to leave. The line of customers was moving along and had now cleared the dining area. He took a seat on the other side of Kelly and began his interview. "Hello again Miss…"

"Kelly. My name is Kelly."

"Kelly, okay then. I understand you had been talking with the man that sat next to you."

"Yes, that's right. But I didn't really know him." It was clear that she was nervous.

"I'm sorry to put you through all of this, but it is important. I'm sure you'd love to get out of here, and you will very soon. You say you did not know this man, so you had never seen him before this evening?"

"No, never."

"Did he tell you his name?"

"Justin."

"Great, and did you make any plans with Justin?"

"No, of course not. We had just met." She tried to sound offended, but her embarrassment was more evident and she was afraid he knew that she had intended to make plans with him. Still, she had not lied, because she never had the chance to ask.

"Did you talk about anything in particular?"

"No, not really. Mostly just general stuff I guess. We were both alone and decided to talk, you know?"

"Of course, and there's nothing wrong with that. He didn't try to make plans with you for after dinner? Maybe ask you for a ride or try to go back to your place?"

"No, nothing. Is this helpful at all? I'm trying my best." She felt guilty, not for what she had done, but for what she almost did. Not that she had done anything wrong, but she knew that she almost did something stupid. She was embarrassed too because she just knew that the detectives and probably everyone else there that night could sense what she had almost done. She wanted to leave.

"Yes, you're doing great. In fact, if you would just give the officers your contact information, you can go now. Thanks for your time Kelly."

Relieved that her ordeal was over, she stood and walked to the end of the now very short line. There was a fear that crept up inside of her as she looked over at the door, as if there was something dark and ominous waiting for her in the night. She would be walking straight home, and quickly.

The manager reappeared with a drink in a Styrofoam 'to go' cup. He handed it to Jackson and was shocked when he actually paid for it. It wouldn't make up for the loss of business, but it was a start, he thought. "Is there anything else I can do for you?" He asked, now in a slightly better mood.

"We are ready to wrap things up. However, you will not be able to let anyone in the ladies room until we can get a crew over here and clear it."

"So what do I tell my customers?" he was getting heated again by the inconvenience.

"Tell them it's out of order and let them use the men's. You can send them to the gas station if you want. But if you want to open up again, you have to keep that room off limits to everyone until you're told otherwise. If that's going to be a problem, we can just keep you closed."

"No, no, that's fine. No one in the ladies room, I got you."

Seeing the last of the people go out the door, Jackson turned and headed to the ladies room at the back of the restaurant. He found Edwards inside, inspecting the window sill. "I think he used a paper towel or something to open the window. The dust is clearly disturbed, but I don't see any prints."

"By the time he left, he knew we would be searching this room. He was back to being his usual careful self. Fortunately the waitress was slow to clean off the counter. We should get all we need to identify him off of that.

Still, just in case, we need to get this room locked."

"Do you want it taped off?"

"No, not if the manager can lock it up. There's no need to ruin anymore of his business tonight by freaking out the customers."

Giving some last minute instructions to Beck and Ramirez, Jackson and Edwards went back to their car. Jackson started it up and then seemed to go into one of his trance like states, deep in thought. Edwards knew better than to interrupt, but instead just waited for him to come out of it. As he did, he looked at his watch and said "If they haven't picked him up by now, he's left the area. If I know him like I think I do, he's going to try to put some distance between this place and himself so he can regroup, regain control of his 'game'. Call the station and have road blocks set up on every major road in the area. I think he'll try to hitch a ride with someone if he hasn't already. We got too close this time and it threw off his plans."

"Do you want a patrol sent to your ex's place?"

"No, we can't spare the man power."

Though he was still confused by how well Jackson was handling everything, Edwards was finally in his glory. First he got to be in charge of the canvas operation. Now he was calling in road blocks and hot on the trail of a serial killer that now had a name. He dared to dream that maybe before the night was over, he would be placing the cuffs on Thomas Reardon. Then in the morning he would be standing before the press, ready to receive his department citation and who knows, maybe even a promotion. He shook the thoughts from his head and picked up the radio as Jackson pulled away from Denny's and rejoined the man hunt.

****

Trevor drove on at a speed uncharacteristic for him, not because he was in a hurry to get home, but because he wanted to put space between that woman he had approached at the restaurant and himself. Then a realization came to him that caused him to slow down and assume his normal pace just above the speed limit in that unspoken zone that was illegal, but not enough to warrant the attention of most police officers. He always figured that if you were not going too much over the speed limit, it would take a pretty desperate cop to give up his hiding space along the highway to pull you over. No, they would sit and wait for the ones that were really speeding, the ones that would pay more. Trevor slowed down because he realized he was trying to outrun something he could not outrun, his own thoughts and feelings. No matter how far away from the woman he got, it was how she made him feel, and the thoughts in his own head that bothered him. Those things were not easy to get away from.

As someone who travels for a living, he had had plenty of opportunities to learn to deal with and attempt to control his own thoughts. However, this was one of those times when the only way to break the endless cycle of thoughts was from some outside stimulus. He thought over his options and though it was getting late, and he had considered stopping for the night, that might not help. After all, once he had a brief conversation with the desk clerk at the motel, he would then be resigned to his room, with nothing but the TV to keep him company. It would most likely be a night spent staring at the ceiling, counting the tiles, or the holes in the tiles. If he wasn't going to sleep, what would be the point in stopping?

What he needed was someone to talk to, not about his feelings or problems, but just someone to elicit spontaneous thought, someone to offer a voice to listen to other than the one in his head. That decided, there was the matter of who and where. It was clear that he did not feel like talking to another woman, certainly not tonight and maybe not ever, on a social basis anyway. No, it would have to be a man. How do you go out in a strange town and find a man to talk to and have it not be strange or awkward? There was always the bar scene. Even the smallest of towns has a bar. But they were loud and full of other depressed people and would most likely just make things worse. There had to be a way, but in the meantime, Trevor was encouraged that the thought of solving his problem was at least a new thought and therefore a solution to his problem in and of itself, though only a temporary one.

Thomas Reardon had made it several blocks from the Denny's. After leaving the main street, hidden among the crowd of pedestrians that were out and on their way home from work or out to a bar for a drink, he had slipped into the shadows of the suburban streets where the overhead lights were much farther apart. Winding his way through the quaint little neighborhood he eventually found himself standing next to a fence that ran along the top of the hillside embankment next to the highway. The fence was about five feet tall and although not barbed at the top, he could not run the risk of catching his clothing or skin on the exposed wire endings. At some point it was possible that the police would pick up on his trail and he was now back in careful mode, not willing to leave behind even the slightest incriminating clue. He had been more than generous enough with those offerings as it was. He needed to put some space between himself and the police and regain control of the game, his game, before it got too far out of hand.

He started walking along the fence in search of a place where he could safely get to the other side. His best move would be to hitch a ride. This might solve two problems at once. The police, being ahead of schedule, had interrupted him when he was poised on the opportunity to kill and this left him wanting. It was almost excruciating for him to get so close and have to walk away unfulfilled. Perhaps if he found just the right person to give him a ride, he could get away and then strike.

About a mile down the fence he found a place where the fence was curled back, probably by kids that didn't know they weren't supposed to play near the highway. Careful not to get caught on anything, he bent down and swung through the opening. On the other side he tried to keep his balance as he walked down the steep embankment. At the bottom, among the discarded trash and dead animals, he stepped over the guardrail and continued on his way along the shoulder of the road. Loose gravel and broken glass crunched under his feet as he side stepped the various cans, bottle and cups that travelers had carelessly flung out their windows as they drove by. Fortunately he found himself on the side of the highway that led out of town. For whatever reason, people tended to be more willing to help someone leave town. Perhaps there was a romantic empathy for the lone wanderer that just wanted to leave the city for greener pastures. Whatever the reason, it would work out best for him if he could get the right person to stop. Ideally, what he wanted was another lone traveler, desperate for conversation. He never minded talking to his victims. There was a special thrill getting to know someone before he killed them. It wasn't a matter of making it more personal, he cared nothing for his victims, but the more he knew about their lives and the people in them, the more people he knew would suffer by his actions. It was an added bonus that he didn't always achieve, but enjoyed when he did. It was strange the chain reaction of pain that could be set into motion by the death of just one person.

Though traffic was fairly light, there was a steady stream of cars passing by, and that was exactly what they were doing. Swirling the wind around him as they passed, the garbage at his feet disturbed as the flaps of his jacket and ends of his hair shook, leaving behind the faint smell of exhaust. He had walked along the highway for what must have been an hour now. It was getting to the point of frustration and he began to consider how hitch hiking was much like fishing. Fishermen went to the best spots and used the right bait and the best fishing rods, but when all was said and done, they could do nothing but wait and see if the fish decided to bite, it was all up to them. He had chosen the best road, the appropriate direction and looked desperate and friendly at the same time. Still, it was up to the drivers whether or not they chose to stop and pick him up. There was nothing more he could do, and that lack of control was disquieting to his soul.

A strange phenomenon seemed to be at play. The more desperate he was, the more he needed a ride, the harder it was be to get one. It was as if his desire were a cloak, a force field that kept everyone at bay. Soon he would have to give up. The open ground of the highway and the bright lights overhead left him too exposed for his own comfort. It would be all too easy for the police to spot him, especially because he was sure his description had been sent to every police agency in the surrounding area by now. In addition, there was probably a frantic man hunt underway after they had come so close to catching him. That kind of near miss would lead to serious action, feeling that he was within their grasp at last.

Looking around at his options, he determined there were not many. He had walked far enough that the neighborhoods had thinned and faded along the side of the road. Now there was a great deal of nothing. Though leaving the highway would afford him the cover of darkness, it would not lead him anywhere he wanted to be. He needed another victim and if that were not possible, a place to sleep would suit him, but not until he was much farther away. He was out of the hot zone, but not outside the search area. They would not be giving up so easily on this night. They had tasted victory and were in hot pursuit. On the other hand, he was not yet ready to end the game.

Before he was forced to make a decision, the unmistakable sound of a car slowing down captured his attention. The glow of the red brake lights shown bright before him as the tires of the car came to a stop on the shoulder of the road. From what he could see, the driver was alone and appeared to be wearing a suit. The license plates were from out of state, another traveling salesman in need of companionship, perfect.

Cautiously he approached the car on the passenger side, bent down and looked into the half open window. "Where you headed buddy?" the driver asked him.

"For the moment I just need to get out of town" Thomas was more honest than he intended to be, but hoped that would win him favor with this lonely traveler.

"Good enough for me. I could use the conversation. If you're up to it, hop on in."

"I think I can handle that, thanks." Thomas opened the door and sat down, grateful for the soft cushion of the seat. After closing the door and putting on his safety belt, he looked over and saw the driver had extended his hand. Politely shaking it, he introduced himself, quickly trying to think up an appropriate persona for the occasion. "Thanks again for stopping, my name's Josh."

"Josh, it's a pleasure. My name is Trevor."

Chapter Eighteen

Road blocks were a strange departure for police officers. Used infrequently, most officers never got quite used to them. They were full of danger and yet could easily bore someone into complacency. The danger came from several scenarios. To begin with, much like a construction worker holding a sign beckoning drivers to go 'Slow', officers were standing on the side of active roads, hoping people had the common sense to obey their commands. If a driver failed to pay attention or his car failed to respond properly, it could mean disaster for those helplessly standing in the way.

Another danger came from those drivers that, though not being sought after themselves, were involved in illegal activities. If someone in the car was in possession of drugs, firearms or stolen goods, they would likely become jumpy, feeling that the roadblock was there for them. In that case, anything could happen. The worst part was, the police were often caught off guard, looking for someone or something else entirely. The element of surprise could prove fatal.

Then of course there was always the possibility that they would run across the very car they were looking for. Though they would likely be more alert and ready to handle the situation, it could turn into a real battle, depending on who they were dealing with. This final situation was the one everyone hoped for and dreaded. When properly resolved there was certainly a feeling of satisfaction that made it all worthwhile.

Though Officer John Simpson was aware of, and had dealt with all of these scenarios in one way or another, his reasons for hating road block duty were altogether different. He dealt with some element of danger every day as a patrol officer and though the special circumstances of a road block made him uneasy, it was not the primary reason for his complete and utter disregard of them. No, his reasons were much pettier. What bothered him most was the inconvenience of it all. It never failed that the call would only come when he had long standing plans that could not be put off. Road blocks mysteriously never seemed necessary when he was actually on duty. Requiring extra help, he would be called in on his off time. As if his hours of service were not strange and inconvenient enough, working all hours of the day and night at some time or another, to be called in when he was supposed to be able to spend time with his wife was just too much.

This night was no exception. John Simpson had purchased tickets to a stage show months in advance. He had planned a wonderful evening with his lovely wife of five years that would include dinner, a show and dessert at their favorite intimate spot. Normally it would include drinks as well, but recently she had announced that she was pregnant. This gave them all the more reason to take advantage of the opportunity for a date, knowing soon their lives would revolve around a tiny, helpless life.

The rate of divorce among police officers was alarmingly high and John Simpson was determined not to fall prey to those statistics. He did his best to place his wife ahead of his job, and the baby would become his highest priority. He would not be an absentee father. It was nights like this that made it difficult to hold it all together.

Dressed up beyond the casual date they were accustomed to, complete with jewelry, perfume and a few sparkles on her neck, his wife was radiant. He could not deny a sense of pride in being seen with her. Perhaps it was her pregnancy, but she had a glow about her that made her even more beautiful than he was used to. Ever thankful that she agreed to marry him and always wondering what he had done to deserve her, he never took her love for granted. They arrived at the restaurant, one that required advanced reservations, and had been seated at a secluded table near the back. Soft music played in the background and the chandelier above shimmered making the whole room appear as if right out of a fairy tale.

A worried expression came across her face as her eyes went from the delicious food selections, to the prices next to them. "Don't worry about the prices. Tonight is a special night. Order what you want" he assured her with a wink and a smile. My how he loved her. They placed their order and watched as the waiter retreated to the kitchen. Suddenly John's cell phone rang.

"Don't answer. Please, just don't even look at it" she pleaded, knowing that her fairy tale evening was about to come crashing to the ground.

"You know I have to. I'm sorry, but I need to check it." He flipped open the phone as he saw that it was headquarters. "This is Simpson."

"Officer Simpson, we need you to come in for a road block. We need the extra man power."

"But I'm right in the middle of something."

"Sorry, this comes from the top."

He closed his phone and the disappointed look on his face said it all. "What is it now?" she asked him, knowing enough, but wanting to hear it anyway.

"They need me for a road block. I have to go."

"Wonderful. What about dinner? What about the show?"

"You can go without me I guess. If you don't want to stay and eat alone, I guess we can have them bag it up and take it with us."

"I don't want to do anything alone. This was supposed to be our special night. I hate your job!"

"I know and I'm sorry. Please go to the show though. Maybe you can get someone else to go."

"Who? Everyone else is busy with their own plans. Plans they get to keep. No, I'm not going without you. Let's get the food and then you can take me home."

And so his wife sat at home eating their over priced dinner and watching TV instead of the show she had wanted to see so badly. The tickets and the money he spent on them would just go to waste and if he was lucky, there would be left over food in the fridge for whenever he was able to go home and eat it.

Until then, he stood on the passenger side of the road, flashlight in hand, bored out of his mind. Though the danger lingered in the air, what he dealt with mostly were people that were indignant about the infringement of their rights by being stopped and questioned when they had other places to be. Occasionally there would be the concerned citizen wanting to 'help in anyway I can'. Others were nervous either because they felt guilty about something or because they had the creepy sensation that a dangerous killer might be in the car behind them, and in this case that could be true.

Generally the way a road block worked was to have patrol cars on the road forming a V shape and forcing all traffic to be routed through one lane. As the cars pulled up, one at a time, they would be asked to stop as one officer would approach from each side. The job of the officer on the drivers side was to ask a few general questions and distract the driver while the officer on the other side searched the vehicle for anything suspicious or matching the search criteria. Then there were often other officers that stood back and kept an eye on the scene as a whole.

John was on the passenger side and without direct interaction with the passengers, was falling into a dangerous state of mind. He was thinking more about the speech he would get when he got home about how his job had once again interfered with any hope of a normal life, and with a baby on the way. Boring as it was, he was responsible for the safety of the other officer as he would likely be the first to become aware of any threat. He could ill afford to not pay proper attention.

Waving on the next car he looked down the line and saw what he thought might be something they all dreaded. One of the cars was weaving strangely, even at such low speeds. If the driver was driving under the influence, it would be a whole new set of problems. They could not just let him go, a danger to themselves and anyone else on the road. However, processing a DUI can take as long as four hours. They hardly had the time or man power to deal with that. It was going to be a long night.

As the next car pulled up, John noticed it was a young couple, probably on a date. Lucky them, he thought, and his mind briefly returned to the date he was supposed to be on and how lovely his wife had looked. She won't look so lovely when he gets home.

He could tell that the driver was nervous and was brought back to the situation at hand. The young man rolled down his window and used the word officer. This generally had two meanings. Some in the criminal element used the word officer as a way of showing contempt for those that interfered with their way of life. Others used it because they were nervous, felt guilty or were genuinely trying to cooperate. From what John could tell, this young man fell into one of the latter categories.

Before long he began to wonder if the driver was afraid of them or his date. Through the glass he could hear her say, "How long is this going to take?" as she leaned over the driver and addressed the officer directly, clearly unhappy at the delay. He seemed to be rather embarrassed by her actions and quickly tried to regain control. In response she merely rolled her eyes and began inspecting her fingernails to show her boredom. Clearly this was not the man they were looking for and so he was waved on and replaced by the next car.

John looked over at the other two officers and longed to be in their place. His heart was definitely not in this and he didn't want to endanger himself or anyone else by being complacent. Perhaps he could convince them to switch places with him soon. They stood there, leaning against the car, sipping coffee and laughing. Sure, this was worth him giving up his plans. The next car full of teenagers was ready for his careful inspection.

****

Trevor drove along, trying to get a look at his new companion without being too obvious about it. He had a strange smell that seemed like a combination of body odor and pine trees. Without thinking, he looked up at his rearview mirror to see if there was an air freshener hanging there that he had forgotten about, but of course there wasn't. This man Josh looked like he had been on the road for some time. His clothes were dirty and tattered, his hair greasy and he hadn't shaved or showered in the recent past. Still, he was grateful for the company. He had already stopped thinking about the events at dinner and was ready to hear what this man had to say about life. Even in his condition he might offer some good advice. "So what has you out on the road tonight?" he asked.

"Just time to move on, you know? I can't stay in one place for too long or I go nuts. It's time for a change of scenery. How about you, where are you headed?"

"Home."

"You don't sound too happy about it."

"I guess I'm not. I travel a lot as part of my job and I've been out of town. Not much to hurry home to. Sounds like you don't really have a home though, is that right?"

"Not really. I left home, if you could call it that, when I got out of high school and never looked back. I've never had a real job, a real family or a real home. I guess I don't fit into the 'normal' way of life, at least as most people see it."

"Interesting." Trevor was truly fascinated by this man already. He was suddenly full of questions and wanted to know more about this free existence. "I see quite a bit of the country through my travels, although not the most interesting parts. But you...that's really something. I mean it's like a grand adventure, not knowing where you're going to sleep or eat next. You wake up in a different town with no roots, no ties or obligations to anyone or anything. That's really incredible."

"Yeah, I guess in a way it is. It can be tough sometimes though. Money is hard to come by and often it's not a matter of where I'll eat, but if. And it's not easy to find a place to sleep when you can't shower regularly. Finding a ride is getting tougher too. People don't pick up hitch hikers like they used to."

"Still, the freedom of just picking up and moving on to a new place whenever you want, getting a fresh start, that must be so liberating." His mind was fast at work. He had never considered such a life. He had followed what everyone told him was the right way to live. He went to college, got a degree, found a good job, bought the house...that was what he thought everyone did. It never occurred to him that he could make his own decisions and break free of the mold.

"Oh, don't get me wrong, I wouldn't change my life for anything. I'm just saying, it's not for everyone. Most people need something a little more stable."

"Do you ever get lonely?"

"Not really. I meet lots of people, like yourself for instance, that I would never meet if I stayed in one place, working year after year. Plus the fact that I don't stay too long allows me to leave before things get all messed up and confusing. When I leave someone, it's usually on good terms, as friends."

"Amazing. I feel so trapped by my job. I mean even though I'm out on the road it is so confining. I don't make any decisions; they are in control of everything. Then when I go home, I'm all alone. I'm more alone than you are and I see the same people every day."

"That sounds pretty bad to me. I think maybe you need to make some changes."

"Actually, that's exactly what I've been thinking lately." Trevor's mind was in full gear now. Forgotten was the woman at the restaurant. This whole conversation was just the thing he needed. His sense of hope was restored in grand fashion. As the white dashes sped quickly under his car, he let what this man said sink in. It occurred to him that many times in his life it was difficult to maintain a relationship. At some point, things always go bad. Imagine if you could walk away on good terms and never let that happen. You could have friends that would stay friends forever. It wouldn't even matter if you never saw them again. "Do you keep in contact with anyone that you meet?"

"No, that would ruin the whole thing. I have no ties, no plans, just freedom. Once I say goodbye to someone, that's it."

Exactly, Trevor thought. Say goodbye and walk away friends. "So no one really even knows where you are then, you can just disappear." He said this as more of a statement than a question. "You almost don't...exist." As he clarified this to himself he faded back into his own thoughts. The voice of his passenger and new friend became a distant sound that he found easy to ignore. An idea came to Trevor and just as he had worked things out in his mind, he saw something odd up ahead. Brake lights filled his vision and he could see the blue and red lights of police cars directly in front of the mounting traffic. "What's this now?" he asked, irritated.

"Looks like a police barricade ahead. Traffics all backed up. This stinks."

Thomas was more than a little concerned. What started out as a perfect solution to both of his problems, could become a disaster if he had to try to get past the police barricade. He was sure it was him they were looking for and it wouldn't be too hard to spot him. He felt like a sitting duck, a cow being led to the slaughter house. Suddenly he became claustrophobic in this sedan. He tried desperately to come up with a way to ask Trevor to turn around and avoid the police, but how could he do that without causing suspicion. Out of desperation, he considered waiting until they had slowed down enough and jumping out of the car. Then he may have a chance if he ran into the woods. His hand wrapped around the door handle and he braced for the jump as Trevor slowly applied the brakes, but just before he opened the door Trevor spoke. "This is not what I need, some cop looking at me funny and asking me questions. If you don't mind, I'm going to turn around. I think I know a short cut about a half mile back."

"I don't mind at all" Thomas said, his grip easing and a sigh of relief escaping his lips. "Cops don't get along too well with people like me anyway." Though he was not sure why Trevor had decided to turn around, he was not about to complain. His good fortune seemed to be continuing. Now his heart rate was up, giving him a bonus feeling he had not been anticipating.

Defiantly, Trevor shut off his headlights and while he still had enough room between his car and the one in front, he turned and slipped quietly through the opening in the median, going back the way they had come. It felt good to be taking control of the situation, of his life for once. He was not about to let some cop ruin everything the way that woman had.

He continued on slowly, without headlights, until he saw what he was looking for. Along the side of the highway was a dirt road that led into the woods. It was not marked and was nearly impossible to see if you didn't know to look for it. He turned into it saying "I've been by here many times before in my travels. I had seen this road here and always wondered where it led. A couple of years ago I was bored and ahead of schedule, so I decided to turn in here and see just where it led. Turns out, it winds its way through the forest preserve a while and then comes back out on the highway a few miles ahead. I think that will safely put us on the other side of that road block."

"Sounds good. I'm glad you got bored." Thomas marveled at how sometimes everything just seemed to fall into his lap. In just a matter of minutes he had gone from feeling like he had to jump out of a moving car to avoid being arrested, to being driven into secluded woods, victim on a platter right next to him. It was just too easy. He looked out the window and saw how the canopy of trees came together over the road, completely enclosing them in a series of twisted shadows, where the moonlight fought its way through. He imagined that it was nearly as dark in the daytime. As they drove deeper into the woods, he had the uncanny sensation of being swallowed whole, transporting them into another dimension.

The police were out of sight, but still nearby. They would be able to add to the excitement, but not pose a serious threat. There was tall grass and thick woods on both sides of the road. He would have no trouble slipping away into the night. Following the road would lead him back to the highway and past the police. Finding another ride might prove difficult, drivers being put off by the road block, but he would figure that out later. Right now he had to find a way to get Trevor to stop the car without causing him alarm.

Chapter Nineteen

After another half an hour of searching cars that were not at all relevant, John Simpson needed a break. The thought of walking up to the next car overwhelmed him and he signaled his partner to give him a second before approaching the car that was pulling up to the search zone. "Hang on a second will you? I need a break. I'm going to see if one of those guys will switch with me for a while."

"Yeah, alright. Go ahead."

Turning off his flashlight, he stepped in front of the stopped car and crossed over to where the other two officers stood, coffees in hand and smiles on their faces. Trying his best to look wiped out, he let out a big sigh as he came close to them. "Hey guys, can one of you take my place for a while? I'm asleep on my feet and I don't want to become a liability here."

The two looked at each other and shrugged. Finally, as if they decided without speaking, one of them set his coffee down on the hood of their cruiser, straightened himself up and went to work.

John Simpson walked over to his own car, threw the flashlight on the passenger seat and slumped up against the door. Letting out another long breath, he relaxed and wondered just how much longer they would be out here. He looked at the radio and considered calling in for an update, hoping that someone else had already caught this Thomas Reardon character. No sooner had he thought it, when the radio came to life. "Road Block Four, this is Jackson."

John opened the door and grabbed the radio. "Jackson, this is Simpson, go ahead."

"How many are you?"

"There are four of us."

"How many cars?"

"We have two in use as a blockade and I have my own. What's up Detective?"

"I'm starting to think either Reardon never got that ride or he bailed out before getting to the road block. I want you to get in your cruiser and double back towards the original target area. Check every side road no matter how small. If he's past us, he's long gone, but if not, we have to exhaust every possibility. I'm asking the other locations to do the same."

"Understood. We're on our way." John looked over at his partner who was waving the next car up, the car he had seen swerving earlier. It was immediately clear that his suspicions were well founded. He walked over to his partner and got his attention. "Jackson just called. He wants us to start doubling back towards the Denny's. Is this guy as hammered as I think?"

"Yeah, he's flying pretty high. There's no way we can let him slide."

"Is there anyone else in the car that looks capable of driving him home?"

"No, they've all been partying."

"Well, if you guys have to process a D.U.I., you're going to need all three of you here to keep things going. I'll take my car and start heading back."

"You sure? Maybe we should call Jackson and let him know."

"No, that's alright. I need to get out of here anyway. "

"Alright, but be careful."

As John walked back over to his car, he saw them waving the drunk driver over to the side. He didn't envy them. One of them was going to be busy for the next few hours, regardless of how the search went. Happily, he sat down behind the wheel and drove off. Heading back on the other side of the highway, it was only a few moments before his searchlight caught the dirt road entrance that led into the woods. It was not easy to see because the way the tree branches intertwined gave it more the appearance of a cave opening than a road. He stopped his car and debated with himself. A chill ran through him like a cold winter breeze that bites to the bone. There was something evil about this place that he couldn't explain. Shaking off as paranoia, he turned the wheel and entered the shadowy world of the road-side forest. Searchlights on both sides of the road ate away at the darkness that hung over the tall grass like a blanket. He began to second guess his quick decision to come alone.

Thomas Reardon looked out the window, not seeing much more than varying degrees of darkness. He still had not come up with a good enough reason to ask Trevor to stop the car in the middle of the woods. Out of desperation he was about to pretend to be sick when once again, things suddenly turned his way.

"I hate to do this to you, but I really need to take a leak. Do you mind if I stop here for a second?" Trevor asked.

"No, not at all. I could stand to go myself" Thomas replied, fighting off a smile. There was no way things should be falling into place for him so easily, but again, he was not complaining.

As the car came to a stop, he waited for Trevor to get out first. As he heard the other man make his way through the tall grass on the other side of the car, he stood up and quietly removed his leather belt from around his waist. He walked around the back of the car and entered the grass directly behind Trevor, careful to stay out of his peripheral vision. His heart rate sped up as he closed in on his prey.

John continued on, slowly following the road deeper into the woods. All external light was blocked out. His heart nearly stopped as his searchlight showed something among the trees. Stopping the car, he shone his spotlight in the direction of the shape that had caught his attention. Red glowing eyes reflected back at him. Just as he thought his heart would leap from his chest, the shape moved, exposing itself as a mother possum. He collected himself, noticing that his hand was wrapped around the handle of his firearm. He took a deep breath and continued on.

As he moved his way into position, Thomas was careful to step in Trevor's footsteps, taking advantage of the trampled grass to make his approach quieter. It would also leave less evidence, making the crime scene slightly more confusing. In this darkness, that could count for a lot. It would be difficult to figure anything out before daylight, and with this tree cover, that wouldn't help much either.

Closer and closer he got, hoping Trevor would keep urinating for just a few more seconds, while he got into position. As he was finally within

211

reach, something struck him as odd. Though Trevor stood in place as if he was still busy, there was no sound, merely silence. Strange as it was, he was not about to let it stop him from doing what he came here for. Slowly and silently he raised the belt over Trevor's head, ready to throw it around his neck, when suddenly and without warning, Trevor spun around and with a flash of something in his hand, he stood looking Thomas in the eye. It took him a moment to feel the sensation of warm liquid pouring down his chest, followed by a stinging pain. Thomas placed a hand on his own throat and watched it come away covered in what he could tell even in the darkness was blood. He looked down at Trevor's hand and saw the glint of a knife. As he felt his life draining from him, he noticed Trevor staring intently into his eyes, a smile creeping up on his face, then everything went black.

Trevor stood over the now collapsed body of his companion. "Now my friend, as you said, I can leave you on good terms, friends forever." Knowing that anytime he had tried to get close to someone, take that next step in the relationship, it always went bad. This guy was right. Why give people the opportunity to hurt you. End things when they are still good and don't look back, ever. He would have a friend forever now. He looked at the blank, staring eyes that still looked shocked at what happened and he tried to remember the man's name, but he couldn't. It didn't matter. Like he said, "No ties, no plans, just freedom."

He was a new man, living a new life. All the former things had passed away. It was a rebirth of epic proportions. His eyes turned from the limp, lifeless corpse at his feet to his own hands. He saw there was blood on the hand that held the knife and on the front of his shirt from the spray. Next time he would have to find a way to make less of a mess.

The sound of a slowly approaching car snapped him back to reality. He made his way back to the car, turned off the lights and quietly drove away. With any luck, whoever was coming behind him would not notice the body among the tall grass. His heart would not stop pounding in his chest. Is this what it felt like to be alive? Is this what he had been missing his whole life? It seemed only fitting to him that the one who opened his eyes to a new life should be the one to help him cross over to it. He looked in the rearview mirror, and said "Thank you my friend."

As if the darkened forest was not unnerving enough, seeing those red eyes staring back at him had given him a seemingly permanent chill. To ease the tension, John Simpson turned on the radio. The sound of music filled his squad car and made it easier to drive deeper into the woods. In fact, it wasn't long before his mind was drifting to his wife, sitting at home, probably drinking a glass of wine after finishing the food they brought home, the food they were supposed to eat together.

His mind distracted by his thoughts and the music, he began to find it funny that a hardened, big city police officer should be afraid of a few trees and an oversized rodent. He hadn't been afraid of the dark since he was a child. This road began to feel like a useless dead end and he was about to look for a place to turn around, when his eye caught something unusual in the illuminated searchlights.

It took him a moment to figure out just what it was that caught his eye, but then he noticed that it was something about the grass. He turned the spotlight in that direction and noticed the grass was pressed down as if trampled in spots. He looked from side to side to see if what had caught his eye was really out of place and did not see anything like it anywhere else. Wondering at first if he should bother calling it in, he then decided against it. It would likely turn out to be nothing and everyone was far too busy tonight to come running for every little thing that looked strange. Instead he got out of the car, reaching back in to get his flashlight. Upon closer inspection, it definitely looked like it could be footprints. He withdrew his firearm, held it up next to his flashlight and moved farther into the grass. After a few steps, he paused to listen for any movement. Only the wind blowing the leaves above could be heard. Continuing on, circling around the impressions in case they were evidence, he followed the trail deeper in. His flashlight caught something on the grass. Reaching out, he felt something thick and wet as he rubbed his fingers together. He turned the light on his hand and saw his fingers were red, covered in blood. Jumping back, he instinctively wiped his hand off on his shirt. Knowing he should definitely be calling this in, he temporarily froze. The desire to know more compelled him to keep going and after taking only one more step, he noticed a flat area in the grass ahead. He focused his light towards the ground revealing what appeared to be the body of an adult male, lying like a rag doll, eyes staring straight up at the sky, shocked to no longer be able to see.

He fought the almost uncontrollable urge to run and instead, using all of his strength, walked carefully back to the car, stepping in his own tracks to preserve the scene. He sat down on the seat and took a moment to regain his composure. After a few deep breaths he picked up the radio. "Jackson, this is Simpson. Come in please."

"This is Jackson, go ahead" the radio crackled to life.

"I'm on a dirt road about a half mile east of the road block, maybe a mile into the woods. Based on the description you put out, I think I found Thomas Reardon."

"Is he in custody?" Jackson asked with notable enthusiasm.

"In a manner of speaking."

"What do you mean? Have you got him under control or not?"

"Well I guess you could say that, he's dead."

Chapter Twenty

A steady wind thrust the cool night air through the trees and caused the tall grass to swirl and bend in all directions. The branches on either side of the road intermingled above, effectively blocking out the sky and any light from the moon and stars. In daylight, this was a place surrounded in green and full of life, but at night, especially this night, it felt like the cold chill of death.

Officer John Simpson stood anxiously by his patrol car, too nervous to sit down and trying hard not to think about the dead body that lay just a few feet away from him. Though it felt like forever, it had only been moments since he had called Jackson to report his findings. He found it was better if he didn't look in the direction of the lifeless form. He fought hard to fight the images that ran through his head, the blood on his hands, the blank staring eyes, the hapless way the body lay like a pile of loose parts that were still connected. Once more he looked down at his fingers, stained with blood that would not wipe off. He desperately wanted to wash his hands.

Staring down at the road and his own feet, almost willing the appearance of another living soul, he heard the distant sound of an approaching car. He briefly considered the possibility that instead of Jackson, it could actually be the killer returning to the scene of the crime. Once again his hand found its way to the handle of his firearm as he stood up straight and looked in the direction of the oncoming car. His heart rate increased as the headlights fought their way through the woods until the car came into view and he was assured that it was Jackson.

Jackson and Edwards had continued to ride together throughout the night and were only a few miles down the road when they received the call from Simpson. Jackson had found another opportunity to show Edwards just how fast he could drive when the situation warranted it. He quickly found the dirt road and was winding his way through the woods. It wasn't too difficult to see Simpson's car, a beacon of light in the darkness. Every light was still on as he stood there, waiting for them to arrive. As he came into view, it was clear that he was more than a little relieved to see them.

Before the car had even come to a complete stop, Edwards flung open his door and jumped out. It was all Jackson could do to put the car in park before he too exited. Though if what Simpson had said were true, it was not what they expected or wanted, he was anxious to find out for himself just what was going on. He would have to decide quickly whether to redirect or even call off the various patrols at work all over town.

"The body's over there about ten feet in" Simpson said to the detectives. "The footprints off to the left are mine. The other set is what led me to him."

"Couldn't have been too easy to spot in the dark. Good job Simpson" Edwards said, showing his maturity.

"Let's have a look shall we?" Jackson carefully followed Simpson's footprints, followed closely by Edwards.

"There's a spray pattern of blood on the grass I came across so be careful" Simpson informed them.

Using flashlights to work their way through the grass and avoid the blood they now saw, they made their way to the body and crouched down next to it. Looking first at the face and then at the clothing and build, Jackson had to agree that the description certainly matched. There was an open wound on the throat that was likely caused by a knife. Though Reardon had shown the capacity to break from whatever pattern he seemed to be following, it was unlikely that he would have changed his method of killing from strangulation to throat slashing. Whether or not this was indeed Thomas Reardon, it was probably not one of his victims, but that of another killer.

"If this is Reardon, maybe someone tried to fight him off and won."

"That's certainly possible. It's not like him to be that careless though." A lingering doubt plagued Jackson's mind. It didn't fit, none of this did. Reardon had been very much in control in every case, it was part of his signature. Was it possible that he wasn't as clever as they thought he was? Maybe he had been lucky at first and then everything began to unravel for him. No matter how hard he tried to make that scenario plausible, it just wouldn't work. As close as they felt like they were getting to catching him at times, it always felt like it was all planned and still under his control. All of his years of experience told him that Thomas Reardon knew exactly what he was doing and had been playing a game of his design, by his rules and it had all gone his way, until now. "If this was somehow a case of self defense, we could get a call at some point from whoever did this, once they calm down. However, with something of this magnitude, I highly doubt anyone would admit to this until they were forced to." He knew in his heart that the call would never come. Something told him that this was no accident, no case of self defense. This was murder. "We need to ID this guy as soon as possible. With Reardon's fingerprints and DNA on file, we should have no problem finding out if this is him. But until we know for sure, nothing changes in the search."

"How about if we send a blood sample back to the lab with Simpson? Then we could keep the scene virtually intact" Edwards suggested.

"That's a good idea. Call the lab and let them know he's coming." Jackson was shaken by this latest development. With all he had seen over the years, he was rarely caught off guard. Whatever happened here tonight, he could not explain it. He was proud of Edwards for thinking on his feet and maintaining his composure. Once again he had demonstrated just how far he had come in the last few days. In some respects, the student was teaching the teacher. Now it was time for him to clear his head and get back in control of things. As he heard Edwards talking to the lab, he waved Simpson over. Though reluctant to get closer to the body, he came over to Jackson. "In my trunk is a case with some collection devices. In one of the side pockets you should find a glass tube. Would you please bring it to me? And don't forget to bring me a stopper."

Happy to be headed back towards the car and away from the body, he found the car still running and the doors open. Reaching in he popped open the trunk and walked around to the back. The first thing he noticed was how neat and orderly the trunk was, everything in its place. This trunk was cleaner than his house. Held in place by Velcro strips sat a soft, black leather case. He unzipped it to find a variety of plastic bags, rubber gloves, rolls of yellow police tape and several metal instruments, all shined to perfection. Along the side was a pocket and he ran his finger inside. He felt the glass tubes lined up and held in place by an elastic band. After removing one of the tubes, he closed the case.

Carefully he made his way back towards Jackson. When he was within reach, he extended his arm to hand the tube to him. Jackson was oblivious to his discomfort and without even looking he reached up and took the tube from his hand. Placing the tube near the wound, wearing a pair of gloves he keeps in his pocket, he put pressure near the opening of the tube and forced the flow of blood to fill it. He did his best to wipe off any excess around the top edge, then held his hand out in expectation. When nothing happened, he said "I need the stopper please."

Whispering an expletive under his breath, Simpson quickly made his way back to the car and again opened the case. Inside the pocket, along the bottom, he found a rubber stopper. He hurried back to Jackson, handed him the piece of rubber and offered an awkward apology. As if he didn't hear him, Jackson placed the stopper firmly in the top of the tube before handing it over to Simpson. "Take this directly to the lab. They'll be waiting for you. Go lights and sirens. Tell them to call my cell immediately when they have the results. While you are waiting for them to run their tests, stop by dispatch and see if any calls came in reporting an incident in this area, anything that could shed light on what happened here. Any questions?" Holding the tube like it was toxic, Simpson shook his head. He gave him a card with his cell number on it." Good, get going then. Oh, and Simpson, good job. It would have been easy to miss that body so far off the road. You did good work here tonight." He knew Simpson had been shaken by what he had seen tonight and hoped that the compliment might in some small way help restore his confidence.

As he walked back to his car, Simpson stood a little taller and had a look of determination on his face as he got behind the wheel of his car. He pulled on ahead before turning around. Turning off his searchlights and switching on his emergency flashers, he headed back towards the highway, reserving the siren for when he reached the open road.

Jackson stood up and walked back to the road, joining Edwards who had finished his phone call and was leaning against the side of the car. He removed his rubber gloves and leaned next to his partner. Being so unsure of what he was dealing with was unsettling to him. For now, all he could do was wait for the evidence team to arrive and for that all important call with the lab results. He wasn't sure what to hope for. He couldn't imagine that any scenario would be good news at this point, except perhaps to the officers that might be sent home soon if this was the body of Thomas Reardon. His mind would go over every conceivable possibility until the call came.

Ten minutes after leaving the woods, Officer John Simpson pulled into the parking lot at police headquarters. With the light traffic and the room afforded him by the siren and lights, he was able to travel quickly. He didn't bother parking in a space, but just pulled up next to the back entrance. He was certain he would not get towed. Leaving the car running, he ran up the steps, down the hall and made his way to the basement, where the crime lab was located.

In years past, at this time of night he would have found the door locked and the room devoid of technicians. But these days, when everything needed to be done quickly and most cases hung on lab results, one or two techs were around at all times. As he turned the corner, he could see one of them halfway down the hall, waiting for him. Apparently Edwards had done a sufficient job convincing them of the urgency of the situation. He handed over the tube of blood, happy to be rid of it. "How long will it take to make the comparison?" he asked.

"Not long, a few minutes. I already have the other sample brought up in the system. It will take a few minutes to make a positive ID" she replied.

"I need to run up to dispatch for a minute, then I'll be back."

"I'll be here" she said, sounding like she wondered why she should care what his plans were or when he would be back. Forgetting he was even there, she entered the lab and went straight to work.

Simpson walked as quickly as he could without actually running, back down the hall and up the stairs to the dispatch room. For some reason he had yet to figure out, the lights in the dispatch room were always dim. His best guess was that it helped keep them calm as they dealt with hysterical callers.

Inside were three people sitting in front of computer screens, wearing head-phones. The dispatcher had two primary functions. The first was to keep track of all officers on duty. Wherever an officer went, or whatever activity they were involved in had to be called in. If they were going to step out of their car, they called it in. Part of this function was also to run computer checks on cars the officers pulled over and provide them with any pertinent information they had at their disposal.

The second function of the dispatcher was to answer emergency calls. They would then assess the situation and decide how best to handle it, re-directing the appropriate officers based on location. By most respects, the dispatchers were in control of what went on in any given shift.

Simpson looked on the screens that showed the phone calls received to see if anything looked relevant to the killing in the woods, but saw nothing that fit. Next to the dispatch room was an office that was, by contrast, very bright. Inside was the one person who thought he was in charge of the shift, and technically he was. Simpson was almost certain that this room was kept bright to make sure its occupant didn't fall asleep, though it happened quite often anyway. This was the office of the shift commander.

The shift commander was the highest ranking officer of the shift, usually at least a lieutenant. The function of this position was to oversee everything, make important decisions if a situation came up, give approval for lunch breaks and do paperwork. Shift commanders were on a rotating schedule and changed shifts every six weeks. There were three shifts to make up the twenty four hour period of each day. Having to turn your life upside down every six weeks was not easy. Trying to fall asleep at different times, never sure if it was day or night, not able to spend time with family and friends consistently made for a difficult life and made most of them more than a little cranky.

Inside the office, Simpson found the Lt. at the desk, making out the schedule for the next month. "We have a situation in the woods off the high-way. Detectives Jackson and Edwards are on the scene now..." Simpson had begun to explain but was cut off.

"I know, they just called in for an evidence team. What about it?" From his tone it was clear that he was offended by the accusation that he was not aware of what was happening on his watch.

"Jackson wanted me to see if any calls came in that might be related" Simpson said a little defensively.

"No, nothing. Is there anything else? I've got work to do here."

"He wants someone to call him if one comes in." Simpson looked down on the desk to see what was keeping him so busy.

"Sure, I'll get my secretary on that right away" he said, leaning forward and covering his papers with his arms. "Now if you don't mind…"

This particular shift commander was especially cranky. Part of it was just his natural personality. However, he had also just taken the detectives test and failed. In response, he took out his frustration on those under him. As for those that were already detectives, he would certainly be in no hurry to help them out. Let them do it themselves, they're the detectives, he would say. Simpson knew that Jackson would not be getting any calls from him tonight, no matter what news came in.

He turned and walked out of the office and back through the darkened room, trying hard to sympathize with the man. As he stepped back into the hallway, he suddenly remembered that he was waiting on the lab results. Though he tried to keep under control, in a matter of a few steps, he found he had already broken into a jog.

Within a few seconds he was back at the lab and standing behind the tech as she sat at her desk. He was determined to be the one to call Jackson with the results. It always paid to impress the detectives, especially one with Jackson's reputation. He had done it once tonight already, twice would certainly make an impression. "So? Anything yet?"

"Just a second and you can see for yourself." They both looked at her computer screen and waited for something to happen. She began to nod slowly. "Yep, There you go."

"Where?" he asked, not seeing what she was. She pointed to an area at the bottom of the screen. He leaned in and read it over three times to be sure he knew just what it was telling him. He stood up silently and picked up the phone on her desk. Retrieving Jackson's phone number from his pocket, he let out a breath and an expletive.

Chapter Twenty One

Jackson stood, leaning against his car, calm and lost in thought. He reflected on this latest twist. He was in unfamiliar territory now. Usually when he saw something he had a good sense for what happened. His knack for seeing a crime scene unfold in his mind like he was watching a replay made him one of the most valuable detectives around and had helped him put many killers behind bars, saving an unknown number of lives. This scene however had him puzzled. Rarely did a series of crimes, especially murders, take such an odd and drastic turn.

Next to him in silence, Edwards thought anxiously about the phone call they were waiting on. The entire case hung in the balance and from what he could tell, there were three possible conclusions that could be drawn from the dead body that lay just a few feet from where he stood. The first, and what he considered least likely possibility, was that this victim was unrelated to the case they were working on. If that were true, they would likely hand it over to other detectives and get back to the manhunt. This was not an ideal conclusion, but it would mean they still had a chance to catch their man.

The second scenario was that this was Thomas Reardon's latest victim, which just happened to resemble him. If that was the case, it could be the newest way for him to mess with them, trying to confuse them and throw them off his trail long enough to get away. If that was his intention, he had likely succeeded. This made him a little fidgety about just standing around doing nothing. He wouldn't put it past Reardon to try something like that, but it seemed unlikely for him to change his method of killing to the use of a weapon. He was definitely a hands on killer, literally, and to kill in this latest fashion would completely change the profile they had developed for him. The best part of this conclusion was that again, they would still know who they were looking for, though he might have eluded them once again.

It was the third possibility that truly bothered him. If this was the body of Thomas Reardon, that would mean they were robbed of the chance to catch him and bring him to justice themselves. That was the moment he had been dreaming of his whole career. The press taking photos, his name mentioned on TV and in the headlines of all the biggest newspapers, that was what he used to motivate him on the days that he just didn't feel like being a cop anymore. He was sure that catching a serial killer would instantly advance his career.

It had also become personal for him. He knew that Reardon had toyed with them, taunted them and strung them along. He pictured him sitting in a room laughing at their ineptitude, wondering how it could be so easy to fool the police and get away with murder. He pictured the victims and their blank stares and how the last thing they saw was him, staring at them with pleasure in his eyes as their souls left this world. But what bothered him the most was his personal threat to Jackson and his family. He wanted to bring Reardon in and make him pay.

The thought that was on both of their minds was that if this victim was also their former killer, that would mean starting all over again. A new killer would have emerged, one that they knew nothing about. This killer would have outsmarted the man who had outsmarted them for so long. That thought gave them both the chills. The sound of Jackson's phone ringing startled them both out of their thoughts and brought them back to the present. "Jackson" he answered.

As he listened to the voice on the other end of the line, he walked back to the body laying in the grass. He turned on his flashlight and stared down at the victim, nodding slightly. Edwards stood rigidly watching Jackson in anticipation. He didn't want to interrupt the call, but desperately wanted to hear the other half of the conversation. He certainly couldn't figure anything out from Jackson's half. After a few seconds, Jackson closed the phone and stood silently looking down at the body.

"Well?" Edwards asked when he could wait no longer.

"According to the lab, this is the body of Thomas Reardon."

"You've got to be kidding me." Until this moment, Edwards was not sure what he was hoping for. He now knew that this was not it.

"No, I'm afraid not. Get on the radio and call off the search. There's no point in tying up half the department when we no longer know who we are looking for." Jackson was walking back towards Edwards when he could see that his anger was boiling over like a tea kettle about to blow, he knew he needed to say something. "Listen Bill, I know this isn't what either of us wanted, but unfortunately it is another part of the job."

"What is?" he asked through clenched teeth.

"Disappointment. You can't take cases personally, even when the killer does, and you can't get so involved that you get frustrated beyond your ability to let go. We work hard on these cases and for a while they are a big part of our lives, but if you can't let go at a time like this, you will literally lose your mind. This job is not worth your health."

"Are you telling me you have already let go of your frustration and disappointment?"

"No, I wouldn't go that far. It takes time. But the truth is, there are more unsolved cases than solved ones. This chapter is closed and the killer was brought to justice, even if it wasn't by our hands."

"Yeah, but you can't tell me that you didn't want to bring down this scum yourself, especially after he made it personal. I mean, think of those victims and what he did to them, and for what, the fun of it? And you with your psychic ability or whatever it is that it lets you see what he did better than the rest of us, you have to feel cheated."

"I'm only human and I know what you are saying. Yes, if I had my choice I would have been the one to stop him. But this is exactly what I'm talking about. If you let yourself get too emotionally involved, you will not make it in this job for long. I guess that is where my faith really helps."

"Right, about that. If like you say, you are doing your part, following God's master plan by chasing down the bad guys, why would he deprive you of the opportunity to finish the job yourself instead of robbing you of the satisfaction?"

"*Vengeance is Mine sayeth the Lord.* It's not my place to question Him, but to trust Him. When you think about it, what Reardon or any other criminal does is more offensive to God than to anyone else. He can end it however He chooses. Besides, in the end, it is still an answer to prayer. The killer was stopped and before reaching my family, if indeed that was ever his plan. Now, the tech crew will be here any second. When they get here I'll drive you back to your car and you can head home. I'll need you fresh and alert tomorrow, we have a new killer to catch."

"Wonderful." Edwards slumped back against the car, harder than he intended. Staring angrily in the direction of the body of the man they had tried so hard to find, he tried to make sense of it all. In his mind he ran through everything that had brought them up to this point. Was there something they could have done better or different? Could they have foreseen this somehow? One question led to a dozen others and finally he had had enough. Maybe Jackson was right. You had to keep it all at a distance, put up a mental and emotional barrier. Maybe it was time he found something to help him get through besides alcohol and one night stands. He was turned off by the whole religious idea. He was too young to stop having fun. If he became a Christian, he would have to change his whole lifestyle, right? No more hanging out in bars all night, bringing home strange women. That made him happy, or at least he thought it did. Still, it wouldn't hurt to just ask a few more questions and find out a little more about the whole Christian thing. After all, it seemed to work for Jackson, a man he had come to greatly admire. Suddenly and without explanation, a calm came over him. His anger was gone.

****

Jimmy Falcon was not his real name, but he felt that it was at least partially responsible for getting his foot in the door as a reporter for a major newspaper. The name sounded like something out of a comic book and, truth be told, it was. Taken from the geeky reporter that worked with Clark Kent in the Superman comics, Jimmy Olsen, and the some time sidekick of Captain America, The Falcon, one DC and one Marvel. The name had a certain ring to it that was just fun to say.

As an investigative reporter, it was up to him to come up with stories that would sell newspapers. He was fortunate enough to get a good one, right out of the gate. He had heard rumors of a possible serial killer at work and decided to look into it further. He hit the jackpot and was rewarded with a large article. In fact, he felt it was probably his article that had got the police to finally do their jobs, because he received a call in the middle of the night saying the killer had been found.

He was now on his way to his desk, before the sun was even up, because he had a follow up article to write that would really make his name known. He would even work it in that he was personally responsible for bringing it to an end. As he understood it, there were some mysterious circumstances at play that brought an end to the story, but that would have to wait for part three in his series. He was determined to get this latest story in the next addition.

Coffee in one hand, his notes in the other and a big smile on his face, he rounded the corner and came to his desk. To his surprise, there was a man sitting at it. Looking around to see if there was anyone else around, he asked "Can I help you?"

"My name is Detective Jackson."

"Is that supposed to mean something to me?" In truth, the name sounded oddly familiar, but he was too caught off guard to place it.

"Well it should." Jackson set a piece of paper down on the desk in front of Jimmy.

"Oh, I see you read my article. And that seems to be your name there, circled in red."

"That's right."

"Well if you came to thank me for making you famous, a phone call at a decent hour would have sufficed."

"Do you know where I got this?"

"Hard to say, it's sold all over town."

"Do you know where I got this particular copy?"

"Why don't you go ahead and tell me so I can get to work. I have an article to write."

"It was left for me by the serial killer. He is the one that circled my name and the fact that I have a daughter and ex-wife."

"Gosh, that's weird" he said sincerely.

"You see, he wanted me to know that my family was now involved and that if he wanted to, he would make them his next victims."

"Man, I am really sorry. I didn't mean..."

"He was able to make it personal, because you told him who I was. You endangered my family with your careless writing."

"It was never my intention. Please forgive..."

"Don't ever do anything like this again."

"I won't."

Jackson stood up and let Jimmy Falcon take his seat. He started to walk away, knowing his point had been made. Though he knew he was justified in what he said, he didn't feel right walking away before saying one more thing. "You have a great future as a detective if you decide to go that way. You're quite an investigator." And with that he was gone.

"Thanks" Jimmy shouted after him. As he thought about what had just happened, his article took on a new shape in his mind. He would make sure to write how well the police detectives did their jobs, despite the danger they and their families live with on a daily basis. They put their lives on the line, to protect the lives of others and deserved our respect. Satisfied with this new spin, he took a sip of coffee, turned on his computer and got to work.

****

Daylight was creeping up on the horizon. Trevor Simmons had driven through the night. His heart pounded for hours as he relived the events of the night over and over in his mind. It felt like someone had removed a wall that was deep inside him, preventing him from fully experiencing life and now he was seeing and feeling for the first time. Strange, he thought, how someone's death could give him life.

He searched his feelings to see if he felt remorse or somehow sorry for the man that had gotten into his car and met his end. He felt no anger or contempt for him, and was indebted to him for showing him the way, but he felt no sorrow. Perhaps it was just time for the free spirit that was contained in that man to flow into a new being, one that desperately needed it, like Trevor.

His thoughts went to the future, the now near future. He had not driven straight home. He wasn't ready for that yet. But soon he would return to his normal life. He couldn't make any drastic changes that others would notice, not yet. Though he was anxious to continue the life that he had just gotten a taste of, his practical side told him to lay low and follow a normal routine until he was sure that there was no one looking for him. As far as he knew, there were no witnesses, no way to connect him to the victim. Though it was possible, however unlikely, that they could prove he had traveled through the general vicinity, there should be no way to directly connect him to anything. If he just played it cool for a little while, everything would be fine.

Before long, he would be back on the road again, another business trip, another chance to meet a stranger, make a friend and send them on the road to forever.

Made in the USA
Charleston, SC
08 July 2015